The Truth Within Me

Book two in the Within Me Series

Rozia Bell

Banks & Bell Legacy

This is a work of fiction. Names, characters, businesses, places, events, and incidents are either the products of the author's imagination or used in a fictitious manner.

ISBN:
979-8-9989231-5-9 (Paperback)
979-8-9989231-6-6 (Ebook)
979-8-9989231-7-3 (Audio)

Cover design by Samantha Sanderson-Marshall
Edited by Laurie Chitennden
Published by Banks & Bell Legacy, LLC
www.roziabell.com

First edition 2026
Printed in the United States of America

Dedication

This book is dedicated to my dear Karma.

For me, it was real.
Real in my bones.
Real in the way my heart still reaches for you
before it remembers why it shouldn't.

And if love were only about feeling,
I would choose you, again
and again
and again.

But I have learned that loving you
and loving myself
cannot live in the same house.

So I'm walking away,
even as my heart still whispers your name.

For me, this was real.

Trigger Warning

If you have ever apologized to someone who owed you an apology, stayed too long, left too late, or eaten cold food because you didn't want to wake him up…

This book is for you.

Trigger warnings include: emotional abuse, coercive control, pregnancy loss, and recognizing yourself on every other page.

If you're in a tender place, please take care while reading.

And if you find yourself saying, "I've been there before…"
Just know…you're not alone.

The Phone Call

"What the hell…you're married?" The words burst out before I can think.

I press the phone harder against my ear, like pressure might change what I'm hearing.

My heart is breaking.

But his voice is steady.

Part 1: His Side

Karma

There are three things you should know about me.

1. *I am very good at reading people.*
2. *I never do anything without a reason.*
3. *I loved her.*

Everything else is a matter of perspective.

Chapter 1

1 Year After The Phone Call

She's laughing again.

That sound, it cuts through the noise of everything else. The waves, the seagulls, the wind, it all folds beneath her laughter like it knows its place. Even nature bends to her when she's happy.

God, it's a beautiful thing to witness. The way her head tips back just slightly, the way her eyes close before the sound escapes, as if even her body hesitates to give the world something that belongs to me.

That's what her laughter is…

Mine.

Sometimes I make her laugh just to remind myself that I can. It's not about the joke; it's about the response. About knowing that beneath the softness she pretends to own, I'm the one who orchestrates it.

"Stop staring at me like that," she says, nudging my knee with hers.

The corner of my mouth lifts, not enough to be called a smile, but I don't answer. She wants the sound of my voice, but silence holds more power.

I study her instead. The sunlight slipping across her cheekbones, the faint shimmer on her lips that catches every particle of light like it's trying to impress me. There's a birthmark beneath her left eye that she hates. She covers it with concealer when she thinks I'm not looking. I never told her that's the thing that keeps her human.

She laughs again, nervous this time. "Karma, I'm serious. You're creeping me out."

The wind shifts and her braids slide over her shoulder, long and deliberate, reaching almost to the curve of her waist. They move like they have their own rhythm, catching light as the ocean throws silver against them. She always wears them down her back like that. Controlled. Neat. Intentional.

I reach for her wrist.

My fingers find her pulse, steady but quick. I trace it with my thumb, feeling the thrum beneath her skin.

Still here, it says. Still beating for me.

Her glasses slide slightly down the bridge of her nose when she tilts her head. The frames make her face look smaller, softer, almost delicate. But I know better. I know the sharpness behind them.

Her skin is that deep almond shade that drinks in the sunlight instead of fighting it. And the tattoos crawl up her arms, wrap around her ribs, disappear beneath her shirt like secrets only I get to see. Script, symbols, ink layered over scar tissue. They don't just tell a story.

They testify.

Every mark says she survived something.

Every piece of ink says pain won't scare her away.

She calls them art.

I call them proof.

"Don't you like being watched?" I ask.

She gives me that look that is half amused, half wary. Her lips curve, but her eyes hesitate behind the glass. Still, she leans into me, unconsciously puts her hand over her stomach like she is hiding her imperfections.

Of course she likes being watched.

There are a thousand ways to measure love.

But for her? I measure it in surrender.

And Reya surrenders so easily now.

That's what time will do to a person: erode the edges, file them down until even defiance sounds like affection. Break them down, build them back up in your image, and they'll call it devotion.

I shift my gaze. The ocean is cruel in the most beautiful way.

It breathes like it is alive, each inhale dragging the world closer, each exhale spitting it back out, stripped of what it tried to keep. Salt cuts through the wind, the wind cuts through the heat, and everything folds into something raw, something that strips the world to its bones. The ocean never lies. It moves because it must. It drags what it loves under, keeps what it can hold, and spits out the rest like a confession. People call that chaos. I call it honesty.

Reya sits there like she belongs to it, eyes soft, pretending the waves are singing her peace. She clings to the sound the way the drowning cling to air, convinced it is mercy instead of warning. She doesn't understand that peace is just what destruction looks like when you've stopped fighting it.

That's what she never sees.

I am not the storm against her.

I am the tide.

And the tide doesn't chase. It waits. It pulls. It teaches you that coming back is not a choice; it's a current. And no matter how far she drifts, she will always return to me.

She calls it calm. I call it surrender.

"I forgot to tell you." She says, glancing toward the waves. "I bumped into someone the other day."

My grip on her wrist doesn't tighten. Not exactly. But it changes just enough to remind her I'm listening.

"Who?"

Her smile falters, just for a second. The smallest crack in a polished lie.

"Some guy at the grocery store. Nothing weird. He just asked how we were doing."

The name drifts between us, light but irritating. Like grit between teeth. I wait. I've learned silence makes people confess more than questions ever will.

She fills the silence with noise, something soft and harmless. A joke, maybe. Something about the guy's cologne. She's always talking when she's nervous. Always patching the air between us with words that mean nothing.

But people who have nothing to hide don't talk so much.

"I told him I was happy," she adds, turning back to me. "That I'm doing really, really well."

The repetition, *really, really,* it's a tell. She doesn't realize I notice things like that.

I study her, the way her throat moves when she swallows, the way her fingers twitch before settling on her lap.

She wants me to believe her.

And I do.

Because she's here.

Because she still tells me everything.

Even when I don't ask.

Especially when I don't ask.

She brushes sand from her thigh, and I watch the motion, absent-minded and familiar. Then she rests her hand on my leg, like she's staking claim. As if this is equal.

As if she is trying to convince herself that she made the right choice.

And Reya Carter has never liked to admit when she's wrong.

The waves crash again, pulling back with a sound like breath being stolen. She looks at the horizon, but I watch the reflection in her eyes instead.

She stands and reaches for my hand. I hold it out and let her help me up from our spot.

I step closer. The air between us smells like salt and her shampoo, and something I can't process. She doesn't look at me when she says it, barely above a whisper, like the words are fragile things that could drown if she says them too loud.

"I love you, Karma." She says.

Three words. Soft as sea foam, heavy as the undertow. They hang in the air between us, trembling, before dissolving into the sound of the waves.

I could tell her I love her too. I could give her that balance she always aches for.

Instead, I let silence answer. I let her feel it, the weight of my stillness, the way the world seems to just pause and listen. She glances at me, searching for something in my face, and I watch the exact second she decides to take my quiet as devotion.

That's the moment she gives the ocean to me and doesn't even know it.

Her words sink into me, settling deep, warm, absolute.

Chapter 2

11 Months And 3 Weeks After The Phone Call

We are on the road before the sun has fully clawed its way over the mountains. The city shrinks in the rearview mirror. The hotel towers dissolve into the heat and the neon signs are traded for desert.

The highway hums beneath the tires, a long-unbroken note that fills the car when she won't. The air outside is dry enough to taste; it scrapes the throat like sandpaper and sunlight. Mirage water dances ahead of us, blue for a second then gone.

Reya sits toward the window wearing a grey oversized hoodie despite the heat, knees pulled up to her chest despite the length of her legs. Her cheek pressed against the glass, her reflection stares back at her, solemn and double-exposed.

"You're quiet," I say.

"Just tired," she says as she shrugs her shoulders. She puts a smile on her face as she turns to me.

"Can you wipe the window where your face was? I hate the oil smudges." I reply to her as I turn the radio on low and allow a song from another decade to fill the space. The O-Jays singing us into a stillness.

The desert is endless here. Endless and flat and shimmering and biblical.

I've always liked it. The way it burns everything unnecessary away. Out here, you can see what survives.

I glance at her profile, at the small line between her eyebrows. "You'll feel better once you smell the ocean."

She nods, but her eyes don't change.

Hours later the air begins to thicken with salt. The wind through the cracked window carries something dam, something living. The sound of the waves is still miles off, but I can hear it already in my head, that slow collapse and pull.

The last time we went, she said the ocean made her feel free. I remember thinking, *then maybe I'll take her here again.*

She reaches for the dial, turns down the music. "Can we stop soon?"

"Soon," I tell her. "But in the meantime, tell me a story."

She turns her head toward me. "A story?"

"Yeah, you're always asking me for one. Now it's your turn."

I reach for her hand on the console, let my fingers rest on top of hers. "Tell me something good. Something that will get you out of that head of yours."

She watches the road ahead, eyes half lidded against the glare. I can see her thinking, reaching for words she wasn't prepared to find. When she finally speaks, her voice sounds far away, like she is telling the story to someone who isn't here.

"Once upon a time," she begins softly, "there was a moth who fell in love with a flame.

"Every night, she would fly close enough to the flame to feel the warmth. Not too close, but just enough to see if she could survive it. The flame told her she was special, said no other moth had ever made it that far without burning. So, she believed him.

"But the flame was never hers. It belonged to a candle that lit everyone who came near. And one night, when the moth finally got brave enough to touch him, the flame flickered higher. She thought the intensity was love. But it was just the wind."

Her voice fades, but she keeps looking at the road. Almost as if she is choosing her words carefully.

"The next morning," she says quietly, "all that was left of her was a small piece of ash stuck to the wax. People thought the candle had gone out for good, but it was just hiding the smoke, until the next moth came along."

She exhales through her nose. A thin-almost laugh. "Not a very good story, huh?"

I study her. "It's dramatic," I say. "Sounds like one of those books you like to read."

"Maybe," she says. Her mouth twisting a bit. "But I like to think the moth didn't die. Maybe she was just pretending to burn so she could see what the world looked like in the dark. What the world would look like without the flame."

I shake my head, smiling, but she doesn't see it.

She is talking in riddles again, weaving metaphors like spiderwebs.

Still, something about it unsettles me. The way she says *the flame wasn't hers.*

The sky outside deepens to orange, and the horizon starts to blur. Her hand slips from mine and she places it in her lap.

***

By the time we check into the hotel, she is quiet again. The kind of quiet that fills every corner of a room. She sits on the edge of the bed, still in her travel clothes, hands folded over her stomach like she is afraid of disturbing something invisible between us.

I watch her in the mirror while I wash my hands. The reflection makes it easier. I can study her without her knowing. She looks smaller here. The room is too big, the light too soft, like even the lamps know she doesn't belong to them.

"Long drive," I say. "You should lie down."

"I'm not tired."

I turn the water off and dry my hands slow. "What do you want to eat?"

"Anything is fine."

"Come on, babe," I press. "What sounds good?"

She thinks for a second. "Let's do tacos?"

I nod. "Alright. I'll go grab it." She is always trying to guess what would make me happy. Always trying to sense what I am feeling and bend to my unconsciousness. I love that about her.

She smiles, faint but grateful, and that small curve of her mouth feels like victory.

I take my keys and my wallet. "Lock the door behind me. And take a shower so you can get out of those travel clothes." I say before walking out of the room.

I wait in the hallway until I hear the door and the click of the lock.

Good.

The night air hits different here. It feels cold and alive. The sign from the diner across the street flickers against the car hood, blue and pink like bruises healing under skin. I slide into the driver's seat, start the engine, but I don't pull out right away.

For a moment, I just sit there, watching the hotel window

that faces the lot. The curtains drawn but I can picture her inside.

Pacing.

Maybe calling her mom.

My phone buzzes once on the passenger seat.

A message I don't open. Not yet.

I already know who it's from.

I pull out of the lot and let the thought of Reya Carter follow me down the road.

When I come back to the hotel two hours later, she is sitting cross-legged on the bed, hair pulled into her bonnet, the television murmuring Martin in the background.

I hand her the bag.

"Did you get tacos?" She asks peeking inside the bag.

"No," I say, unwrapping my burger. "That's what took me so long. I was driving for nearly an hour looking for a taco spot. I didn't want to keep you waiting so I settled on burgers. I'm sorry."

"Thank you," she says. Still grateful for the meal even though it isn't what she was craving.

Chapter 3

11 Months After The Phone Call

Reya hasn't been herself.

A little quiet, a little far-off.

Still the same woman sitting across from me at the breakfast table, but her laughter comes slower now, like she has to remember how it sounds.

I tell myself not to think too much into it. Women move through moods. She just needs grounding. Something to remind her who she is.

Who *we* are.

"I won't keep asking," I tell her, watching the way she stirs her coffee without looking up, "but I just want to be sure. Are you okay?"

"I'm okay," she says. Her voice lands light, like it doesn't want to leave her mouth. "Just overwhelmed. And tired. And missing my mom."

I reach across the table, take her wrist, and press my lips against the soft center of her palm. Her pulse flutters against mine. "Maybe we should get out of town," I say. "San Diego. You've always loved the beach."

The suggestion sounds generous when it leaves me. In truth,

she needs air, and I need to handle a few things out there.

She nods. It's small and polite. But not excited.

That's new.

Reya usually leans toward my ideas. She expands around them. This one just lands on her and slides off. I keep my expression soft.

"Or we don't even have to leave the state," I add lightly. "We could just disappear for a weekend. No phones. No people. Just you and me."

Her fingers tighten around the mug. Not noticeably. Just enough.

There's a wall there. Not brick. Not yet. But drywall.

Thin. Hollow.

I smile anyway.

"You know," I say, leaning back in my chair, "this reminds me of that time I said you would survive a zombie apocalypse because you talk too much."

That gets a flicker.

Almost a smile.

"I change my mind, you would definitely die right now."

She rolls her eyes faintly and smiles. There it is.

"But I, on the other hand, would survive. Because I would sing my way out of danger." I start singing, low and dramatic, off-key on purpose. "I would walk five hundred miles…"

She exhales through her nose.

Not laughter.

But close.

I stand, come around the table, slide behind her chair. I let my hands rest on her shoulders. Not heavy. Not claiming. Just warm.

"You don't get to go quiet on me," I murmur near her ear. "That's my thing."

She stills.

I soften my tone immediately.

"Hey," I say, pressing my cheek lightly against her hair. "You're allowed to have bad days. But you don't have to carry everything alone."

That line usually works. Offer safety. Offer partnership. Make her feel seen without asking too many questions.

She leans back slightly into me.

Not fully. But enough and I take it.

I hum again, softer this time. Something stupid. Something harmless. My hand drifts down her arm slowly, steady rhythm. Familiar rhythm.

People don't leave comfort. They drift toward it.

"I love you," I tell her, simple.

If she's pulling away, it's because she's tired.

Or thinking.

Or being influenced.

I can fix tired.

I can outlast thinking.

I just need her close again.

And once we're in San Diego, once it's sun and salt and no one interrupting, she'll remember.

She always does.

Chapter 4

10 Months 2 Weeks After The Phone Call

She's been gone longer than she said she would.

No text. No call. Just the ticking of the clock and the stripes of sunlight cutting through the blinds, shifting inch by inch across the floor like they're keeping time better than I am.

She told me she had a dentist appointment. Just a cleaning. Said she'd be in and out.

I didn't think much of it…except that I did.

Reya knows I love her smile. She keeps up with it for me. The whiteness. The symmetry. The way her lips curve when she laughs. That's not something you neglect. And I know she's insecure about it, she covers her mouth when she laughs too big, like joy should be rationed.

I picture her in that chair, head tilted back, mouth open under that blinding overhead light. A hygienist leaning in too close wearing latex gloves and making small talk.

"So are you married?" He might ask her.

"Not yet, but soon." She'll say it like that. Confident. Claimed.

The TV hums in the background. I flip channels without seeing any of them. News. Sitcom. Sports. Static. Back to news.

Three hours now.

A cleaning doesn't take three hours.

I stand. Sit back down. Stand again.

I check the appointment confirmation in her email. 10:00 a.m. Cleaning.

It's 1:17.

My phone vibrates.

Dad.

"Hey, old man."

"You sound tired," he says. "You workin' too hard or lovin' too hard?"

I grin despite myself. "A little of both."

He laughs, deep and easy. "When you gonna give me more grandkids, son?"

"Soon," I say. "Me and Reya are always trying."

It's the truth. In a way because I am trying.

Trying to have a child with Reya.

Trying to build something permanent.

Trying to create a reason she can't just wake up one day and decide she's different and wants to leave.

But she's scared. Always has been. Says she'd be a bad mother. Says the world doesn't need another version of her. That she already has a daughter and that was enough.

So, I told her I was fixed. Said I couldn't have any more kids.

Let her believe it was safe so she'd let her guard down.

Fear makes Reya hide. But trust makes her stay.

"If she gets pregnant," I tell him, half-laughing, "it would be a miracle."

He laughs. "Well, hurry up. Reya ain't getting any younger. And neither are you."

We hang up but the room is too quiet now.

I check her location.

Loading.

Loading.

Nothing.

She must've turned it off.

My jaw tightens.

She never turns it off.

Something doesn't feel right.

And when something doesn't feel right, it usually means something isn't.

I grab my keys before I consciously decide to.

The sunlight outside hits like accusation. I tell myself I'm clearing my head. But before I reach the car, I'm already typing "Reya dentist office" into my phone. Just to double check the address. Just to confirm I remember correctly.

The drive is short. I know every turn between our house and that office. I know where the light lags too long. Where she complains about the pothole near the corner. Where she always parks because it's "less crowded."

My grip on the steering wheel tightens at every red light.

I don't speed. I don't need to. I just need to see.

As I turn onto the street, I scan the lot before I fully pull in.

There.

Her car. Parked exactly where she always parks.

I don't pull in. But I slow.

I Watch.

I Count.

Ten seconds.

Twenty.

Thirty.

Nothing suspicious. No unfamiliar car idling beside hers. No movement.

I let out a quiet laugh. Of course it's there.

Of course she's there.

All that doubt. All that noise in my head. Gone. The world settles back into alignment. She's exactly who I thought she was. Exactly where she should be.

I drive past the office slow enough to see through the glass and I almost convince myself I see her silhouette in one of the chairs.

Almost.

Good enough.

I keep driving.

My pulse evens out. My shoulders loosen.

That's the thing about trust.

You don't give it once.

You test it.

And when it passes, you reward it.

When she gets home, I'll kiss her forehead. Tell her she looks brighter already.

And I won't mention the drive because love doesn't need to announce itself. It just needs to make sure everything is where it belongs.

Chapter 5

10 Months After The Phone Call

Reya thinks I don't hear her when she tiptoes out the door.

She thinks she's quiet.

She's not.

Every movement she makes has a sound. Her hesitation, her guilt, the way she stands too long in doorways like she's waiting for permission she won't ask for out loud. Even the silence she leaves behind has volume if you know how to listen to it.

And I do.

I sit on the edge of the bed for a minute after she's gone, thumb tapping absently against my leg. The house feels bigger without her in it. Too big. Like the walls lean back and breathe differently when she's not here.

I don't like it.

I don't like the shift.

I don't like the way the quiet changes shape when she's not filling it.

I tell myself she's only going to the store. Nothing dramatic. Nothing suspicious. Just groceries. Bread and milk or whatever she thinks we need.

But my chest still refuses to relax.

She's been too quiet lately. Too internal. Too far away inside her own head. Sometimes she looks at me like she's trying to remember who I am, like she's comparing me to some version of myself she prefers.

I hate that look.

It makes me feel…replaceable.

I grab my keys.

I don't want to sit here waiting like some man who doesn't know his place in the world. The house is too still without her hovering around in that soft way she does, always half anxious, half grateful. I don't want to think too long. Thinking turns into noise.

Noise turns into doubt.

And doubt turns into her creating problems I didn't give her.

I get in my car, but I don't go to the grocery store.

I go to the gas station down the street instead, the shitty one with flickering lights and pumps that move slower than my patience. I pull into an empty stall and let the engine sit there idling, vibrating softly under my hands.

I'm not getting gas.

I'm letting the minutes pass in a place she doesn't know to look.

I watch people come and go. Men in neon vests, women with messy buns, teenagers buying snacks. Everyone has somewhere to be. Something to do. Someone waiting on them.

Reya has me.

And that should be enough.

I unlock my phone and check the messages even though I already know what I'll find.

Nothing from her.

I scroll up our thread, reading old messages. Her long ones, the ones full of softness and apologies and "I'm sorry if I upset you" and "I just miss you." I stop at the one where she told me she didn't deserve me.

That one always hits good.

Not because she's right.

Because she believes she's right.

Reya doesn't understand she needs me more than she loves me.

Most people don't get the difference.

When she finally texts me that she's at the store, I smirk.

Of course she checked in.

Of course she told me without me asking.

Of course she reached for me the way she's supposed to.

I take my time typing back: Don't forget I like the wheat bread. The white stuff is pointless.

I picture her standing in the aisle, second-guessing whatever she originally picked. Putting something back. Reaching for what I like instead. Fixing the mistake before I even see it.

Reya is different because she listens, she learns, she adjusts.

My phone buzzes with one more notification. Not from her, from someone I've been ignoring.

I swipe it away.

That's the thing people don't get about me, I build order. Structure. Predictability. I make systems. People fit into them or they don't. Reya fits into them.

Reya was born to fit into them.

When she cries or spirals or asks questions that make her

doubt me, it's not because she's unhappy. It's because she's scared of disappointing me. That fear is healthy. Fear keeps people anchored.

Fear keeps them loyal.

Fear feels a lot like love when you mix it with longing.

A siren passes somewhere behind me, loud and distant. I check the time.

I shouldn't have to wonder what aisle she's in.

I shouldn't have to wonder who she's talking to.

She doesn't cheat. Not anymore, at least. I know that.

We both had our "oops". Our one "I'm sorry I lied to you".

I tap the steering wheel twice, start the engine, and pull out of the lot. I drive slow as I pass the grocery store, not stopping, not turning my head. I let the car keep moving while my eyes flicker toward the parking lot.

I don't want her to be scared of the world. I want her to be safer with me than without me. I want her to understand that I know how to take care of her in ways she doesn't even know she needs yet.

I circle the block once, then twice…then I text my brother: You out?

He responds immediately: At O'Malley's.

Of course he is, but I need to talk to him in person. Get a feel for his relationship with Reya. I need to know if he is the one that's been in her ear.

The bar smells like old wood and citrus cleaner. Low lights. Televised game nobody's really watching.

He's at the far end of the bar still holding onto the 90's like it's a personality trait.

His hair freshly shaved, low.

Interesting.

I don't acknowledge it, but I peep it. Put it in my pocket for later.

His white T-shirt is crisp. His oversized jeans are bunched at the ankles. His Timberlands, that have no business being worn in the Las Vegas heat, are wide and center of attention.

He looks like he stepped out of a time capsule, except his eyes don't match the nostalgia.

They're sharp. Present. Calculating in a different way than mine.

He grins when he sees me. "Karma! Look who escaped."

I slide into the seat across from him.

"I leave the house," I say.

"Without her?" He asks.

Not accusatory. Just curious.

The bartender sets down a whiskey without me asking. I nod once.

"She's fine," I say. "Just emotional."

He snorts. "They all are."

Not wrong.

"Reya is different, now." I add. "She's not weak. She just needed structure."

He leans back, slow, studying me the way he studies everything. He doesn't rush responses or tries to fill the silence.

"Structure," he repeats.

"She spirals," I continue. "Questions things that don't need to be questioned. You give them too much room, they start inventing problems."

He lifts his beer. Takes a sip. Watches me over the rim.

"Or," he says evenly, "you could just answer the questions. Unless she is asking questions because something doesn't add up."

I don't blink. "It adds up," I reply.

"For you," he says.

There it is.

Not advice. Not accusation. Just a mirror.

"She parked on the far side of the store the other night," I say casually. "Sat in the car ten minutes before going in."

His eyebrows lift slightly. "You watching her now?"

"I pay attention." I say. And I watch him for any shift in his body language. There isn't one.

He nods once. Not agreeing. Just logging it.

"The difference between attention and surveillance," he says lightly. "One makes people feel safe. The other makes them feel small." He takes a sip of his drink.

"She doesn't feel small." I argue. But I know there is no point.

"You sure?" He asks.

No edge. No heat. Just a question placed gently on the table between us.

I take a sip of whiskey instead of answering.

He drums his fingers once against the table. "You ever think you work too hard?"

"Work too hard for what?"

"To make sure nobody leaves."

I smile faintly. "People don't leave me."

He tilts his head. "You say that like it's a fact."

"It is."

He shrugs. "If you have to manage someone into staying, that's not staying."

I let the silence stretch. He doesn't rush to fill it. He never does. Maybe we get that trait from our father.

"You love her?" He asks finally.

"Yes." And I mean it. Reya is different. She is my favorite adrenaline rush. My storm when I ask for peace.

He nods. "Then why you always sound like you're strategizing?"

I inhale. "I'm not."

He looks at me for a long second.

"You are," he says calmly. "You just call it something else."

I don't react.

He leans forward, elbows on the table. "You don't gotta answer me. Just…think about why you need her to feel smaller than you in order to feel secure."

I don't flinch.

I don't defend.

I don't explain.

"She needs me," I say instead.

He studies me again. That same sharp, quiet gaze.

"That's what you told yourself about the last one."

I finish the whiskey in one swallow. "And she came back," I say as I slam the glass on the table, a little harder than I intend.

He doesn't smile at that. "Yeah," he says slowly. "They usually do."

There's something in his tone. Not judgment. Not approval. Just pattern recognition.

I check my phone.

No messages from her.

Good.

I stand and he doesn't stop me.

"Don't ruin this, Karma." He says as I walk away.

I glance back at him. "I won't ruin it."

"I actually like this one." He yells to me, but my mind is already somewhere else.

He just watches me leave. Like he already knows something I haven't admitted yet.

When I walk into the house later and see her unloading groceries, wheat bread on the counter, everything lined up neat, I feel a calm settle over me.

I kiss her forehead, warm and soft, and I look in her eyes.

She looks tired.

Small.

Grateful.

Good.

A woman who relies on you is a woman who stays.

And Reya?

She's staying.

She always will.

She's too deep into me to climb out now.

And even if she tried…I'd be right here.

Waiting.

Pulling her back where she belongs.

Her phone buzzing takes me out of my head. It causes me to jerk up at her. She hardly gets notifications, so it imbalances me.

"Who is that?" I ask. Not accusatory. Well, not exactly. But interested.

"Ava," she says casually.

"Oh," I say. Showing no reaction. "Is she still pushing that girls trip thing?" I ask. "Ya'll are too grown for that, Reya."

"She was just checking on me." She says it in a way that tells me I shouldn't care. And I don't care. Not really. Except for the fact that Reya's family is toxic. From her abusive father, to her emotionally unstable mom, to her selfish sister. But it's family, so I play along.

"People only check when they want something." I say. Ava hadn't been there for Reya for years. I had to hold my composure every-time she would tell me a story from her past. I had to pretend that it didn't affect me as much as it did. But in reality, they all could have done a better job at protecting something so fragile. Now I'm here picking up the pieces. Molding her into a woman.

She is filling the space with pointless pleasantries.

"You don't have to defend her," I interrupt her before she spirals. "I know you care about her. I'm not saying cut her off. Just be careful. You've been doing well not letting other people get in your head. Don't go backwards."

I say it like a true therapist. Like a man who really wants what is best for her. What is best for us.

She decides not to text back, and I pull her in close.

"That's growth," I say as I let the silence fill the air.

Chapter 6

9 Months After The Phone Call

We need a storage bucket.

That's it. That's the whole errand. A five-gallon bucket for the garage, maybe two, something with a lid that actually seals. Reya has been reorganizing the garage for three weeks in her head and apparently today is the day her head decided to make it real.

I didn't need to come.

She didn't need me to come.

But she made that face when she mentioned it. Not asking, just mentioning, the way she does when she wants company but won't say so, and I grabbed my keys.

The store is the usual Saturday chaos. Flatbeds cutting corners. A child sitting inside a display bathtub while his mother pretends not to know him. The particular smell of lumber and something chemical underneath it. Reya walks beside me easy, no agenda.

She is an Electrician, she belongs in hardware stores the way some women belong in the nail salon.

We find the storage aisle without needing the signs.

"Okay," she says, stopping in front of the display. She crosses her arms and surveys it like she's making a real decision. "Five gallon or six."

"Five."

"What if I need six?"

"For what, Reya?"

"I don't know yet, *Karma*. That's why I'm asking about the six."

I look at her. "You don't know what you need the bucket for."

"I know I need a bucket." She picks up a lid, checks the seal, puts it back. "I just don't know how much bucket I need."

"Get the five. If you need more space, get two fives."

She considers this with more gravity than it deserves. "That's actually smart."

"I know."

She cuts her eyes at me and I almost smile.

She's reaching for the five-gallon when I notice him.

Plain clothes. Older guy, maybe fifty, moving with that particular stillness that isn't browsing. He's in the next aisle over, visible through the shelf gaps, and he's got his phone up at an angle that has nothing to do with checking a shopping list. His eyes are tracking someone further down the row.

I follow the line of his attention.

A younger guy. Maybe twenty-five. Hoodie despite the heat. He's got three or four drill bits in his hand and he's doing that slow, casual drift toward the end of the aisle that isn't casual at all.

"Hey," I say quietly.

Reya looks up from the bucket lids, fidgeting with the bracelet around her wrist.

I cut my eyes toward the aisle without moving my head.

She follows the look. Takes it in. The plain clothes. The younger guy. The drift.

Her whole face changes. It's instant. Eyes lighting up, lips parting just slightly, like she just found something worth rooting for.

"Oh, he better run," she whispers.

I lean in closer without thinking, my shoulder brushing hers. "What?"

"He needs to go. Right now. Pick up the pace, baby." She says it under her breath like she's coaching him from the sideline.

I huff out a quiet laugh, shaking my head as I angle myself beside her, close enough that our arms stay touching. "You're rooting for the thief."

"I'm rooting for the underdog."

"He's stealing drill bits, Reya. That's not an underdog story."

"You don't know his life, Karma."

"I know he's got four drill bits in his hand and no basket."

She waves this off, her shoulder bumping mine like she's brushing my logic away with her whole body. "Maybe he forgot his basket."

"He didn't forget his basket."

"Maybe he didn't *need* a basket."

I look at her for a long moment. "Of course he doesn't need a basket, he is stealing." I let my lips curl into a smile at the audacity of it.

She ignores me and turns back to the aisle, watching through the shelf gap with her arms still crossed, invested now. The younger guy has slowed his drift. He's clocked something. His eyes move.

"He knows," I say.

"He doesn't know."

"He knows."

She makes a small pained sound, leaning forward like she can will the outcome to change. "Just walk normal. Walk normal."

The plain clothes guy shifts his angle slightly. Still hasn't moved in. Still documenting.

"He's going to get caught," I say.

"He's not going to get caught."

"Reya."

"He just needs to commit. You can't half-commit to something like this, that's how you get caught. You either go or you don't go, there's no…"

I turn and look at her fully, not even pretending to watch the aisle anymore.

She stops.

Looks back at me.

"What?" She says.

"That's a very specific philosophy you have there."

"I'm just saying."

I tilt my head slightly studying her, closer now than I need to be. "You sound like you have personal experience."

She opens her mouth. Closes it. Picks up a bucket lid she has no interest in. "I watch a lot of documentaries." She laughs, and I can't help it…I smile with her, because everything she does feels like something I want more of.

"What kind of documentaries?"

She doesn't answer.

I step a little closer, lowering my voice just enough to make it ours. "Reya."

"…True crime."

I nod slowly. "Right." I put my hand at the small of her back, breathe her in.

She sets the lid down. "Can we focus please?"

"I am focused," I say. "I'm very focused."

She cuts her eyes away from me, but her mouth is doing the thing it does when she's trying not to react. That small war between her face and her dignity that she loses every time.

And I let myself watch it happen.

Back in the aisle, the younger guy has gone still.

He puts the drill bits back.

Every single one.

Slow. Deliberate. Back on the hook like he was just looking all along.

Reya makes a sound like air leaving a tire. "Oh, come on."

I glance at her, amused. "Justice," I tell her.

"That's not justice, he didn't even try."

"He absolutely tried."

"He didn't follow through."

"That's the point."

She turns to me, offended now, stepping closer like she needs me to understand. "You don't half-do something like that. You either do it or you don't do it."

"You're very passionate about this."

"I just don't like wasted potential."

"Wasted potential," I repeat.

"Yes."

"For drill bit theft…"

"You're missing the bigger picture."

I shake my head and reach for the bucket she was about to grab, my fingers brushing hers for just a second longer than necessary.

She watches me for a second and I don't look away.

Then, slowly, her eyes move up toward my face.

She squints.

"What," I say, already shifting my attention fully to her.

She leans in slightly. Not touching. Just looking.

I don't move. "What? What? What is it?"

"You have one rogue ear hair."

I blink.

"That's not true…"

"It definitely is." She nods, satisfied. "It's doing its own thing. Completely independent."

I huff out a quiet laugh, shaking my head. "That's not real."

"It's very real. It's committed, too. More committed than drill bit guy."

I stare at her.

Not because I don't believe her. But because she's looking at me like that…like she found something worth keeping.

She smiles like she's proud of herself.

"You should let it live," she says, already turning back to the buckets. "It's cute, and it has personality."

I grab the five-gallon bucket and drop it on the flat cart.

She watches me.

Then grabs another.

Drops it in next to it.

"I thought you only needed one," I say.

"I did."

"And now you need two?" I ask her. More interested than angry.

"I evolved."

"That happened fast." I smile.

"What can I say, your ear hairs convinced me." She laughs.

And I laugh a little too, quieter this time, like I'm still caught on the way she said it.

We start toward the front, walking close without thinking about it.

She's still smiling to herself.

That quiet one.

The one she doesn't perform.

As we walk toward the register, she leans against the cart and glances at me again, like she is still halfway in whatever moment just happened between us.

"By the way," she says casually, "if we're talking about things that shouldn't exist…"

I already don't like where this is going.

"You eat ramen noodles like a college freshman," she finishes.

I look at her. "Ramen is good as hell."

"You put hot sauce in it."

"That makes it flavorful as hell."

"You eat it out of the pot."

"That's fewer dishes." I say as I point to my forehead.

She shakes her head slowly. "You are a fully grown man."

"And you're emotionally invested in a stranger stealing drill bits."

"That's different."

"It's not different."

"It's completely different."

We are moving toward the cashier when I say it.

I don't plan to; that's the part I notice later.

"You want to know something about me that nobody knows?"

She looks up at me. Something in her face goes careful, like she is afraid to react too big and scare it off.

And for the first time since we walked in here, she's not joking.

"Yeah," she says. Quiet. Like she's been waiting for this without knowing she was waiting.

I keep walking, but slower now, just enough that she stays right beside me. Eyes forward. "I don't sleep well." I tell her. "I haven't in years. At three, four in the morning I'm just…up. I can't shut it off. I never could."

She doesn't say anything. She's smart enough to know I'm still talking.

"But lately…" I pause. Not because I'm searching for words. I know exactly what I am about to say. I've been deciding if I should say it since the drill bit aisle. "It's quieter. Since you chose me, I don't wake up the same way."

I feel her looking at me.

I don't look back.

"I've never told anyone that," I add.

And then I put the bucket on the belt and start unloading the cart.

She's still for a moment beside me. I can feel it without looking. The way she is holding the words, turning them over, deciding what they mean. Deciding what she means.

I let her decide.

We step out into the parking lot and the air hits different out here. It's a little warmer. A little quieter.

She pushes the cart with one hand, the other tucked into her sleeve.

Still smiling.

On the drive home, she puts her feet on the dash.

She hums along to something on the radio like she's exactly where she's supposed to be.

I glance at her, then back at the road.

I thought all we needed was a bucket. But standing in that hardware store with her, somewhere between debating thievery and laughing about ear hairs, it felt easy. It felt like us. And for a second, that felt like enough to make me believe I could do this with Reya.

Chapter 7

8 Months After The Phone Call

Reya moves differently when she feels eyes on her. She moves softer, like she's performing peace instead of actually feeling it. She's been drifting around the house all morning with that careful energy. Quiet energy. Measured energy.

Thinking.

I don't like when she thinks too long.

So I keep my eyes closed and let my breathing even out. Pretend sleep. It's amazing what people reveal when they believe you're unconscious. When they think judgment is offline.

I slide my arm around her waist before she can decide to move away. Protective. Women love protection.

She stiffens for half a second.

She thinks she's subtle.

I tighten my hold just enough to remind her where she is. My chin rests near her shoulder. My mouth close enough to her skin to feel the warmth.

I let a few minutes pass before I speak.

"Morning."

She startles.

Not dramatically. Just enough.

She wasn't expecting me to be awake this early. She was somewhere in her head. Somewhere I'm not invited.

That's new.

I open my eyes slowly and study her profile. She avoids looking at me. That's not fear.

That's calculation.

It doesn't feel like I'm losing her.

It feels like she's trying to understand me.

That's worse.

When a woman thinks she understands you, she starts asking questions she isn't ready for answers to.

"Can I ask you something, Karma?" She says. Her voice is light. Casual.

It's never casual.

"Always," I say.

Inside, I'm already mapping contingencies.

If she says Talia: confusion first. Then offense. Then distance.

If she says Ava: I pivot to exhaustion. Make her feel dramatic for asking before coffee.

If she brings up the past: I soften. Make it about trauma. Trauma buys time.

"What is something about you that nobody knows?"

I almost laugh.

Not because it's funny.

Because she thinks there's still something left to discover.

I close my eyes briefly not to think but to decide.

I have told so many versions of myself over the years that the original draft barely exists anymore. Before Reya. Before the nickname. Before Talia. Before anyone.

There was a boy once.

But he learned quickly.

People only love what they can control.

So I became controllable. Then I learned how to reverse it.

I inhale slowly, letting her scent settle into me. Cocoa butter. Vanilla. Soft things.

"Reya," I murmur against her shoulder, letting a smile lace my tone, "why do you wake up with questions?"

She shifts. Slight irritation. Slight embarrassment. Good.

"What kind of question is that, anyway?" I ask. Half joking, half serious.

"A normal one."

I turn my head and finally look at her.

"You know everything about me that matters. If there was something important," I continue softly, brushing my thumb against her hip, "don't you think I would've told you?" That's how you do it. You make them feel unreasonable for wanting more.

You make them feel special for knowing what they already know.

You give just enough warmth that they question their suspicion.

She studies my face for cracks.

There aren't any.

And whatever I was before Karma…stays buried for a reason.

I feel her watching me, searching. She's trying to line up the version of me she knows with the version she's starting to question.

I let my hand move slowly up her arm, not rushed, not hesitant.

Her breathing changes. It always does because the body is easier to influence than the mind.

I lean in, press my mouth lightly to her neck, just a ghost of contact. Enough to remind her I'm here. Not enough to satisfy anything she's feeling.

She exhales like she's been holding something in.

Good.

I shift closer, letting her feel the weight of me without giving her direction. No rhythm.

No pattern. Just presence. Unpredictable presence.

She turns her face toward mine.

Instinct.

I stop just before our lips meet. Close enough that she can feel my breath. That's all she gets.

Her lips part slightly. She leans in but I don't move.

That moment, that small hesitation, is where everything shifts.

"I love you, Reya," I say, low, steady.

Her breath stutters. "I love you too, Karma."

There's something different in it now. Less certainty. More need.

She tries to close the gap again, like if she can just reach me, she can settle whatever's building inside her. But I keep my hand at her chin. Not tight. Not forceful.

Just enough.

I hold her there.

Right on the edge of getting what she wants.

People show you who they are in that space.

In the waiting.

In the almost.

Her breathing gets uneven. Her body shifts closer without thinking, like she's trying to solve something that isn't meant to be solved.

I watch it happen.

I let it happen.

Because this is where she forgets the question.

This is where whatever she was about to ask, about my past, about Talia, about anything that requires clarity, starts to dissolve.

Not because I answered it but because I replaced it.

Attention is currency.

And I decide where it's spent.

She leans in again, softer this time.

Careful.

Like she's asking without asking.

Just long enough for doubt to creep in.

Just long enough for her to wonder if she did something wrong.

Then I close the distance.

Finally.

And the way she exhales into me tells me everything I need to know.

Relief.

Not just desire.

Relief.

That's the part that matters.

I keep it slow and controlled and let her settle into it like it's something she earned instead of something I allowed. Because if she believes she earned it, she won't question why I held it back.

My hand drifts along her side again, grounding her. Re-centering her. Rewriting the moment.

By the time I pull back slightly, her eyes are softer.

Clouded.

The question is gone.

Replaced with something easier to manage.

I brush my thumb along her jaw, watching her carefully.

She doesn't ask again.

She won't.

Not right now.

And whatever I was before this, before her, before the stories, before the versions, stays exactly where it belongs.

Out of reach.

Chapter 8

7 Months And 3 Days After The Phone Call

She's off.

Not emotionally but structurally.

Her responses lag by half a second. Her eyes track something internal before they land on me. She's conserving energy.

That's new.

I don't confront change while it's forming. I let it finish building. Then I decide whether to dismantle it.

She thinks I don't notice.

That's almost sweet.

She's on the couch pretending to scroll but the phone screen hasn't moved in forty-seven seconds.

I sit beside her slowly. Not touching. Presence before contact.

"What's going on with you?"

"I'm fine."

Too quick.

Too prepared.

I nod like I believe her.

Then I let silence expand.

Silence is uncomfortable for people who are hiding something. It forces them to fill it.

I don't look at her immediately. I study the edge of the coffee table instead. Slow breath in. Slow breath out.

"Babe." I say, softer. "I'm losing you."

Her body reacts.

"What?"

"I feel it," I say evenly. "It's like you're slipping away from me."

Not accusation. Observation. "You're quieter. Your energy's different." Then the pivot. "And I don't know what I did wrong."

That line never fails.

Guilt is faster than logic.

She leans toward me immediately. "Karma, I didn't mean to..."

I interrupt gently. No sudden movements.

"No. Don't apologize." I drag my hand down my face like I'm steadying myself. Let my voice thin slightly. "For once, I wish you'd just let me in."

That's the hook, *let* me love you.

Her eyes gloss over.

Tears form exactly when I expect them to.

"I don't want to lose you," I continue. "You're my peace, Reya."

Peace is important. People will destroy themselves to preserve what feels like peace.

"You're the only thing in my life that feels right."

That lands.

She collapses inward. Reaches for me and I let her.

Not immediately.

One second.

Two.

Three.

Then I close the distance because timing matters. Three seconds of cold makes warmth feel like salvation.

She melts into me.

"I'm here," she says. "I didn't leave."

"I know," I murmur. I wrap my arms around her. Restrictive enough that she feels held. Not enough to feel trapped.

"Don't do that again." Soft tone. Hard instruction. "I need you more than you know."

Need sounds romantic. It's leverage.

The rest of the day unfolds predictably.

Overcorrection.

More affection. More effort. More touch.

She folds herself smaller.

This is the part most men get wrong.

They demand reassurance.

I don't.

I let her offer it.

Rewarding effort without acknowledging it is more effective than praise.

"There's that laugh," I tell her when she laughs too hard at something that isn't funny. "I've missed you."

She dissolves into it like putty.

Later, I rest my head in her lap eyes closed. Not because I'm tired. Because vulnerability disarms suspicion.

Her fingers move on my shoulder.

Ownership disguised as tenderness.

Her phone buzzes then her fingers freeze.

Interesting.

She moves carefully, easing out from under me.

I don't open my eyes, but I make sure my breathing stays steady.

I listen. Footsteps to the kitchen.

Stillness.

No crying.

No pacing.

Just silence.

Longer than it should be.

Something is wrong.

But not catastrophic wrong. Not yet.

When she returns, her breathing is different. More controlled. More forced.

She slides back beside me like nothing happened.

Her hand rests on my chest but I feel the trembles.

I don't react.

Not tonight.

Tonight, I let her think she won.

Tomorrow, I'll measure the damage.

If someone is speaking into her ear…I'll find out who.

People who interfere with what's mine tend to regret it.

Chapter 9

7 Months After The Phone Call

It's a good day.

Not the loud kind.

She's softer when nothing feels wrong. Less vigilant. Less curious. More devotional.

My head is in her lap. She's tracing the side of my face like she's memorizing something sacred.

I let her.

"Tell me a story," she whispers.

Of course.

She always wants stories when she wants reassurance without asking for it directly.

"You and these damn stories," I mutter, but I don't move.

"Then tell me one I haven't heard."

I know exactly which one she wants. She wants to know more about Chaniece. She wants to know about the scandal. She wants to know about who made that FB post.

"Like what?" I say casually. I won't offer any information; I will let her ask me.

She kisses my forehead.

That's strategic. She thinks affection buys access.

"Tell me how you got your nickname."

I stop scrolling. That is not the story I thought she would want to hear. But I let the pause sit long enough to feel meaningful.

Then I smile slow. The way a man smiles before telling a story about how he built something with his bare hands.

"You really wanna know?"

She nods.

Of course she does.

Everyone wants to believe they're getting the origin story.

I shift slightly, still in her lap, but angled so I can look up at her. Eye contact from below disarms people. Makes the story feel confessional.

"They call me Karma," I begin, calm and steady, "because people who hurt me always get what they deserve."

I don't rush it.

"Jobs lost. Relationships implode. Friends turn on them. Accidents happen. Promotions disappear."

I shrug like it's coincidence.

"I don't have to do anything. Life just…balances itself."

I watch her face carefully.

The word *balances* always lands. I've used it before. On coworkers. On guys I've mentored. On women who needed to believe the universe was fair.

"And the crazy part?" I continue. "It always happens when they try to leave me."

There it is.

She stiffens.

Good.

I take her chin gently between my fingers and kiss her, slow and reassuring.

"It's not revenge," I say softly. "It's alignment."

That sounds better. It sounds more evolved.

More intelligent.

"I've always been like that. Even back when I was helping people through their messes…or managing guys who thought they were smarter than me."

I let that sit.

Ambiguous.

Professional enough to be convincing.

Vague enough to mean anything.

"You learn quickly who's loyal and who isn't. And the ones who aren't?" I smile. "They always circle back."

Her fingers hesitate on my head and I feel the shift.

Before she can spiral, I pivot.

"Speaking of circling back…" I sit up slowly. "You were at the store a long time last night."

Her face drains.

I keep my tone calm. Observational.

"And you parked on the far side. You never park there." I don't blink. "And you sat in your car for ten minutes before going in."

Her breathing gets shallow.

"How do you know…"

I laugh softly.

"It was simple math. It takes 7 minutes to get to the store. But it took you 17 minutes to text me you were actually inside the store." I lean closer. "So, I assume you sat in your car?"

"I did. I had to double check the grocery list."

"Babe, I pay attention."

That's what I call it.

Attention.

Not control.

Attention.

I touch her cheek.

"I just want to make sure you're safe."

She nods, slow, like she's letting it settle. "I know," she says softly.

"And one day," I continue, letting it sound like it just came to me, "I want to have a baby with you."

Her pupils dilate.

Fear and longing look the same at first.

"A baby grounds people," I continue, almost thoughtful. "Gives them something real. Something permanent. Something to be proud of."

Permanent is important.

People behave differently when something is permanent.

She swallows, then gives me a small smile. "You've been thinking about this?"

"About you?" I tilt my head. "Always."

I brush a strand of hair behind her ear.

"You'd look beautiful carrying my child." I pause, then add lightly, "I know I had a vasectomy." I let her relax.

Then, "But miracles happen every day."

"Yeah…they do," she says quietly.

I stand, stretching.

"I'm gonna shower." I look back at her. "Don't go anywhere."

Soft tone. Clear instruction.

I close the bathroom door behind me, but I don't turn the water on. Not yet.

I allow the house to go still. Silence does interesting things to people. It stretches their nerves thin. I stand there, hand resting lightly on the sink, and listen.

For a moment, nothing.

Then, a shift of fabric.

Her breathing changes.

Faster.

A phone vibration.

Soft, but distinct.

I don't move.

I count in my head.

One.

Two.

Three.

The couch creaks. Then footsteps.

Light and careful. Moving away from where I left her.

I smile.

Not wide.

Not obvious.

Just enough.

Because now I know. If it were nothing, she would have ignored it. If it were harmless, she wouldn't have needed distance.

The water finally turns on, and steam fills the room slowly. But I lean closer to the door, not touching it. Just listening through the hollow wood.

No crying.

No raised voice.

Just quiet panic.

Processing.

Good.

Panic is workable.

Panic makes people predictable.

I step into the shower and let the water hit the tile instead of me.

There's no rush.

Whatever has her attention, I'll find it.

People always slip when they think they're alone.

And I've never had trouble uncovering what someone thinks they're hiding.

When I turn the water off, I wait an extra ten seconds before opening the door.

Timing matters.

By the time I walk back into the bedroom, towel low around my waist, she's exactly where I left her.

Sitting.

Composed.

Too composed.

I tilt my head slightly.

"You okay?"

Her answer comes half a beat too late.

Chapter 10

6 Months And 3 Weeks After The Phone Call

Our home is dark when I unlock the door.

She's waiting for me.

I can feel waiting in a room. It has weight.

I step inside, keys still in my hand.

She's on the couch. Still. Too still.

Then she starts crying. Not subtle or quiet or cute. The kind of crying that rehearses itself before the audience arrives.

Interesting.

I close the door behind me.

"What's wrong?"

"I know you had a family emergency," she cries. She wipes the tears away, but I stare at her. She launches into a messy, frantic mess about my family emergency. Trust. Facebook group. Dating someone else.

"I didn't question you," she continues. "I trusted you…"

Ah, so there it is. That's the fire.

"I should have known from the late nights, the times you didn't come home at all. I should have fucking known." She punches me in the chest. Trying to release all the pain that has been pinned up inside her. Trying to punch away the tears.

But I am completely lost. "Whoa, what are you talking about, Reya?"

I take the phone from her and look at the screenshot.

I look at the picture. It is one I've sent before. Careless of me.

Or efficient of me. I'm not sure yet.

But my brain moves quickly.

It is an anonymous post that says something about "Are We Dating The Same Guy".

How does this come up twice in less than a week? It's peculiar, but no time to dwell on it now.

Who posted it? Doesn't matter yet.

What does she know? Not enough.

What does she need? Reorientation.

I let my eyes narrow slightly, not guilt.

Annoyance.

Annoyance works better.

"You really believe this shit?"

Her face shifts immediately.

Doubt creeps in. Good.

"I know who posted this," I say casually.

I don't. I haven't a clue who posted it.

But confidence fills gaps.

Some girl I used to talk to.

Timeline? A year ago.

Place it during conflict. That gives it logic.

"Reya, we were fighting all the time. You were living two lives. One with me and one with…" She blows her nose in her sleeve. "We weren't having sex…" That's it, shift history.

Make it mutual.

"So, I hung out with this girl Chaniece."

Pick a name that sounds real.

Neutral. Unthreatening.

"We went out a few times. But nothing happened."

Always say nothing happened. Never defend too hard.

"I ghosted her. Because I was in love with *you*."

That part I deliver smoothly. Like it costs me something.

And there it is, she melts a little.

"And now she's trying to get information." I hand the phone back like it's beneath me.

Then I laugh.

Light.

Dismissive.

"I can't believe you fell for that bullshit."

That's the pivot. If she fell for it, she's the one who made the mistake.

I know Reya hates when I drink, but I pour myself a glass anyway. Not because I need it. Because it signals calm. Unbothered men don't rush.

She's shrinking already. Her shoulders fold in. Her breathing softens. The fight drains out of her.

I walk toward her slowly and forgiving. I wrap my arms around her and rest my chin on her head.

"Babe…what do I have to lie for? I only want you." Then I add the closer. "I'll call her tomorrow. Tell her to cut the bullshit. She knows I'm done with her."

Done with her.

I say it casually. Like deleting a contact. Because that's what it is.

If someone becomes inconvenient, I remove them.

She grips my shirt tighter.

Reassurance through disposal.

She relaxes and we move to the couch.

I pull her in first. Physical containment after emotional disruption creates bonding. Her legs drape across me. She wants proximity now.

Good.

I let silence settle. She asks about nicknames. Interesting pivot. Deflection from the Chaniece story. Or something else?

"I started calling Delilah, Lyla…" She says soft. Innocent.

She asks if I've ever had a nickname.

I exhale lightly.

"Yeah." I say, although I'm trying to figure out why she's asking. "They call me Karma."

Her body stills.

"Who calls you that?"

I don't elaborate yet. I let her sit in it.

"Everyone who knows me," I add.

That part is intentional.

"Why do they call you that?"

I lean back and smile. Pride seeping through my pores. "Because I *am* Karma."

Simple.

Confident.

I don't explain further. People fill in their own mythology. I watch her face shift. She internalizes it immediately.

That's what fascinates me about her. She doesn't question the warning. She absorbs it. She reframes it. She turns it inward.

That's rare.
Most people want to run from the idea of consequence.
She leans into it.
Presses closer.
Like she deserves me.
That's the moment I know she's not leaving.

Chapter 11

6 Months After The Phone Call

My brother, Big Mike picks the place.

Low lighting. Exposed brick. Music loud enough to blur conversations but not drown them. A place that still thinks it's trendy.

He's already there when we walk in.

White T-shirt, as always. Oversized jeans, per usual. Timberlands planted wide. Cornrows braided straight back, parts sharp but thinning toward the crown where time has started collecting interest. The braids start strong at the hairline and thin out halfway back where the recession refuses to cooperate. He's got maybe three solid rows in the center and faith doing the rest of the work.

He looks like 1998 refused to let him go.

He grins when he sees me.

Then he sees her.

And his eyebrows lift just slightly.

Reya's wearing her braids down tonight. Long. Glossy. Sliding over her shoulder when she laughs. Her almond skin glows under the amber lights like the room was built around her tone. Glasses perched high on her nose. Tattoos peeking from under her sleeves like inked secrets.

She smiles at him before I can introduce them.

"Big Mike?" She says, arms extended like she's known him her whole life. "I've heard so much about you."

Her smile is open.

Too open.

Mike pulls her into a hug, amused. "All good things, I hope."

"Depends," she says, leaning slightly into the joke. "Your brother said you still think Jay-Z hasn't made a bad album."

Mike barks a laugh. And just like that, she has him.

I watch it happen.

The way she makes eye contact. The way she listens like the answer matters. The way she tilts her head just slightly when someone's talking.

She makes people feel seen.

It's a gift.

It's dangerous.

We sit and the drinks come.

Within ten minutes, the bartender knows her name.

Within fifteen, the couple at the next table is laughing at something she said about childhood trauma and Capri Suns.

She doesn't overshare. She calibrates.

That's what makes it impressive.

She knows exactly how much vulnerability to give without making anyone uncomfortable.

Mike leans back in his chair, watching her over the rim of his glass.

"Is she always like this?" He asks me quietly.

"Like what?"

"Shiny."

I glance at her.

She's laughing now. Full smile. Head slightly thrown back. She covers her mouth for a second, habit, then drops her hand when she remembers she doesn't have to hide it.

A man at the bar glances over.

Then again.

I feel it before I think it.

Heat.

Not anger.

Assessment.

I shift my hand to her knee under the table. Not squeezing. Just resting there.

A reminder.

She doesn't move it away.

Instead she glances at me and smiles, softer this time. Private.

I like that smile better.

The one meant only for me.

"She's good with people," I say to Mike.

"She's good with *herself*," he corrects.

There's a difference.

Reya leans toward Mike now, asking him about the braids.

"How long you been wearing them like that?" She asks, as she moves her hand close to his head.

He smirks and leans into her. "Since before you were probably born."

She gasps theatrically. "Rude."

He laughs again.

She laughs with him.

"I'm only asking because it's time to let them go. I see more scalp than braids." He pushes her shoulder and they laugh together again.

"I'm serious. I think you would look handsome if you embraced the bald." She says.

"And if you're wrong?"

"I'm a woman…I'm never wrong."

And for a second, something sharp twists in my chest.

Not jealousy. Calculation.

She doesn't even try.

That's the problem.

She doesn't even try, and people orbit her anyway.

The bartender refills her drink on the house.

"For the storyteller," he says.

She beams.

"See?" Mike mutters to me. "Shiny."

I take a sip of my whiskey.

She turns back to me suddenly, resting her hand on my chest like she needs to anchor herself.

"You okay, babe?" She asks softly. The way she looks into my eyes like she can see my soul, makes something soften inside me.

She always comes back to me.

"Of course," I say.

She smiles again, smaller, warmer.

But I notice something: When she laughs like that, big, loud, vibrant, she belongs to the room. When she looks at me like this, intentional, reserved, measured, she belongs to me.

And I prefer the second version.

Mike studies me. "You good?" He asks.

"Yeah," I answer.

But my eyes are still on her.

I don't want to dim her.

I don't.

I just want to make sure the warmth stays where it belongs.

When we leave, she slips her arm through mine, still buzzing from conversation.

"That was fun," she says. "I like your brother."

"I can tell," I reply. She doesn't hear what I mean by it. She leans her head briefly against my shoulder.

Satisfied and unaware, but I make a quiet decision. Next time, *we* pick the place.

Somewhere quieter.

Somewhere smaller.

Somewhere she doesn't have to shine so hard.

Not because I don't love her light.

But because light attracts attention.

Chapter 12

4 Months After The Phone Call

It happens in the quiet. Not during arguments. Not during drama.

Those are easy. This is subtler.

She's on the couch scrolling when I come out of the bedroom. Her posture is different. Folded inward. Thoughtful.

I knew this would surface eventually. She hasn't called her daughter in three weeks.

I noticed on day six.

By day ten, I stopped wondering if she would.

By day fourteen, I understood something important: If I didn't mention it...she wouldn't either.

Now it's day twenty-one. And it's finally caught up to her.

"Baby," I say lightly, dropping beside her. She slides into me without hesitation. Her body still trusts me. "You okay?"

She hesitates.

"I'm just thinking about Lyla. I feel like I haven't talked to her enough."

There it is. Mother guilt always arrives late. But when it does, it hits hard.

I nod slowly.

"She's good," I say. "She's with her dad. She's surrounded by love."

Validate the child.

Then elevate the woman.

"And you needed this time." My hand moves down her arm, steady. "You needed space to grow. To find yourself again."

She exhales.

Relief and resistance fighting each other. "You can't pour into her if you're empty."

"I know," she whispers.

She doesn't fully believe it, so I reinforce it. "Don't punish yourself for healing."

I kiss her forehead.

She's still tense.

So I reward. I reach behind the cushion and pull out the bracelet. Timing matters.

"I got you something."

Her attention shifts immediately.

From guilt to curiosity.

"Why?"

"Because you canceled that girls trip," I say. "Because you chose us."

Chosen feels powerful.

"Because you've been present and focused."

I brush my thumb over her wrist.

"You've been so…mine."

She softens instantly. Of course she does. I fasten the bracelet around her wrist slowly.

"I like knowing you're here," I tell her. "Even when you're in another room."

She hears romance. I hear tether. I lift her wrist to my lips.

"Thank you for loving me, Reya."

That's when it happens. The guilt dulls. Not gone. Just quieter.

And here's the part she'll never understand: If she calls her daughter right now, she'll feel torn. If she waits until tomorrow, she'll feel intentional. Tomorrow becomes easier. And easier becomes habit.

I hold her close.

Not tight. Just secure.

She relaxes fully into me.

The hierarchy rearranges itself without either of us saying it out loud.

Motherhood will always be there.

But right now?

Being here feels lighter.

And lighter is addictive.

Chapter 13

2 Months 2 Weeks After The Phone Call

They say dancing shows you who a person really is.

If that's true, then I'm in trouble.

The studio smells like fake plastic and candles trying to disguise sweat. The lights are low and golden, the kind that makes everyone look softer than they probably are.

Reya stands beside me like this was her idea to infiltrate my dignity.

"I can't believe you talked me into this," I mutter, adjusting the cuffs of my black button-down out of habit. I dress for order. Not for hip movement.

She grins at me.

The instructor claps. "Leaders on the left, followers on the right!"

I hesitate for half a second.

Committing to the left side of a dance floor shouldn't feel like signing paperwork, but here we are.

Reya bounces on the balls of her feet like she's about to win something.

"I should warn you," she whispers, "I dance like I'm allergic to rhythm."

I lean closer. "And I have two left feet."

"Perfect. We'll cancel each other out."

I don't think that is how it works, but before I can protest, the music starts fast, brassy, and unapologetic.

She steps forward when she's supposed to step back and collides straight into me. Instinct takes over. My hands land on her waist before I think about it.

Warm and solid and real.

"Wrong direction," I whisper in her ear, closer than I intend.

"I'm improvising." Her eyes are wide. Innocent. Mischievous. And just a little too pleased with herself.

That look.

That look has gotten me into more trouble than I'd ever admit.

"That's not what this is," I say, but there is no weight behind it. Not anymore.

I start counting under my breath. "One-two-three. Five-six-seven..."

Control the pattern. Control the frame.

She watches me for half a second then deliberately spins the wrong way. I catch her again, my grip tightening just enough to steady her.

I sigh. She laughs.

And something in me breaks open.

It starts as a breath through my nose. Then my shoulders shake. And suddenly I'm laughing.

Actual laughter.

The kind I haven't heard from myself in a while.

"You're impossible," I tell her.

She steps directly on my foot. "And yet," she says, "you're still here."

I look down at our tangled feet, then back at her.

"Because I like it." I tell her.

"Like what?"

"*You.*"

It comes out simple. Unpolished. No performance. I lean forward and kiss her nose before I can overthink it.

The instructor passes by and adjusts my hand higher on her back. "Relax your shoulders."

Reya immediately grabs my shoulders and shakes them. "Relax, sir. Like this."

She does some kind of exaggerated shimmy that should embarrass me.

Instead, I laugh again.

When did I start laughing this easily?

She is still holding on to me when it fades, her hands lingering like she forgot to let go, and I don't move them.

We try again.

One-two-three.

Five-six-seven.

This time, I stop forcing it. Instead of directing her like a project, I guide her and I can feel the difference in my hands.

Guiding is listening.

Directing is deciding.

She focuses on my chest instead of her feet. I focus on her breathing instead of the mirror.

When I spin her, she actually completes the turn.

Her face lights up like she just discovered fire.

"Did you see that?!" She shouts.

"I did," I say, ridiculous pride swelling in my chest. "Don't let it go to your head."

Too late.

The song shifts. Slower. The lights dim slightly and couples drift inward.

My hands settle at her waist again, but this time they don't feel rigid. They feel…natural.

"You're not counting," she says.

"I gave up," I admit.

"Good." She rests her forehead against my chest.

My heartbeat is steady. So is hers.

"Are you embarrassed?" I ask quietly.

"Never," she says. "Life is too short to be cute about it."

I study her.

"You don't care what people think," I say.

"I do," she replies gently. "I just learned to not let it stop me."

That lands somewhere deep. In a place I don't usually let things reach.

The song ends and we're slightly sweaty, completely off-beat, and smiling like idiots.

And I realize something uncomfortable.

I didn't think about work.

I didn't think about control.

I didn't think about outcomes.

I only thought about Reya Carter.

On the drive home, the windows are down. The night air rushes in cool and alive.

She sings at the top of her lungs. Loud. Dramatic. Off-key.

I shake my head.

Then I join her.

Worse than off-key.

She laughs mid-verse and keeps going.

At a red light, I look over at her.

"What?" She asks.

"You're going to be the reason I loosen up, huh?"

She leans back, satisfied. "That's the plan."

I reach over and lace my fingers through hers. Being with her doesn't feel like something I have to manage, it feels like something I get to enjoy.

Chapter 14

31 Days After The Phone Call

It's the night after the argument and the air has settled.

I can feel it before I see her, the way tension lingers in a room after it's been handled properly. Not gone. Just absorbed. That's how these things should work. No dramatics. No rehashing. Just time doing what it does best.

She's on the couch when I come out of the bedroom. Knees tucked under her, phone in her hand, not really looking at it. Waiting. I can always tell when she's waiting. Her body gives her away before her face does.

I don't rush.

I sit beside her, leaving a small space between us. Enough distance to let her notice the shift when it closes. She notices everything when she's unsure. That's not a weakness. It's attentiveness.

I sigh, slow and deliberate, rub my hands over my face like I've been carrying something heavy.

"I didn't mean to be short with you yesterday."

I watch her carefully when I say it. The way her shoulders lift, just slightly. The way relief reaches her before logic does. She starts apologizing immediately, taking responsibility before I've asked her to.

Predictable. But still…sincere.

I stop her gently. Say her name. Keep my voice soft. I don't want this to feel like a correction now. I want it to feel like reassurance.

"You didn't do anything wrong."

That's the part she needs to hear. I can see it land. The way her eyes gloss just a little, like something tight finally loosened. I lift her chin, meet her gaze. People need eye contact when they're being forgiven, even if they didn't technically do anything wrong.

"I'm human," I tell her. "I get frustrated. I mess up. That doesn't change how I feel about you."

It's true. Or at least, it feels true in the moment. Feelings are contextual. They respond to behavior.

She relaxes under my touch almost instantly.

I pull her legs across my lap, start massaging her calves, slow and steady. Touch is the fastest way to reset someone.

"You've been amazing," I tell her. And she has been. Thoughtful. Trying. "Most women wouldn't do half the things you do."

That's not a comparison meant to threaten, it's a distinction meant to anchor. I watch her chest rise as she takes it in. She wants to be different. She wants to be chosen. This confirms it.

"I just want to make you happy…"

"And you do," I say, and I mean it. Happiness doesn't have to be loud to be real. It just has to be consistent.

I kiss her knee, then her thigh, slow enough that she feels the intention. Gratitude works better when it's demonstrated. She melts into the cushions like tension was never there at all.

When I pull her into my chest, I feel her settle. This is the part she clings to. The softness after friction. The warmth that feels earned.

"See?" I murmur. "We're good. We always come back to each other."

She nods against me. I can feel her believing it.

She asks me to tell her a story.

She always does that, asks for stories when she wants closeness without interrogation. It's easier to listen than to ask directly. I tease her lightly, then agree. There's no harm in a story. Stories let you say things without committing to them.

"There was a man," I begin, keeping my voice even, rhythmic. Calm enough to soothe. "A man who lived a long time believing nobody could really know him."

I feel her react immediately. Her body tightens, then softens. She's already mapping me onto the story. That's fine. That's what stories are for.

"He had everything," I continue. "Attention. Admiration. People who thought he was strong and put together."

My hand traces her shoulder, grounding her while the idea settles.

"But none of it felt real until one day he met someone different," I say. "Someone who made him feel…less empty."

That part always works. Everyone wants to believe they're the exception. Her breath changes. I can feel it against my chest.

"He likes that she needs him. That she trusts him. It makes him feel important in a world that has always been cruel to him."

That's honest. Importance matters. Anyone who says otherwise is lying.

I tell her the man isn't used to feeling exposed. That some truths are dangerous if shared too soon. That timing matters.

"So he lies?" She interrupts.

I correct her gently. Not lies. Timing.

That distinction matters more than people realize.

In the story, the woman doesn't question him. She protects the feeling. She lets him be who he is. And because of that, he loves her more.

I let the silence stretch after I finish. Silence is where meaning settles.

She nestles back into me, tells me she likes the story. I believe her. Discomfort means she's paying attention.

I stroke her hair slowly, steady, like nothing important has happened.

From where I'm sitting, the story lands exactly how it's supposed to.

She feels chosen.

She feels like understanding me is part of loving me.

And she believes, at least for now, that whatever I haven't said won't matter.

That's enough.

For tonight.

Chapter 15

30 Days After The Phone Call

It's been a month with Reya by my side. One month since the night my wife called her.

Thirty days, and things already feels settled again. That's the word that comes to mind when I watch her move through the house like she understands the space, like she belongs in it. She doesn't hover. She doesn't ask permission for every little thing. She fits herself into this life without needing to rearrange it too much.

I like that.

She laughs easily. Sometimes too easily. But it's real. She's present in a way most people aren't. When I say something, she reacts to me, not just the words. That kind of attentiveness is rare.

"You always do that," I tell her.

"Do what?"

"Answer like you're trying to get it right."

She tilts her head. "Maybe I am."

"You don't have to," I say.

She watches me for a second, like she's deciding if that's true.

"Okay," she says finally. "Ask me something then."

I don't hesitate. "What scares you?"

She smiles at that, but it's smaller now. More careful. "Dang. You don't waste time, I see."

"I'm interested."

She looks down for a second, then back at me. "Being... misunderstood," she answers. "Like people think they know me, but they don't actually see me."

I nod slowly. "That happens a lot?"

"More than I'd like."

"Yeah, I can see that." I soften my tone.

Her eyes flick up to mine, searching.

"What do you want?" I ask.

She laughs again, a little breathless this time. "Like...right now, or in life?"

"Both."

"Right now?" She begins, glancing at me. "To not say anything that makes you think I'm crazy."

I smile, "Too late for that."

She nudges my arm, "See? This is what I mean."

"And in life?" I smile at her.

She takes a second longer with that one. "I want to feel... settled. Not stuck. Just...like I'm where I'm supposed to be."

I nod. "That's not crazy, I feel that way at times too." I place my hand in hers and we sit.

I let the silence lead me.

"If your soul had a color, what would it be?"

She laughs, shaking her head. "That's not a real question."

"It is to me. I want to know everything about you, Reya." I say, squeezing her hand just a little tighter. "We've known each other so long, but we never *really* talk. And you fascinate me."

She looks at me again, longer this time. "Green," she finally says.

"Green?"

"Yeah, like...alive. But also calm. Like it can grow, but it's not rushing."

"I think that fits you perfectly," I say.

I tell her enough about myself to keep the exchange balanced. Just enough to feel mutual. Shared, but not exposed. I've learned that people don't need details to feel close, they need permission to talk.

She confuses listening with intimacy.

That's not a mistake. That's how most people are.

When she looks at me like I've unlocked something in her, like I've asked the questions no one else ever has, I let her believe that. It makes her feel understood.

When I get quiet around other people, when I notice her mentioning someone else too casually, too often, I can feel her clock it immediately. She studies my reactions, now. Adjusts herself without me asking. That's not a flaw. That's awareness. That's emotional intelligence.

Some people would call that walking on eggshells.

I call it learning.

Today is nothing special. A Tuesday. No plans. No expectations. I'm on the couch, scrolling through my phone, tying up a loose end from earlier when Reya says she's running to the store. She asks what I want.

"Something sweet, something crunchy. Maybe something chocolatey." I tell her.

Clear. Simple. There's no reason to complicate it.

I hear the bags before I see them. Too many. Paper rustling. Movement that takes up space.

She sets them on the counter like she's presenting something. Smiling. Proud.

"I got options!" She beams. "Six, actually."

Options.

I don't look up right away. I don't need to. I already feel the irritation settle in. Small, contained, precise. I told her what I wanted. She decided to interpret instead of listen.

When I finally look at the counter, it's exactly what I thought. Ice cream sandwiches. Gummies. Chips. Cookies. A whole spread of effort aimed in the wrong direction.

"I said chocolate," I say.

She blinks then starts explaining. Tells me what she thinks I said. And that's the part that bothers me. Not the snacks. The rewriting.

"No," I say, calmly. "I said chocolate."

I keep my voice even. This isn't a fight. It's a correction. I watch her face as it shifts. Confusion first, then that little flicker of panic she tries to hide. She doesn't like disappointing people. Especially me.

"I don't know why you make things harder than they need to be," I add.

The sentence lands exactly where I intend it to. I can see it in her posture, the way her shoulders dip, the way she immediately starts looking for a fix. She offers to go back to the store. Apologizes. Takes responsibility.

I let it sit for a moment longer than necessary, then I wave it off. "Forget it. It's fine."

It isn't, but that's not the point. The point is that she understands now. The discomfort will do the rest of the work for me.

I walk into the bedroom and close the door behind me. Not slamming it, just enough to change the air. Enough to mark the moment.

I don't think about it again until she knocks. She's holding a cookie. An offering. A repair. When she opens the door, I soften my expression. Let the edge drain out of my voice.

"Thanks," I say as I take the cookie and kiss her cheek. Light. Brief. Not indulgent. Just enough.

She relaxes instantly. Like a switch flipped back into place.

I watch it happen and feel the balance return. This is how it works when two people pay attention.

She learns me.

And I make sure she knows when she's doing it right.

Chapter 16

The Phone Call

I pat my pockets; left, right, back.

Nothing.

"Shit."

The wheel jerks in my hands as I snap the U-turn. Tires shriek. The hum of the engine deepens under my foot, vibration running up my leg. My pulse is in my throat, pounding like someone's knocking from the inside. I can't remember if I deleted my messages or not.

Either way, Talia knows better than to touch my phone. Took years to make her the woman I needed: eyes down when I say, smile when I want, silence until I'm done talking.

Years to train her.

But still…women are nosey.

I roll up the driveway too fast, gravel spitting under the tires. The car stays running like a low growl in the background. When I hit the porch steps two at a time, my palms are slick but my face is stone. I fix my jaw before I turn the knob, because the last thing I'm doing tonight is walking in here looking guilty.

"I thought maybe you'd have the decency to own up to it, Reya. But I guess I was wrong." I hear her say the second I push the door open. Talia is holding one phone to her ear, while holding another phone in her hand. *My phone.*

Shit. Nosey ass.

The air smells faintly of lavender from one of her candles, and underneath it, her perfume.

My gaze does a quick sweep: her stance, her hands, the angle of her shoulders. My mind files away the little details without thinking. Where is my phone, how close she is to the door, the way her weight shifts on her heels.

I cross the living room in three long strides. My shoes scuff the hardwood, sharp against the quiet. I take my phone from her hand; slow, deliberate, my eyes lock on hers like I dare her to pull back.

My wife's eyes do not flinch. They just…look. Not wet with tears, not sharp with fury. No heat at all. Just a blank, steady stare that makes my gut shift. I've seen her hurt. I've seen her mad.

I've never seen her gone.

"Reya? Really?" She asks, voice flat enough to cut.

"Talia, I told you not to go through my phone." My tone drops low as I step forward, closing the space until the tips of our shoes touch. "It's an invasion of privacy."

She tilts her chin up, her breath brushing my jaw. "You always do this to me." A small shake of her head. "And I'm tired of it."

My jaw ticks. I catch her wrist, not hard, but enough to feel the quick flutter of her pulse. "Whatever she said is a lie."

"She didn't say anything," she says, steady as glass.

She slips her wrist from my grip. No yank, no struggle. Just gone.

I follow her out to the car, catch her by the arm before she can get in. My voice is low, urgent. "Don't do this. You're the only one who understands me, Talia. You're my anchor. My peace."

She meets my eyes, soft but unshaken. "You love her," she says quietly. "I can tell by the messages. You never felt that way toward me. Just let me go."

I drop to my knees and wrap my hands around her waist. I bury my face into her stomach, the stomach that is so familiar, so warm. "Don't walk away from me."

She puts a hand on the back of my head and the subtle pressure makes me bury my face deeper into her. I smell her. I kiss her.

"Not this time, Karma." She says. Still no tears. Still no emotion.

I lean closer, fingers tightening on her arm until I feel the muscles tense under my grip. "I will never let you go, Talia."

Not a promise. A sentence.

***

The click of the front door echoes behind me.

Talia's perfume is already thinning in the air. I look at the phone in my hand, three missed calls from Reya glaring up at me.

She's still there. Waiting.

Talia, though…that look in her eye says she might not be.

I step into the kitchen, leaning against the counter. My thumbs move fast: Where are you? I fire off to Talia.

No read receipt yet.

I call Reya and she answers so fast it's like she's been holding the phone in her hand.

"What the hell, Leven! You're fucking married?" Her voice comes sharp, almost shaking.

"First of all," I say, letting my voice drop into that slow, steady tone I know makes her second-guess herself, "Calm your tone. Who are you cussing at?"

There's a pause. "Sorry, I was just..."

"I don't care if you're mad or not. You know you can't talk to me like that."

"Sorry," she says again, quieter this time. "You're married? And you failed to mention it?"

I roll my eyes, exhaling through my nose. "I didn't think I had to mention it because me and Talia are through."

There's silence on Reya's end. I know she's thinking, weighing her options.

"I know I should have told you," I add, softening my tone, "but I didn't think it was necessary since me and her haven't been a thing in years."

"But..." she starts, then stops herself.

I don't give her the space to build momentum. "I have no reason to lie to you, Reya."

"True," she says, and there it is, that little drop in her voice that tells me she believes me.

Enough for me to know that the tide is already turning back to me.

Part 2: Her Side

Reya

I have made the same mistake twice.
Once with my eyes closed.
Once with them open.
I'm only telling you about the second time.

Chapter 1

1 Year After The Phone Call

I stopped laughing long ago.

But today, I laugh. Mostly at him, though.

The wind is sharp, carrying salt and something sour, like old seaweed baking in the sun. The sand grinds between my toes, dry and stubborn, clinging to skin that doesn't want it. The ocean stretches in front of me like a secret I've already learned the hard way: vast, cold, and always pulling something under.

I stopped calling him by his name many months ago when his nickname suited him so well.

Karma.

And Lord knows he is my karma.

He's watching me again, trying to read me the way he used to.

"Stop staring at me like that," I say, nudging his knee.

He doesn't answer. He just smiles, and Lord help me, I love that smile. I love that smirk. I still love everything about him: the way his jaw clenches, the way he's always curling his hand into a fist like he's holding back the world. I love everything about him, but I know he's danger.

"I'm serious, you're creeping me out."

"Don't you like being watched?" He asks.

The sound of his voice slides under my skin like a memory I can't scrub out.

He looks away, pretending it's playful, and that moment, those few seconds of space, are enough for me to breathe again. To pull myself back. I press my hand to my stomach, aware of it in a way I wasn't seconds ago.

He's forty-eight. Old enough to know better. Old enough to feel safe.

His beard is salt and pepper, trimmed close along his jaw, sharp enough to look intentional but soft enough that I've memorized the way it scratches my skin when he kisses my neck. It makes him look distinguished. Grounded. Like a man who has already lived through storms.

His head is smooth and bald, the shape of it strong and clean. When the light hits it just right, it gleams. I used to run my palm over it absentmindedly, like it was a lucky stone.

And when he smiles, really smiles, the small gap between his front teeth shows. Not big. Just enough to make him imperfect. Just enough to make him *human.*

His eyes disappear when he laughs. They narrow into warm slits, crinkling at the edges, like he's holding back secrets or joy or both.

He is always groomed. Always put together. Crisp shirts. Clean shoes. Beard lined up. Nails trimmed. He moves through the world like presentation matters.

Except for his ears.

Tiny stubborn hairs curl out of them, impossible to tame. I used to tease him about them. He'd pretend to be offended, run a finger along the edge like he might shave them later.

He never does.

And for some reason, that's what I love most.

Because it reminds me, he isn't invincible. He isn't carved from marble. He isn't a god watching from above.

He's a man.

A flawed, aging, breathing man.

And somehow that makes him easier to forgive.

But I know I shouldn't let him in again.

My brain knows he's poison, but my heart?

My heart still drinks from the same cup. Still loves him with the same reckless hunger I had the day I met him.

And that is a dangerous game.

He is always watching. I learned that the hard way.

I actually did come to love it, the security of being watched, the illusion that I was precious enough to be guarded.

The wind shifts, tossing my braids across my face. It smells like salt and change. I dig my fingers into the sand just to ground myself, to remind my body where I am, not where he wants me to be.

"I forgot to tell you," I say, fidgeting with my sleeve. My voice sounds steady, but my stomach knows better. "I bumped into someone the other day."

His grip on my wrist changes. Not tighter, just heavier. Intentional.

I can feel his mind working through his skin.

He's cataloging the moment, deciding what it means, deciding if he needs to lie, deciding if this is the beginning of the end.

And maybe it is.

I caught him off guard. For once, he doesn't know what to do.

That small shift in his hand tells me everything I need to know.

I learned to sense the small changes in him. The shift in his breathing. The faint tension that rides up his arm before it reaches his voice.

"Who?" He says.

"Some guy at the grocery store. Nothing weird."

Breathe, Reya. Control yourself. "He just asked how we were doing."

The air between us thickens. The ocean keeps thrashing in front of me, waves colliding with the shore, over and over and over, relentless and loud. I pause, eyes on the horizon, pretending to watch the tide pull back. He reads my silence the way a hunter reads tracks in the dirt.

I can feel his stare tightening against the side of my face. The sunlight glints off the water, too bright to look at. I force a smile, but it doesn't reach my eyes.

"I told him I was happy," I say softly. "That I'm doing really, really well."

Breathe.

Just breathe.

I rehearsed this a hundred times in my head. I thought I was ready. But I'm not.

I had to tell him, though. He always finds things out. Always manages to turn a coincidence into a confession.

And now he's watching me, measuring me, the way he measures everything.

He always told me that guilty people talk too much.

And right now, I am proving him right.

So instead of explaining, I fidget with the bracelet on my wrist. Let my thumb trace circles on the charm that is shaped like the moon. My fingers move before my brain does. I brush sand from my thigh, slow, deliberate, like maybe it'll look natural. The grains cling to my skin, glimmering in the light before falling away.

I keep my gaze fixed on the water, even though the motion of it makes me dizzy. Each wave folds into another, unstoppable, untamed.

I rest my hand on his leg, squeeze just enough to steady the tremor in my wrist. I can feel him looking down at my hand, studying it.

He brought me to the beach because he thinks this is my happy place.

He thinks this is where I'm softest, calmest…where I'm still the girl who once believed the ocean could wash her clean.

But he's wrong.

The chaos of the waves, the sting of salt on my lips, the way the gulls scream over nothing.

This isn't peace.

The wind snaps against my skin, cold and wild. I don't flinch, I just let it hit me. I let it remind me that I still have a body, still have a choice.

If he really knew me, he would know this isn't my happy place.

"I love you," I whisper.

The words taste different this time. Not sweet, not safe. Just necessary. I need him to know that for me, this feeling is real. For me, this all-consuming love made me feel alive.

He doesn't answer.

He uses the phrase as control, never as a reply.

The silence between us hums with the sound of the waves devouring themselves, over and over, like they're trying to erase proof they ever touched the shore. Like they ever touched my heart.

The wind stings my eyes, and I tell myself it's the salt.

I turn toward the water so he won't see me cry.

The tide knows how to leave.

Chapter 2

11 Months And 3 Weeks After The Phone Call

"Can you wipe the window where you face was..." I hear his voice interrupt my thoughts.

I don't answer, I just move. My hand is already there before my brain catches up, dragging my sleeve across the fog like it's something I've always done.

And then a thought flickers in my mind.

Back to that trail, to that hike. To a version of me that felt too wild to be tamed.

I remember how the dust was kicking up with every step. The heavy, familiar heat of home wrapping around me.

And two paths.

The hot springs to the left. Easy choice. Obvious. Expected.

And the river to the right. Colder. Longer. *Uncontrolled.*

I remember standing there. Not asking. Not waiting. Just choosing what felt right to me.

"*You don't have to follow me...* "I had said, my voice light and teasing and mine.

In the car, the desert slides past us in hot, wavering waves. The sky is wide and empty, the kind of emptiness that makes you aware of how full your head is. I keep my body turned toward the window.

Karma clears his throat. "We'll stop soon," he says. Then, softer, "But in the meantime...tell me a story."

My fingers tighten slightly against my thigh.

He never asks me for stories.

That's always my thing.

He wants to draw me out.

He wants to read my insides again.

I inhale through my nose, slow and steady, letting the heat seep through the glass onto my forehead. Then I shift just enough so he can see the side of my face, the obedient angle of my chin.

Inside, something sharp curls up my spine.

You want a story? I'll give you one.

One you won't understand.

I wet my lips, keep my voice airy, almost embarrassed.

He glances at me. He likes when I talk soft. He likes when I sound unsure.

Good.

Let him think this is softness.

Let him think this is surrender.

"Once upon a time," I begin, letting the words settle between us like dust. "There was a moth who fell in love with a flame. This moth lived at the very edge of a quiet forest. A place where trees whispered to one another and shadows moved like sleepy ghosts."

The desert outside the window melts away in my mind.

I let myself slip into the story.

Into something bigger than this car.

"The moth was small," I say softly, "smaller than all the other creatures. Her wings were thin as pressed petals, fragile enough that a harsh wind could tear them. She spent her nights drifting between the trees, lighting up only when the moon touched her. And though her glow was faint, it was her own."

I don't look at him.

"One night, while she was out wandering, she saw a light in the distance. A warm, golden pulse, bright enough to make her pause mid-flight."

My voice lowers.

Gentler.

More reverent.

"She'd never seen anything like it. It flickered and danced in one place, steady as a heartbeat...It was a flame."

I swallow, letting the moment hover.

"The flame lived atop a candle on the windowsill of a grand old cottage. People came from far away just to light their lanterns from him. He was bold and tall and beautiful. The kind of beautiful that promises warmth even as it promises ruin."

The car grows quieter.

"At first, the moth only watched from afar. She knew flames were dangerous. She'd heard stories about tiny bodies that were swallowed whole, wings swallowed by heat. But this flame seemed different. He leaned toward her. Reached for her. Spoke to her in crackles and sparks."

I pause, tracing the window with my eyes as though I can see the story painted across the morning sky.

"He told her she was special. That no other moth had ever dared to get so close. He said he liked the way her wings shimmered in the dark, how she glowed for him when the forest had nothing left to give. And she believed him. But the flame was never hers. It belonged to a candle."

My heart begins to race because of how true it is.

"The moth came back the next night. And the next. And every time she came, she flew just a little closer. The warmth felt good. Safe. Like something she'd been searching for without knowing she was searching. The warmth was consuming. Different. Interesting. Addicting. She…"

I let my fingers curl in my lap.

"She didn't notice that her wings were thinning." I say, quieter now. I give him an unsure look. "She didn't see the tiny singes along the edges. She just thought love was supposed to hurt a little."

My voice cracks. Soft, almost imperceptible, but I let it.

"One evening, the wind picked up. Harder than before. Strong enough to push the little moth forward, closer to the flame than she ever meant to go."

The desert road stretches ahead of us.

But my mind sees a hand-drawn world of ink and gold.

"The flame roared higher, just for a breath. A sudden, wild leap. And the moth…she thought it was love. She thought it meant he needed her."

I pull a slow inhale.

"But the flame wasn't reaching for her. He was reaching for the wind."

Silence expands in the car.

"And when the wind stopped," I whisper, "the flame settled back down. Unbothered. Unchanged. But the moth fell. Her wings were charred; her glow was gone. She landed on the windowsill. Tiny, trembling, almost ash."

I can feel Karma watching me now.

But I still don't look at him.

"People who passed by the cottage said the flame burned her. Some said she was foolish. Some said she deserved it. They thought the flame went out, but it was only hiding the smoke until the next moth came along."

I finally lift my eyes to the horizon.

"That…wasn't a very good story, huh?" I whisper, letting a shaky laugh slip out. "Kinda childish?"

My voice cracks just slightly.

Karma gives a small, dismissive laugh.

"Dramatic," he says. "Sounds like one of those books you like to read."

I keep my head bowed for another breath. Then, slowly, I straighten. Just enough for me to feel it, not enough for him to notice.

"Maybe. But I'd like to think the moth didn't die," I say, stronger now. "I think she pretended to die. I think she pressed herself into the wax, let her glow dim on purpose, and waited. Patiently."

I sit up straighter.

Very slightly.

Just for me.

"She waited until the flame stopped paying attention to the windowsill. Until he forgot she was there at all. And then one night, when the cottage was quiet and the moon was full, she pushed herself free from the cooling wax."

My voice softens, but there's steel beneath it.

"Maybe the moth lost a little of herself along the way, but she didn't go to another candle. She didn't look for warmth ever again."

I breathe in the last line.

I let the story end there.

I blink slowly and give a small, self-deprecating smile, turning my face toward him like a girl embarrassed by her own imagination.

But inside?

Inside, I am smiling.

Because the moth just told the flame the truth.

My heart thumps once. Hard. Not from fear but from clarity.

Silence fills the car.

Karma looks back at the road. Jaw tight now. Clenching. Unease creeping in like fog under a door.

He doesn't understand the story.

Not really.

He heard a moth.

He heard a flame.

He heard longing.

He didn't hear the moth start to think for herself.

Or maybe he did.

***

When we finally make it to the hotel, my mind refuses to quiet.

It buzzes with thoughts, heavy and tangled, like a swarm of bees trapped behind my ribs.

My head knows I have a decision to make.

My heart…still wants to love him through it. Through all of it. Through the way he presses too hard, loves too sharply, watches too closely.

There's a part of me (a small, broken part) that keeps thinking about the little girl inside me who needed to be loved through her faults, her insecurities, her loudness, her softness, her everything.

And sometimes I look at Karma and wonder if some small boy inside him needed the same thing.

If maybe he pushes me just to see if I'll stay.

If maybe he needs me to prove love can be endured.

If maybe the breakthrough is always just one more day away.

He makes hope feel like a treadmill with a hot dog dangling just out of reach. Close enough to chase, never close enough to catch.

Every now and then, I leap for it, arms stretched, lungs burning but I always fall short.

And he always watches.

"Long drive," he says, snapping through the noise in my head. "You should lay down."

The hotel room is cold, the kind of cold that seeps into your ankles first.

The air smells faintly of bleach and ocean air trapped in the curtains.

The bedspread crackles when I touch it.

"I'm not tired."

My hands shake, part energy drink, part anxiety.

He watches my hands.

He always notices weakness first.

"You shouldn't sit on the bed with your travel clothes," he says casually, like he's correcting a child.

I stand immediately.

My body reacts before my brain catches up.

"Your bag needs to be unpacked. It looks sloppy," he adds, nodding toward my suitcase still upright by the door.

I nod, even though the knot in my throat is forming fast.

The sound of the zipper is too loud in the quiet room.

"What do you want to eat?"

His tone is soft, but I know better. This is not a question. It's a test.

"Anything is fine," I say. I keep my voice soft, even. But we both know it doesn't matter what I ask for.

If I say sushi, he brings back steak.

If I say burgers, he returns with fish.

If I say tacos, he returns with something no one asked for.

I could really use a burger.

A greasy, messy, real burger.

But I can't say that.

"Let's do tacos?" I ask, pretending to be unsure, to defer to him.

I even tilt my head the way he likes.

"Alright," he says. "I'll go grab it. Lock the door behind me."

He always says that.

Lock the door.

As if protection and confinement are the same thing.

He walks out, and I hesitate.

Then I follow. Quietly.

My bare feet barely whisper against the carpet as I go to the door.

Through the peephole, I see him.

Still there.

Standing in the hallway.

Waiting to see if I'll obey.

Of course I obey.

My throat swells. I know the script. I know the answer. I lock the door. Loud enough for him to hear.

I turn away from the door and almost break. This room feels too small, too bright, too full of sharp corners.

I rush to the window, part the curtain just enough. Thin enough for me to see him. Thick enough for him not to see me.

When he makes it to his car, he just sits in it. Engine running. Headlights off. Watching the hotel door like a hunter watching a snare.

He always waits.

Always checks.

He won't leave until I've obeyed every invisible rule.

Finally, the headlights flare to life and the breath I've been holding collapses out of me all at once. Sharp, broken, panicked.

I can't do this.

I can't do this.

God, I can't…

I clutch my sleeves to my face and cry into the fabric, muffling the sound. My knees buckle, and I sit on the floor beside the window. The carpet is rough under my palms. The air tastes like cold salt. But then, then I think about the moth.

The wax.

The flame.

I think about the nights I pressed myself small enough to survive.

And I force air back into my lungs.

Breathe, Reya.

The ocean is close.

With shaking fingers, I reach for my phone.

I dial the only number my heart could memorize in the dark.

Ava.

The ringing barely lasts a second before she picks up.

"Ava?" I breathe, except it isn't breathing. It's choking. It's drowning on dry land.

"Reya?" She says immediately. "What's wrong? What's going on?"

And just like that, just hearing my name in a voice that isn't demanding anything from me, I fall apart.

I press my forehead to the cold hotel wall, clutching the phone like it's the only solid thing in the world.

"I can't..."

The words are airless.

Ugly.

Bare.

"I can't do this, Ava. I can't, God, I can't..." I breathe fast and hard and unfulfilling. I can't catch my breath.

"Slow down," she says. Her voice smooth, steady, low. Like she's trying to soothe a wild animal. "Where are you?"

"In a hotel."

I swallow hard.

The lump in my throat is a stone.

"He took me to San Diego. I don't...I don't know. The room feels small. He watched the door. He...he waits. He always waits..."

"Reya."

"He always watches." I cry. "He always…"

Her voice sharpens. Not angry, precise. "Are you safe?"

I nod before remembering she can't see me, and a broken little laugh punches out of me.

"Am I safe?"

Another laugh.

This one wet.

"Depends who you ask."

"Reya."

I squeeze my eyes shut. The tears spill hot, uncontrollable.

"Ava, I love him," I whisper, the confession ripping straight out of my chest. "I love him so much. It's stupid. It's insane. I know I should leave him. I know I should. But…but my heart doesn't know how to stop…it just keeps…"

"Loving him," she finishes gently.

I sob, an ugly, choking sound, and bite down on the sleeve of my shirt to muffle it.

"It's like he's in my blood," I cry. "Like I only feel alive when he's close. And I hate that. I hate myself for it. I hate that I'm this weak."

"You're not weak," Ava says, firm. "You're human. And you're in love. And those two things together can wreck anybody."

I sit on the floor and bring my knees to my chest, the phone trembling against my cheek.

"He's the only thing that's ever felt like… like magic," I whisper. "Even when he hurts me. Even when he scares me. It's like…when he looks at me, I feel like I matter. Like I'm chosen."

"Reya," Ava says, pain breaking through her steadiness. "You don't have to be chosen. You have to be free."

The words hit hard, like a wave slamming into a sandcastle I thought would survive the tide.

"I don't know how," I confess. "I don't know how to leave him and still breathe."

"Yes, you do," Ava says. "You're already doing it. You're calling me. You're whispering truths you've never said out loud. That's the beginning."

"I feel sick," I whisper. "I feel like I'm betraying him."

"You're not betraying him." Her voice drops to a calm whisper. "He betrayed you first."

My breath steadies.

She knows.

She knows more than I told her.

And I'm not ready to know how much she knows.

"Ava…what do I do?"

"You leave, Reya," she says. "You walk. You run. Hell, I don't care if you crawl. I don't care how slow it is, but you get out. Even if you still love him. *Especially* if you still love him. Love is not a leash."

I press the heel of my hand to my chest, trying to quiet the shaking.

"I'm scared."

"I know."

There's rustling on her end, like she's pacing.

"You can be scared. You can cry. You can hate it. But you cannot stay."

I swallow.

"He'll come back soon."

"Then listen to me carefully," Ava says.

"When he walks back in that room, be whatever he expects

you to be. Not because you're weak. If he knows you're going to leave him, he will pull you back in."

A beat.

"And then, when you get home…you call me again. And I will help you pack. If you leave him stranded, he will be mad enough to let you go. Let's make a plan, right now."

A sob tears loose, but it's softer now.

My pulse slows.

The room doesn't feel quite as small.

"Karma thinks I'm still his," I whisper. And maybe he is right. Leaving my fiancé, Tim, was easy. This feels worse. This feels like I'm leaving part of me. The best parts of me, behind.

"And he's wrong," Ava says. "He just doesn't know it yet."

I sit there with the phone still in my hand long after Ava hangs up.

The dial tone has faded, but her words haven't. *You can be scared. But you Can. Not. Stay.*

The room feels different now.

I place the phone back on the nightstand. My palms are still trembling, but it's the kind of tremble that comes after a storm, not during one.

The kind that says: you survived the wave you didn't think you could survive.

I wipe my face, take a shower, unpack my suitcase, straighten the hem of my shirt, and breathe.

Not deep.

Not confident.

Just enough.

Headlights sweep across the curtains.

Karma.

The sound of the car door closing is soft but unmistakable.

I stand.

Brush invisible wrinkles from my pants. Wipe under my eyes again. And then, I put the mask back on.

The quiet girl.

The soft one.

The agreeable one.

The door opens.

He walks in with a plastic bag looped around his wrist.

"Tacos?" I ask gently.

He sets the bag on the table. "No," he says, like it's the most normal answer in the world. He tells me a lie about driving for hours looking for a taco spot then he pulls out a Styrofoam container and some napkins.

It's burgers.

"Thank you," I say. My voice comes out small, careful.

He nods. Satisfied.

Then his eyes brush over me. My hair, my posture, the way my hands are folded.

He sees something in my face.

Something I didn't hide well enough.

"You okay?" He asks, stepping closer.

I nod quickly. "Yeah. Just tired."

He studies me for a long moment.

Too long.

My stomach knots.

Then he touches my cheek with the back of his knuckles, and I feel my resolve flicker.

And just like that, my body remembers him.

The warmth of his hand. The gravity of him. The space he fills without even trying. He smells like outside air and cologne and something unfamiliar that makes my heart ache.

He leans down.

Kisses me.

And I let him.

Not because I want to, but because some ancient, broken part of me still melts the second he touches me.

Still thinks love might win if I just hold on longer.

His lips are soft but certain.

His hands frame my face like I'm something precious.

He pulls me closer by the waist, and I inhale for a different reason entirely.

I hate that I still respond. I hate that my body doesn't understand what my mind knows. I hate that something in me still feels chosen when he touches me like this.

We move together in the dim hotel light, guided more by muscle memory than desire.

Nothing explicit.

Nothing messy.

Just the kind of closeness that's built on wanting and wounding each other.

When it's done, I lie there beside him, the blanket tangled around my legs, the air heavy with that familiar post-storm quiet.

His arm drapes across my stomach, warm and heavy.

Possessive and comfortable.

He breathes evenly, like everything is perfect.

Like nothing is wrong.

Like he didn't just pull me back into the gravity I've been trying to escape.

And as I stare at the ceiling, a soft realization blooms in my chest: I am tied to him in more ways than one.

This love is killing me slowly.

I turn my head, look at him sleeping beside me.

His lashes soft.

His jaw relaxed.

His body warm against mine.

He has never looked more beautiful.

Or more dangerous.

A single tear slips down the side of my face and disappears into the pillow.

He will never let me go.

Chapter 3

11 Months After The Phone Call

Love should soften a person, make them bloom, make them brave.

But with him, love feels like holding my breath underwater. Beautiful for a moment, unbearable the second I remember I need air. The world blurs at the edges, and then…panic. Heat. Silence.

Karma thinks I have been distant. He thinks I'm overwhelmed, or sad, or drifting toward the edges of myself where he can't reach me.

But the truth is quieter than that.

Smaller.

More dangerous.

Something in me has started to shift. Slowly, like a tide pulling back from the shore, taking pieces of sand with it. It's not loud enough for him to hear it yet, but I feel it.

In the stillness of the mornings when the house is cold and my thoughts finally stop whispering in his voice.

In the way my hands tremble before I touch him.

In the breath I hold before answering his questions.

I'm trying to listen to my own thoughts again. They're faint, fragile, almost shy. But they are there. Like a seashell you press to your ear, nothing but the ocean at first, until suddenly there is a voice buried in it.

My voice.

It tells me the truth I never wanted to face: I can love him with every piece of my soul and still know I have to leave.

"I won't keep asking," he says. His voice cuts through the quiet like a knife cutting soft fruit. I jerk subtly, hating that I didn't notice him sooner. I need to be aware of him. Of his presence. Of the way he moves, the shadows he casts. Not because I'm afraid of him, but because my thoughts have sharp edges now, and I need to keep them hidden. I can't let him hear the shift inside of me. If I stay too long in Karma's orbit, I'll start mistaking the pull of gravity, start forgetting who I am.

He steps closer to me. Deliberate. "But I want to be sure. Are you okay?"

I have to steady my breathing.

God, I love him.

"I'm okay," I say with a steadiness I didn't know I could muster. "Just overwhelmed. And Tired. And I miss my mom."

I miss her so much. She is only a phone call away, but I can't bring myself to pick up the phone. I know if I call her, she will hear it in my voice the second I say, "Hello".

He reaches across the table and grabs my wrist. Not hard. Not soft. He presses his lips against the most tender part, and my pulse jumps against his mouth betraying me. My heart flutters.

I silently beg it to stop.

This. This moment is what I have been fighting. Not him. But us.

Karma has the power to make me forget every bad moment in a single breath. He can wipe out days of sadness with a single touch, erase doubt with murmur.

"Maybe we should go out of town. You've always loved the beach."

I know Karma. He wouldn't suggest a trip unless he needed to go there.

He always had reasons beneath reasons.

But he's not the only one who can use distance.

He is not the only one capable of strategy.

The beach isn't my happy place.

It never was.

But maybe I can make it my freedom place.

Chapter 4

10 Months And 2 Weeks After The Phone Call

I have to remind myself to unclench my jaw.

Lately, I wake up with teeth marks in my tongue from grinding in my sleep. I live in a constant state of tension, always remembering, always calculating.

How he likes his eggs: runny yolks, never scrambled.

How the bottles in the shower must face forward, labels perfectly aligned.

How every move he makes is deliberate, like a chess player who never plays to lose.

Karma isn't the kind of monster who leaves bruises you can photograph.

He's the kind that shrinks a woman until she barely fits inside her own skin. The kind who makes you question every thought until you start speaking in his voice.

Some days I almost wish it was physical.

Bruises fade. A black eye heals.

But this?

This rewires you.

"You don't want the father here?" The nurse interrupts my spiral.

I glance at her badge.

Washington.

Like a president. Like something steady. Founding. Historic. I think of Hamilton and almost laugh. *Who lives, who dies, who tells your story.*

I hum a line under my breath to steady myself.

"No," I say. "He...doesn't like hospitals." The lie tastes thin.

The paper gown crinkles as I pull it tighter around me. The ties feel like ribbon. Decorative. Useless. The slit down the back leaves me half-exposed, half-erased.

The air smells like antiseptic and latex. Sharp. Unforgiving.

A drawer slides open.

Metal against metal.

Gloves snap into place.

"I know how that goes," she says lightly. "My son hates hospitals too. But he would've still been there."

She smiles like it's harmless.

It isn't.

I stare at the ceiling tile above me. There's a crack running through it like a fault line.

I sit on the cold table, feet resting on metal stirrups, toes already numb. The paper beneath me crackles when I shift, too loud in the small room.

I do wish someone had come with me.

But no one can know.

Not my sister, Ava.

Not my mom, Clara.

And not *him*.

Especially not him.

Because if he knew, this wouldn't be my decision anymore.

I press my hands flat against my stomach. Sad. Confused.

But certain.

I cannot have a child with this man.

"But God…I want this baby," I whisper. "I want this baby more than I want to breathe."

The nurse looks at me, eyes wide. Like she heard something she doesn't hear often. Remorse, in the middle of tragedy. But I can't take her sympathy right now.

I think about my daughter, Delilah. About all the moments I pretended I didn't want her, convincing myself I was protecting her when I was really protecting me. And in that pretending, I missed so much.

"You don't have to do this, you know."

"I know." I say as I lay back further into the bed surrendering to the inevitable.

She takes my movement as final and continues.

I have to do this even though I know I'd be a better mother now. I know I'd hold this one differently. And still, I'm about to let them take her from me.

The nurse's voice is gentle, practiced. I nod as she speaks, but her words float above me, muffled by the hum of machinery starting up. I don't know what each sound means, only that soon, one of them will mean it's happening.

The air grows thinner. My heartbeat grows louder.

I lay back, and a tear escapes before I can stop it.

My hands move to my stomach.

Protective.

Instinctive.

Like I'm already guarding what I'm about to lose.

Breathe. In and out.

In and out.

I picture myself holding her.

The weight of her warm and new against my chest.

I imagine the doctor placing her there the way they placed Delilah. But this time I would cry the way her father, Dorian, cried: full-bodied, unashamed, tears spilling over for something that feels like salvation. This time I'd pull her close enough to breathe her in.

That clean, impossible scent of something untouched by the world.

Something that hasn't yet learned about disappointment.

But when I imagine looking up at Karma, the image shatters.

I see his eyes. Dark, unreadable. And in that darkness, something sharp.

Something that would shape this baby the way he shaped me until she's smaller, quieter, frightened of her own reflection.

The thought twists my stomach. I press my palm against it, whispering a prayer that I don't finish.

"God, I hope I don't regret this." I whisper to no one in particular.

The nurse doesn't leave my side. She takes my hand and says, "I'll be here for you, even if no one else is."

Her grip is firm. I didn't realize how much I needed it until she almost let go.

The doctor's voice drops lower, clinical and calm. Words blur together: speculum, cramping, suction. My body tenses before I can process them.

The paper crinkles more under my fidgeting body. And the faint metallic clink of instruments being laid out consumes my nostrils.

"What's your name?" The nurse asks.

"Luma," I answer. I give her a made-up name, from a made-up story. A name that was invented to escape the giants of this world.

The air tastes metallic, like blood and bleach.

I hear footsteps outside. A phone rings at the front desk.

Normal sounds, colliding with the most unthinkable moment of my life.

Then another sound joins it: a low, mechanical hum. It isn't loud, but it cuts through me because I know what it means.

"Are you okay?" She asks me as she feels my trembling hands.

I nod. I can't say anything. If I speak…if I speak in this moment, something inside of me might shatter, and I might run out of the room. I might break under the pressure of wanting this baby growing inside of me.

Instead, I close my eyes, and let the sound burrow deeper, until it's everywhere.

The doctor says something about starting.

I nod.

Cold. Pressure. Then pain, sharp and deep, like my body is trying to hold on.

I bite down hard to keep from crying out.

And in that moment, my mind betrays me.

It gives me a picture I can't bear: a little girl running barefoot through the yard, her laugh wild and whole and mine.

The hum deepens.

It's almost over.

It feels like both a mercy and a crime.

I call an Uber back to the dentist's office, where my car waits like an alibi. I made sure of that, just in case Karma decided to check that I am where I said I would be.

I hold it together the whole ride. Stare out the window, hands folded tight in my lap, watching the world move like nothing's changed.

But the moment I step out of the Uber, my knees weaken.

Just make it to the car.

Just make it to the car.

Each step feels heavier, the pavement rising and falling like waves.

By the time I reach the door handle, my vision blurs. The moment I drop into the driver's seat, the sob rips out of me so violently it startles my own body.

It's not a cry. It's a breaking.

The kind that comes from the gut. The kind that leaves your chest sore.

I wanted her.

I wanted her more than I wanted to be safe. I wanted to protect her.

I prayed for a do-over with Delilah. I swore I'd do it right this time.

The tears don't stop. I bite the sleeve of my sweater to muffle the sound.

Salt floods my mouth. My eyes burn.

I hate him.

How cruel the universe can be…to give me Delilah, a child I forced myself to believe I didn't want, a child Dorian took far, far away, and then, to hand me another baby on a silver platter.

My second chance.

I had an opportunity to adore the sound of her cry, only for it to be sucked out of me before it ever had the chance to exist. Only for me to bury it before it felt the joys of my love.

"Here is my card, reach out to me any time," the nurse said as she gave me a piece of cardboard my eyes were too blurry to see. I'm sure her intentions were in the right place, but my heart was with my baby.

I look at the card in my hands now; she scribbled a message on the back. Something about family dinner. I throw it in my purse; I can hardly see the writing through the tears.

The sun bleeds low across the sky as I sit in my car, painting the streets gold and soft. I cradle my belly, palm open, though there's nothing left to protect. The ache there isn't just physical, it's spiritual. A phantom heartbeat that once dared to believe it belonged here.

If it were a girl, I would have named her Clarabelle, after my mother.

A name that feels like forgiveness.

A name that feels like home.

And if it were a boy…

I rub my stomach again and close my eyes at the thought of him.

Brandon.

The man I met one day on a hike. Laughing over sunscreen and Harry Potter like we had all the time in the world. Laughter that felt too easy to mean anything, and somehow meant everything.

The name breaks something inside me. I bite my lip to stop the trembling, but it's useless. The tears come quietly this time, warm and steady.

I pick up my phone. My thumb hovers over Mom.

But this isn't something a phone call can fix.

This is the kind of pain that needs a mother's arms, not her voice.

But I've already been gone too long, away from the house longer than I said I would be.

Tonight, I will let myself feel it. Every shard, every echo, every what-if.

The city blurs through the window as I turn toward home, and for the first time in a long time, I don't fight the tears.

I let them fall.

I think I deserve to let them fall for what I no longer carry inside of me.

Chapter 5

10 Months After The Phone Call

I don't realize how quiet my life has become until the refrigerator turns off.

The hum cut out mid-breath, and the silence it leaves behind feels heavier than the sound had ever been. It presses against my ears, against my ribs, against the soft place at the back of my throat where tears always seem to collect but never quite fall.

For a second, I think something is wrong with the power. Then I realize it isn't the house that feels empty.

It's me.

I sit on the edge of the couch, half sunk into the cushion, staring at the grocery list on the coffee table like it is a test I hadn't studied for.

Eggs.

Bread.

Milk.

Soap.

Toothpaste.

Five things.

Five stupid, basic things.

I used to throw them in my cart without thinking. Pick a

brand because I liked the label, or because it was on sale, or because Delilah liked the way the cereal looked in the bowl. Now the list feels complicated and heavy.

Like each item weighs more than it should.

Like each item demands a version of me I no longer remember how to be.

I press my thumb against the word "eggs" until the ink smudges.

I need to go to the store.

I know that.

The refrigerator kicks back on, groaning but the silence it exposed stays.

I stare at the list and mumble, "shit". I'm going to have to ask him.

He is in the bedroom, reclined against the headboard. The TV murmurs sports highlights. His phone glows in his hand, thumb tapping, eyes scanning. He looks relaxed which is the only reason I even try.

"Hey," I say softly from the doorway. "Are you busy?"

His jaw clenches once. Tiny. But I see everything now. "What's up?"

I step inside, the grocery list hidden behind my back, it crinkles loudly in my imagination, I flatten my palm and calm my face. Hating myself for having to rehearse how I can ask him for things. I remember it used to come so easily. Now it's like a chore.

"I'm gonna run to the store," I say. "We are low on a few things."

He looks up, eyes trailing over my face, down my body, back up again. Not lusty. Not warm. Just assessing.

“Like what?” He asks.

I swallow. “Just…the basics. Eggs. Bread. Milk.”

His head tilts. “Didn’t I just give you money last week?”

My mind scrambles through days that all look the same. Waking up tired. Moving through rooms that don’t change. Coffee. Dishes. Silence. Distance. Tests. I can’t find a moment where he handed me anything.

“I…don’t think so,” I say slowly. “Maybe? I don’t know. I can’t remember.”

He smirks like I’m being cute. “You don’t remember?”

Heat rises in my cheeks. “I guess I’m just…tired.”

“You’re always tired,” he says. He doesn’t look away from his phone. “Pretty sure I gave you cash. Check your purse.”

His certainty makes me doubt myself. Makes me wish I were wrong.

“Okay,” I whisper. “Maybe I just misplaced it.”

He doesn’t respond, and I know the conversation is over.

I back out of the room, closing the door halfway behind me so I don’t disturb him. At the dining table, I grab my purse and dig through it fast.

Lip gloss.

Old receipts.

Crumbled tissues.

A key I don’t recognize.

No cash.

I open my wallet. Empty. Of course it’s empty.

I breathe through the sting and walk back to the bedroom.

“You were right,” I begin, then pause because it’s a lie. “I checked. You did give me money, but I spent it.”

He sighs. "How are you always out of money?" He asks. "You're not working. You don't go anywhere. What are you spending it on?"

Shame floods me, even though I know I haven't bought anything for myself in months.

"I thought you were handling everything," I say, voice small.

"I am handling everything," he says. His eyes finally meet mine. "But I need to know where it's going. I can't take care of us if you're careless."

Careless.

The word pierces something soft in me.

"I'm not..." I start, then stop. "I just...don't have access to the accounts anymore. You said it was easier."

"It is easier," he says. "You told me bills stress you out. Remember that? You practically begged me to take over."

Did I?

I remember sighing once. Maybe twice. I remember him saying, "Let me handle it." And I remember being tired enough to say okay.

"When I take something off your plate," he says, "you need to trust me. Not come back asking for more like I'm some ATM."

Tears burn behind my eyes. I blink them away.

"I'm not using you," I whisper.

He looks at me, unreadable. "It sure doesn't feel that way. But don't worry about it. I'll transfer you something," he says. "Just make it stretch, okay?"

I nod, my voice caught in my throat. "Okay."

"Anything else," he asks quietly.

"Thank you," I force out.

He hums, satisfied.

I leave the room feeling smaller than I entered.

My phone buzzes. $60.00 deposited.

Not enough. More than enough. Too much. Too little. I can't tell anymore.

At the fridge, the light glares at me. Half a carton of eggs. Almost-empty milk. Condiments lined up perfectly, the way he likes.

It looks organized.

It feels empty.

I shut the door and lean my forehead against the cool metal.

"Just go," I whisper. "It's groceries."

But leaving the house feels like asking for permission I don't remember being granted.

I grab my keys and purse and head toward the door.

My phone lights up.

Mom.

Her name glows across the screen, soft and familiar and painful. I freeze. If I answer, she'll hear everything in my voice.

Where have you been?

Why haven't you called?

Are you okay?

This doesn't sound like you.

Questions I can't answer without unraveling. I let the phone ring out.

A text follows immediately. Mom: Hey baby. Haven't heard from you. Call me when you can. Love you.

Guilt climbs my throat like a vine. I start typing: Hey, sorry, I've just been…

Been what?

Trapped?

Tired?

Eroding?

I delete it.

I type: I'm fine, I promise.

Delete.

My thumbs hover uselessly.

I hear his voice in my head: Your mom stresses you out. Protect your peace. She is the reason you started going to therapy in the first place.

I lock the phone and put it in my purse.

When I arrive at the grocery store, it smells like cold air and fruit. The lights buzz overhead. Carts rattle. Children cry. A woman laughs near the bakery and the sound rattles something inside of me. One single tear slides down my face.

Shit. I forgot to text him. I pull my phone from my purse and start typing. Thumbs moving faster than the speed of light: hey, I'm at the store.

He likes it when I check in.

I keep my head down.

I grab the cheap milk, eggs with the yellow sticker, the drinks he prefers.

My phone buzzes. The bubbles pulse.

Karma: Don't forget I like the wheat bread. That white stuff is pointless.

Shame stings as I stand there holding white bread. I put it back.

I start over with the list trying to remember what he likes. I imagine every front facing label. Every color. Every part of him that was once an extension of me but now feels like a world away.

By the time I get home, my head throbs. Like something inside of me is trying to get out. I head straight for the medicine cabinet, fingers already reaching for something…anything, when I notice it.

Silence.

Not the soft kind.

The wrong kind.

I turn.

Karma's not here.

My stomach drops so fast it feels like I missed a step.

I don't think…I move.

Fast, but not loud.

Never loud.

My eyes scan the apartment as I walk. Couch, table, counters. Taking inventory without meaning to.

My hands are already shaking when I reach his side of the room. I stop just for a second because I have never been over here like this.

Not really.

Once, I was making the bed and lingered too long on his side.

He didn't raise his voice. He didn't say anything. He just looked at me. Cold and sharp. Like I had crossed something invisible but very real.

I never made that mistake again.

Until now.

I exhale slowly.

Control it.

I can't be frantic. I open the drawer slow and careful and there it is.

The book.

The one I wasn't supposed to ask about. The one I was supposed to pretend not to notice. My fingers hover over it before I touch it, like it might burn. Then I grab it. Fast. Before I change my mind.

The Two of Us.

I flip it over, barely reading it. Just hoping that touching something so forbidden will give me the answers I seek.

A letter slips out. Handwritten.

I shouldn't read it, but I pick it up anyway.

It starts:

My dearest, Karma.

I can feel my head spinning.

My husband.

The words hit like something physical. Like it lands in my chest and stays there.

I keep reading because I have to. Because maybe…maybe there is a version that makes sense.

Writing has been the only way I can get the feelings out of my heart…

My vision blurs. I blink hard.

I hope you understand that you are the best thing that has ever happened to me…

My breath comes out wrong. Too fast. Too loud.

Stop.

Stop.

Headlights cut through the room bright, sudden, final.

He's back.

Shit.

I put everything back perfectly, just the way I found it. I run to the kitchen and stand at the counter taking several large deep breaths to steady my heart.

I unload the groceries in neat lines. Eggs. Bread. Milk. Soap. Toothpaste.

The front door opens.

Karma steps inside, keys swinging, smirk easy. He scans the bags and nods at the wheat bread.

"Good," he says. "We're a team."

"I know," I say. "You take good care of us."

He opens the fridge. The hum fills the kitchen.

"When I open this door," he says, "I know I'm doing my job. Providing. Making sure we're straight."

He says it warmly. Proudly.

It still lands like a warning.

"All I ask," he says, closing the fridge, "is that you be mindful. I don't want you ending up like before. Scraping by. Begging people for help. That's not you anymore."

His hand grips my waist when he kisses my forehead. His lips are soft. His words cut anyway. What he calls begging people for help was me asking Ava to pay for her half of brunch.

"I'm trying," I whisper.

"I know you are," he says. "Come sit with me. I missed you today."

He walks to the living room without checking if I follow.

I follow.

Of course I follow.

The TV flickers. He leans back, arm stretching behind me.

My phone vibrates on the table.

I glance down.

Ava.

Ava: Yo. You know you're in a fucking cult, right?

I miss her.

Her honesty.

Her laughter.

Her ability to see through my bullshit.

For a moment, I think about reaching for the phone.

"Who's that?" Karma asks casually.

"Ava."

His jaw tightens. "She still pushing that girls' trip thing? Y'all are too grown for that single shit."

"She was just checking on me."

He smirks. "People only check when they want something."

"She doesn't want anything," I say carefully. "She just…" Wants to see her sister.

"You don't have to defend her," he says softly. "I know you care about her. I'm not saying cut her off. Just be careful. You've been doing good not letting other people get in your head. Don't go backwards."

Guilt swallows the moment.

I look at my phone. The preview disappears. The screen goes black.

"You gonna text her back?" He asks lightly.

"Maybe later." I say, still trying to steady the shaking.

He nods, pleased. "That's growth."

Chapter 6

9 Months After The Phone Call

We need a storage bucket.

That's it. That's the whole errand. A five-gallon bucket with a lid that actually seals, because the one we have apparently "doesn't commit," which feels like something I shouldn't read into.

I've been reorganizing the garage in my head for three weeks.

Today, I decided to make it real.

Or at least...try to.

My purse sits on the counter, heavier than it should be and still useless. Cards I don't use. Access that doesn't feel like it's mine anymore.

I could ask.

I will have to ask.

I just don't know how today is going to go.

He's in the other room, scrolling, relaxed. That version of him is the easy one. The one that makes things simple if I don't say it wrong.

I lean against the doorway, keeping my voice light and casual.

"Hey...we need a storage bucket," I say like it just occurred to me. Like I haven't been thinking about it for weeks.

I wait. Just long enough to see which version of him I'm getting.

"Alright," he says, grabbing his keys before I finish the thought.

Just like that, relief hits me too fast, too strong.

I smile wider than I mean to. "Okay," I say, already moving to grab my shoes.

He didn't need to come.

I didn't need him to come.

I tell myself that it means something, anyway.

The store is the usual Saturday chaos. Karma walks beside me and I feel it the way I always feel it. That pull. That specific gravity he has. Like the air organizes itself differently when he's in it.

I walk beside him like this is normal.

Like this is just another Saturday.

Like I haven't spent the last month staring at my phone more than I should have. Like I haven't been wracking my brain around Talia, and Chaniece, and the secrets.

I tell myself, in this moment, that a piece of him is better than not having him at all.

We find the aisle without needing signs. I stop in front of the display and cross my arms and try to just be here. Just be a woman looking at buckets with a man that she loves.

"Okay," I say, stopping in front of the display. Arms crossed, like this is serious. "Five gallon or six."

"Five."

"What if I need six?"

"For what, Reya?"

"I don't know yet, Karma." I pick up a lid, check the seal. Put it back. "That's why I'm asking about the six."

He looks at me like I'm being unreasonable.

I am being unreasonable.

"I know I need a bucket," I say. "I just don't know how much bucket I need."

"Get the five. If you need more space, get two fives."

I pause.

Consider it.

"That's actually smart." I say, even though I really want the six gallon.

"I know."

I cut my eyes at him, and he almost smiles.

Almost.

That almost smile is the one I have been cataloguing for moths now, collecting like evidence of something I'm not ready to name. Every time he almost smiles, I feel it in my chest like a hand reaching in and rearranging things without permission.

Stop it, I tell myself. But my chest doesn't care what I know.

I reach for the five-gallon when he goes still beside me.

Not obvious.

Just enough.

I follow it.

A man in the next aisle. Older. Not shopping. Watching.

And a younger guy drifting, holding drill bits like he's not sure if they belong to him yet.

"Oh," I whisper. "He better run."

"What?"

"He needs to go," I say under my breath. My shoulder brushing his as I try to see past the shelf. "Right now. Pick up the pace, baby."

"You're rooting for the thief."

"I'm rooting for the underdog." I laugh, softer this time, like I'm already too invested.

"He's stealing drill bits, Reya."

"You don't know his life."

"I know he doesn't have a basket."

"Maybe he forgot it."

"He didn't forget it."

"You don't know that."

I keep watching anyway.

Because it's easier to care about something small.

Something that doesn't matter. Something that isn't tearing my entire world apart.

"He knows," he says.

"He doesn't know."

"He knows."

"Just walk normal," I whisper, like the guy can hear me. "Walk normal."

The man shifts slightly.

Still watching.

Still waiting.

I feel Karma's attention settle on me again. Not the situation.

Me.

"He's going to get caught," Karma says.

"He's not going to get caught." I murmur, leaning just slightly into him like I need to see better, like that's the only reason I'm this close.

"Reya."

"He just needs to commit. You can't hesitate like that. That's how you get caught. You either do it or you don't, there's no…"

I feel him look at me.

I stop.

Look back.

"What?"

"That's a very specific philosophy."

"I'm just saying."

"You sound experienced."

I pick up the bucket lid I have absolutely no interest in. "I watch a lot of documentaries." I tease him. He is playful today. Not as guarded as usual.

He holds my gaze.

Long enough to make it feel like a question.

I decide to focus on something simple when I see the guy freeze.

Then slowly...puts everything back. Like he was just looking.

I exhale, disappointed.

"Oh, come on."

"Justice," he says.

"That's not justice. He didn't even try."

"He absolutely tried."

"He didn't follow through."

"That's the point."

I turn to him, closer now, like I need him to understand me. "You don't half-do something like that. You either go all in and commit, or you leave."

My fingers brush his wrist without thinking.

"You're very passionate about this."

"I just don't like wasted potential." I say, holding his gaze longer than I should.

Like I'm asking something.

Like I'm hoping he hears it without me having to say it.

He shakes his head and I watch him try not to smile again and I forget how to swallow. Because this is the man I fell in love with. The one in the hardware store on a Saturday who almost smiles at me over stolen drill bits.

This is the problem, I think. *This is exactly the problem.*

Then something shifts.

Not in him.

In me.

I look at his face a little longer than I should.

"Hold still." I say as I lean in closer to him. "You have one rogue ear hair."

He blinks.

"That's not..."

"It is." I nod. "And it's committed, too. More committed than drill bit guy."

He huffs out a laugh, shaking his head, and I feel it...how easy it is, how natural it is to be right here, teasing him like nothing else exists.

I grab the six gallon bucket and put it on the cart.

"Get the five..." He insists.

I consider it for a bit, the argument that could come of this. But ultimately, I put the 6 gallon back and grab the five. But I grab a second one in defiance.

"I thought you only needed one," he says.

"I did."

"And now you need two?"

"I evolved."

"That was fast." He responds.

And as we head toward the front, I'm still smiling.

The quiet kind.

The one I don't think about, and then he says it. Casual, like it just occurred to him.

"You want to know something about me that no one knows" He begins.

I go still inside. Carefully still. The way you go still when something rare lands near you and you're afraid to breathe wrong.

"Yeah," I say like it doesn't matter. Like my whole chest didn't just shift.

He keeps walking. Eyes forward.

"I don't sleep well…" He says and I don't say anything. I just let him talk. Let him get it all out.

"…since you've been around, I don't wake up the same way."

He says it like a weather report. Like he's just noting something factual. And somehow that makes it worse. If he had said it softly, deliberately, like a man trying to be romantic, I could have filed it.

But he said it like he didn't plan to say it.

Like it just came out.

"I've never told anyone that." He says.

And then he puts the bucket on the belt and starts unloading the cart.

You already made the page, I remind myself. *You already know the truth. Don't fall for it.*

But he can't sleep. And somehow, I make it easier for him. And he just told me something he's never told anyone and he said it like it cost him something even though he would never admit that.

"By the way," I say, casual, "if we're talking about things that shouldn't exist..."

He sighs already.

"You eat ramen noodles like a college freshman."

"Ramen is good as hell."

"You put hot sauce in it."

"That makes it flavorful as hell."

"You eat it out of the pot." I laugh because it's true.

"That's efficient."

I shake my head. "You are a grown man."

"And you were emotionally invested in a stranger stealing drill bits."

"That's different."

"It's not."

"It is."

I shake my head slowly. He is a fully grown man. A fully grown man who doesn't sleep and puts hot sauce in ramen and almost smiles in hardware stores.

He is my Karma.

Chapter 7

8 Months After The Phone Call

After Talia's messages, after the "baby" talk, after the story about Karma that felt less like intimacy and more like prophecy, I can't sleep.

He is beside me, breathing slow and heavy, one arm thrown over my waist as if claiming it even in unconsciousness.

But I lie awake. Wide awake.

Thinking.

Not about danger. Not about violence. Not about dying. But about something worse in its own way: Losing myself forever.

Becoming small.

Becoming like my mom, Clara.

I stare at the ceiling, replaying every story he ever told me. Every laugh. Every "me too." Every "I know exactly how you feel." Every moment I thought we were soulmates.

Were any of them real?

Or was he just mirroring me?

A trick?

A tactic?

A way to slide past my defenses and into the softest parts of me?

He pulls me against his chest like nothing is wrong. Like I didn't spend half the night questioning our entire relationship. Like he didn't reveal pieces of himself I can never un-know.

His breathing is slow and calm while mine is tight and shallow.

He kisses my shoulder.

"Morning," he murmurs sleepily.

I swallow. "Morning."

He doesn't hear the stiffness. He never notices emotional distance unless it reflects badly on him. But today…today I need something.

Not comfort.

Not affection.

Not validation.

Truth.

So I stay still in his arms and ask casually, like it's nothing:

"Can I ask you something?"

He hums. "Always."

Liar.

I choose my words slowly.

I need a question he can't turn back on me. One he can't twist. One he can't mirror.

I steady myself.

"What is something about you," I say softly, "that nobody knows?"

His body goes rigid. Not dramatically, just a quiet freeze.

A micro-stillness.

Most people wouldn't notice.

But I've learned his tells.

He smiles into my neck, too quickly, too smoothly. "Reya, why do you wake up with questions?"

I keep my voice light. Unthreatening. Curious.

"Just something real about you," I say. "Something…you've never told anyone."

He shifts. Pulls away slightly. He needs space to craft an answer. He's searching for something that makes him sound deep, interesting, tragic. Something that makes me lean in and feel closer and trust him again.

"Something nobody knows?" He repeats.

I nod. "Yeah. Like…who were you before all the stories? Before your nickname? Before the people who hurt you? Before me?"

His expression flickers.

A crack. A tiny, sharp crack.

Because that's not a question he can fake by relating to me.

It's not something he can mirror because it isn't about us…it's about him.

And Leven only exists in relation to other people. I'm starting to learn he doesn't have a self outside of what he performs.

Finally, he gives me a smile. But it's wrong. It's empty behind the teeth.

"What kind of question is that?" He asks.

"A normal one," I say gently.

His jaw ticks.

"You trying to psychoanalyze me now?"

My stomach drops. "No," I lie. "Of course not. I just…want to know you."

He sits up completely, running a hand on his bald head.

He's irritated. "Reya," he says, tone flat, "you know everything about me that matters."

I quiet myself. But inside, something sharp twitches. Because that wasn't an answer. Not even close.

He glances at me over his shoulder.

"What about you?" He deflects, voice suddenly warm again. "What's something you've never told anyone?"

I swallow.

He's trying to flip it on me. Trying to regain the upper hand.

I whisper, "I wasn't asking so you could copy me."

His eyes narrow.

Just barely.

"What's that supposed to mean?"

I take a breath. "Nothing. Forget it."

His jaw locks.

He didn't like that.

Not at all.

He scoots closer and grabs my chin with two fingers, gentle, but controlling.

"Tell me what you meant."

My pulse spikes. "I didn't mean anything," I whisper.

He studies my face for a long, uncomfortable moment. Eyes scanning every inch like he's searching for disobedience.

Finally, he releases me.

"Don't start acting weird," he says. "I don't like when you get like this."

I nod.

Even though I hate myself for it. He leans back, satisfied

again, and pulls me against him as if nothing happened. But I am no longer inside his arms.

Not really.

I'm somewhere else.

Somewhere quiet and cold.

Somewhere that whispers: He didn't answer because there is no him. Just a collection of mirrors reflecting whatever keeps me tied to him.

His hand slides up my arm. Slow and deliberate like he already knows where to touch. My body reacts before I can stop it.

A shiver, sharp and immediate, travels down my spine.

My body betrays me.

I swallow trying to hold onto the thought, the truth, the proof that is sitting right there, loud and undeniable…

But he's closer now.

Too close.

And my body remembers him faster than my mind can fight him.

He tilts his head slightly, watching me.

Not guessing, knowing he has me where he wants me.

He's done this before.

Not just to me.

That thought should push me back.

It doesn't.

His fingers curl just slightly at my arm, grounding me, pulling me in without pulling me in.

I lift my head, almost without thinking, fingers brushing his chest like I can steady myself there.

Like I can find something real if I just...

He lets me kiss him. He lets our lips touch, then graze. His breath on mine. I moan into him.

I *need* him right now.

"I love you, Reya." He breathes into me.

"I...love you...too...Karma." I say, breathless.

I slip into the living room, sit on the floor beside the couch and pull my knees to my chest. My thoughts whisper: Does he even love me?

I open my phone.

I scroll through old messages.

His old long paragraphs early on: "Everything you say feels familiar."

"You remind me of myself."

At the time, it felt magical. Cosmic.

I thought we were two halves of the same soul.

But now...now it feels like strategy.

I search for signs.

Little inconsistencies.

Moments I ignored. Like when he told me he loved hiking, even though he hates the outdoors. When he said being a grandfather was the best, but I have never seen him with his grandchildren, or even with his children.

When he mirrored my trauma so smoothly it felt rehearsed.

Did he learn me? Or study me? Did he build a version of himself to match me? I scroll through search history.

Old texts.

He was different in those. More like the soulmate he claimed to be. And suddenly, the truth starts to crystallize: He didn't become what I needed. He became what would make me stay.

My throat burns.

I whisper into the empty room:

"Did you ever even like me?"

The silence answers.

Or maybe my own subconscious does.

I feel a tear slip down my cheek.

Not from heartbreak but from clarity. I wipe the tear away fiercely.

Another voice inside me, a quieter, sadder one asks: Why are you still here?

Chapter 8

7 Months And 3 Days After The Phone Call

Leven goes quiet after our conversation.

He watches me out of the corner of his eye.

Tracks my breaths.

Studies the way I move around the room, the way I avoid his gaze, the way my energy isn't bending toward him the way it usually does.

And he feels it.

He feels the shift.

I'm on the couch scrolling on my phone when he sits beside me slowly, carefully, like he's approaching a wounded animal.

He doesn't touch me.

He just exhales.

Soft.

Sad.

Perfect.

"What's going on with you?" He asks quietly.

My heart jumps.

"I'm fine," I say, too quickly. But in reality, Talia, Chaniece, FB, the lies. Everything is swirling in my mind like a tornado that can't be tamed.

He nods, like he expected that answer.

Then he stares at the floor, his jaw working, his chest rising and falling in controlled, measured breaths.

"Babe…" he whispers, voice thickening with something that sounds like sadness.

I tense.

He only calls me "babe" like that when he's trying to pull something out of me.

"I'm losing you," he murmurs.

My stomach drops. "What?" My voice cracks.

He doesn't look at me yet.

He shakes his head slowly, as if he hates admitting it.

"I feel it," he says. "It's like you're…slipping away from me."

My pulse spikes.

He continues. "You're quieter. Distant. Your energy is… different. You're not letting me in."

He swallows hard.

"And I don't know what I did wrong."

Something inside me twists painfully.

Because that sentence, *What did I do wrong?* is the perfect trap.

It makes me question myself.

"I didn't mean to…" I start.

He interrupts, shaking his head.

"No. Don't apologize. I just…" He rubs a hand over his face.

Breath trembling. "For once, I wish you would just talk to me. Let me be here for you. Let me love you."

My eyes sting.

He finally looks at me. Slow, wounded, open.

His eyes are glistening.

"I don't want to lose you," he whispers. "You're my peace. You're the only thing in my life that feels right."

The tears come.

Not his.

Mine.

Because this is exactly the kind of vulnerability that feels real.

The kind that makes me question my doubts about his feelings for me.

The kind that makes me think maybe I misinterpreted, maybe I overreacted, maybe I am the problem.

He reaches for my hand.

Slow.

Gentle.

"Whatever's going on in your head," he says softly, "you can trust me with it."

My voice comes out small.

"I didn't mean to pull away."

He squeezes my hand, closing his eyes like he's relieved.

Like I just saved him from drowning.

"You scared me," he admits. "I thought you didn't want me anymore."

My chest shatters.

I crawl into his lap, burying my face in his neck.

"I'm here," I cry. "I'm here. I didn't leave."

He holds me tight, too tight, arms locking around me like a vise disguised as an embrace.

"Don't ever do that again," he whispers into my hair. "I need you. More than you know."

And with that, my doubts are silenced.

I'm extra gentle with Karma.

Extra affectionate.

Extra good.

I fold myself into him like origami. Making myself smaller, prettier, easier to love. I cook his favorite dinner. I clean the house even though it's already clean. I laugh too hard at his jokes. I touch him constantly, as if my hands alone can prove my loyalty.

He loves it.

He leans back on the couch like a man letting my affection wash over him like praise.

At one point he strokes my hair and murmurs, "There's that laugh. I've missed you."

And I melt. I melt like sugar in hot water. Because it feels like I'm doing something right again. Like I've repaired the invisible damage. Like I've earned him.

Later that night, he falls asleep with his head on my lap, and I sit there stroking his hair, watching the rise and fall of his chest.

His face looks so peaceful.

So gentle.

I feel guilty for even thinking badly of him earlier.

I whisper, "I'm sorry," even though he can't hear me.

And I mean it.

I mean every word.

I'm so deep in the fog of him that I can't tell where he ends and I begin.

My phone buzzes and I freeze.

Carefully, I lift his head and slide out from under him, placing a pillow beneath him so he doesn't wake.

I walk to the kitchen, heart already thudding with dread.

It's a message.

From *Talia.*

I stare at the notification for a long time before opening it.

TALIA: Ashley…I don't know what to do anymore.

A slow chill spreads through me. A part of me feels guilty for creating a fake identity, a fake friend she thinks she can rely upon.

Another message comes through.

TALIA: Every time Karma is around, my head is in a fog. He knows exactly what to say to pull me back in. Every. Single. Time.

My throat tightens.

Another bubble pops up.

TALIA: I've tried to leave him. I swear I have. But I'm not strong enough. I fall apart when he pulls away. And he knows it.

The air leaves my lungs.

She continues.

TALIA: He gives me just enough love to make me stay. Just enough to confuse me. Just enough to make me feel like the problem.

I read the next line twice. *Just enough to make me feel like the problem.*

TALIA: I don't want this baby. I don't want to tie myself to him, again. But he'll never let me leave.

My hands shake so hard I almost drop the phone.

I feel the fog inside myself, the fog she's describing, wrap around my spine.

Because I know that fog.

I *live* in that fog.

I *drown* in that fog.

I scroll back up and reread her words.

He knows exactly what to say to pull me back in.

And suddenly, I'm replaying every time I tried to pull away. Every time I even thought about leaving. Every time I questioned him. Every time I shifted my energy even an inch.

He left. Or went silent. Or sulked. Or withdrew.

And then, he would come back.

With softness.

With affection.

With warmth.

With vulnerability.

With exactly the right tone, the right touch, the right lie.

Only three minutes of cold to make the warmth feel like heaven.

Tears sting my eyes.

Because if Talia is drowning in the same fog…then none of this is unique. None of this is special.

I grip the counter to keep myself upright.

I'm not the exception. I'm just the next one in line.

Chapter 9

7 Months After The Phone Call

Even with the chaos of finding out the truth, it's one of those rare days where nothing feels wrong.

The light is soft in the house.

We've eaten.

We've laughed a little.

We've existed around each other without tension tugging at the edges.

He's lying on the couch with his head in my lap, scrolling, and I'm tracing the side of his face with the backs of my fingers, memorizing him the way a believer memorizes scripture.

I don't want the moment to end.

So, I do what I always do when I want to keep him close.

"Tell me a story," I whisper.

He huffs, annoyed.

Softly, but annoyed.

"You and these damn stories," he mutters, though his tone is warm.

I smile. "Then tell me one I haven't heard."

He rolls his eyes playfully. "Like what?"

I hesitate, then lean down and kiss the top of his forehead. "Tell me how you got your nickname."

He stops scrolling.

Completely.

His fingers freeze mid-swipe, suspended like the world paused with him. For a moment, he's unreadable, and then he smiles. Soft and slow and secretive.

Like he's about to let me into a hidden corner of himself.

He shifts, turning just enough so he's looking up at me from my lap.

Eyes gentle.

Jaw relaxed.

Just slightly.

A shadow flickering behind the eyes. But then, he softens.

Slowly.

Beautifully.

"You really wanna know?" He murmurs.

I nod.

He settles back, chest rising with a satisfied breath.

"They call me Karma," he says, "because people who hurt me always get what they deserve."

The words are soft and casual. But they land like a blade so sharp, I freeze.

He keeps going.

"Stuff happens to them. Jobs lost. Breakups. Fights with family. Accidents." He shrugs, proud. "I don't have to do a thing. Life handles it."

The room shrinks.

"And you know the crazy part?" He says with a small smile. "It always happens right when they try to leave me."

Cold washes through me.

He doesn't let me respond.

He takes my chin between his fingers and kisses me softly.

"It's who I am."

My stomach twists so much I stop listening.

Before I can unfreeze, he adds, "Speaking of leaving…" He reaches for my hand. "You were at the store a long-time the other day," he says calmly.

My throat locks.

"I…I didn't…"

He presses a finger to my lips.

"Don't lie."

A tremor runs through me.

"You parked on the far side," he says quietly. "You never park there. And you sat in your car for ten minutes before going in."

My blood goes cold.

"How do you know…"

He smiles.

Just smiles.

"Babe, it's simple math. It takes seven minutes to get to the store…" he continues.

A lie I used to find romantic now feels like a threat. Because he can time how long it takes me to get to the store, but there is no way for him to know where I parked, unless…

My phone buzzes in my pocket.

He lifts my chin again with two fingers, eyes heavy on mine.

"You know," he murmurs, "it's wild how much you overthink. I love you. I'm here. I always will be."

I swallow, throat raw.

"And I know you're scared…but one day, I want to have a baby with you."

Lightning strikes through my chest.

I can't breathe.

He leans in, voice barely above a whisper.

"A baby would calm you, Reya. Ground you. Give us something real. Something permanent."

My heart starts pounding so loud I swear he can hear it.

He tucks a strand of hair behind my ear.

"You'd look beautiful carrying my child. I know I had a vasectomy, but miracles happen every day."

No.

No, no, no.

I can't have a child with someone I don't even know.

He kisses my cheek and stands to stretch.

"I'm gonna shower," he says. "Don't go anywhere."

His tone makes it clear: *Don't go anywhere.*

When the bathroom door closes, I ease out of the bed, careful not to disturb the sheets.

My phone buzzes again. My hands are numb when I check it.

It's from Talia.

Sent to Ashley Glass.

I open it.

TALIA: I shouldn't tell you this, but I trust you. I've tried to leave him before. He always talks me into staying. Always finds a way to keep me.

And now…my heart stops.

I click the next message.

TALIA: Now I'm pregnant. And I feel stuck. He won't let me go.

My vision blurs.

My stomach drops so hard I feel sick.

Another message.

TALIA: I'm not in that Facebook group, but can you comment and tell that girl she can have him. I just want to be free…Free of *him*.

My pulse roars in my ears.

I step back into the room, slow, careful, listening. The shower is running, but wrong.

The water isn't shifting. There is no movement. No rhythm of a body under it. Just a steady stream hitting tile.

He is not going to let me go.

The future isn't blurry anymore, it's fixed. If I get pregnant, I won't just be with him, I will be *bound* to him.

Chapter 10

6 Months 3 Weeks After The Phone Call

I wait for him.

I wait like a woman who's rehearsed the confrontation a hundred times, practicing every expression, every breath, every crack of heartbreak so it all comes out perfectly tragic.

I sit on the couch with the lights dimmed.

Phone on the table. Body still. Heart sprinting.

When the door finally unlocks, my whole chest goes rigid.

He steps inside and I start crying.

Not the cute cry. Not the single tear. The real kind.

The gut-wrenching, breath-stealing kind I practiced in my head.

He freezes and lets his keys hang in midair. His eyes widen just barely.

Not concern. Not guilt. Not anything tender. Just calculation.

"What's wrong?" He asks, barely a shift in tone.

My voice breaks exactly the way I want it to.

"I know you had a family emergency," I say, wiping my face. "And that's why I didn't call you. But what the hell, Leven?" I cry.

I stand.

Hands shaking. Heart pounding.

"I didn't question you," I cry. "I trusted you. But someone posted you in a Facebook group saying they've been dating you."

I roll my eyes dramatically, right on cue.

"I should've known. The late nights, the times you don't come home at all, when you 'need space' for days...I should've fucking known." I punch him softly in the chest. Weakly. Like I don't have the strength to fight.

He squints slightly.

Not worried.

More...annoyed.

"Whoa," he says. "What are you talking about?"

I grab my phone and show him the screenshot.

I made sure to use a picture I didn't take, one he has sent to multiple people.

One I know he loves. One that has no fingerprints from me.

He takes the phone. Studies it. His eyes dart back and forth between the picture and the caption.

I see the wrinkle form in his forehead.

A sign. A tell. A shift.

I say softly, with perfect trembling pain, "Why, Leven?"

This is my best performance yet.

He exhales sharply through his nose, almost a chuckle.

"You really believe this shit?" He says smirking.

The smirk knocks the air out of my lungs.

He leans back against the counter casually, like this is beneath him.

"I know who posted this. And that's funny."

Funny.

My breath stops. My heart begins racing again. Panic this time, not emotion. Did he see something? Is this a trap?

Before I can think, he keeps going.

"Some girl I used to talk to about a year ago," he says, shrugging. "Me and you were fighting all the time. You showed up with Tim's ring on, and I just…wanted to get away."

The words hit like water thrown on fire. Hissing, cracking, confusing the flames.

"So, I started hanging out with this girl named Chaniece," he continues, picking up the story effortlessly. "We went on a few dates, but nothing happened."

He laughs lightly.

"I ended up ghosting her. Because I was completely in love with you."

The lie is silk. Smooth. Soft. Believable.

It wraps around me until I can't find the edges.

"And now she's posting this trying to get information," he says casually, handing the phone back to me like it's nothing. Like he has nothing to hide. Like he's the victim of someone else's desperation.

He walks to the cabinet, pours himself a drink, and takes a slow sip.

Then he turns to me, smiling with infuriating ease.

"I can't believe you fell for that bullshit."

He laughs.

Actually laughs.

A quiet, confident laugh.

The kind men use when they know they've won.

Because it's a lie so good…I want to believe it.

I almost believe it.

Almost.

But the worst part?

I don't know what to say.

I don't know where to stand.

I don't know which reality is real.

I don't know if I'm brilliant for catching him or pathetic for doubting him.

He watches me for a long second, waiting for me to settle back into the version of myself he prefers. Grateful for his explanation. And I feel myself shrinking.

Because fighting him feels impossible. And believing him feels easier. Believing him feels like love. Or the closest thing to it I've ever known.

After he finishes laughing. Laughing at the story he made up, laughing at the lie so smooth it could be gospel, Leven walks toward me.

He wraps his arms around me and pulls me in tight, his chin settling on top of my head.

"Babe, what do I have to lie for," he murmurs, warm breath against my temple, "I only want you."

The words melt through me like syrup. "I'll call Chaniece tomorrow," he adds, stroking my hair. "Tell her to cut the bullshit. She knows I'm done with her."

Done with her.

The phrasing hits me like a spark.

I grip his shirt, my forehead pressed into his chest, breathing him in.

The scent of comfort.

Of surrender.

Of erasure.

He kisses the top of my head, lingering there, humming like he's soothing a frightened child. Eventually, we move to the couch.

He sits down first, then pulls me beside him until I'm tucked against his side, my legs draped across his lap.

His arm rests heavy around me. Protective, possessive, *perfect.*

After a few minutes of silence, I swallow the knot in my throat.

I snuggle closer, tracing slow circles on his chest.

"Can I ask you a question?" I whisper.

His body tenses almost imperceptibly, just a tightening of muscle under my fingers. Like he thinks I'm about to bring up Chaniece. Or the late nights. Or Talia. Or the six-day silence.

But I don't.

I steady myself and keep my tone soft.

"I started calling Delilah…Lyla," I say, smiling gently. "And I like it. Because I never really had a nickname. Have you?" I ask. "Have you ever had a nickname?"

He exhales through his nose, not a laugh, not a sigh.

"Yeah," he says. "They call me Karma."

I freeze.

"Karma?" I echo.

"Yeah," he says with a grin.

"Who calls you that?" I ask. Intrigued.

He shrugs casually.

"Everyone. Anyone who knows me. Only people at work use my real name…and you."

My stomach drops.

Everyone?

Anyone who knows him?

I become painfully aware in that moment of how little I know this man.

How much he has lived without ever inviting me into any part of his life.

I swallow. "Why do they call you that?"

He smirks, dark, proud, like the name sits comfortably on him.

"Because," he says, leaning back, "I *am* Karma."

The words strike me in the chest. Not cruelly. Not even sharply.

Just…truthfully.

Because suddenly everything inside me shifts. How many times have I lied?

To my ex-fiancé, Tim.

To my old therapist, Dr. Jensen.

To every man who loved me.

To myself.

How many times did I cheat?

Pretend?

Hide?

Run?

How many hearts did I bruise to feel whole? This man, this man who lies so effortlessly, who disappears for days, who breaks me open and pulls me back together, is my consequence.

My mirror.

My reckoning.

My lesson.

My karma.

And instead of fearing that truth, I embrace it.

I lean my head on his shoulder and inhale deeply.

Because if he is my punishment, then I deserve him.

If he is the outcome of all the chaos I've caused, then every jagged edge on him is one I earned. If he is Karma, then I am exactly where I'm meant to be.

I nestle against him, letting his arm tighten around me, letting the lie about Chaniece turn into myth, letting his nickname root itself in my bones. I embrace every bit of him.

Every crack.

Every darkness.

Because in this moment. In this twisted, broken, loving, desperate moment, I truly believe I deserve nothing less…and nothing more…than him.

Chapter 11

6 Months And 2 Weeks After The Phone Call

I sit on the couch, phone in hand, the room quiet except for the low hum of the AC.

The silence has weight. It presses on my chest and makes me bold in a reckless, desperate way.

I open Facebook as Ashley Glass.

I join the Las Vegas "Are We Dating the Same Guy?" group using the fake email I made.

My hands shake, but I keep going. I make a post, "Does anyone know this man?"

I upload a picture of Leven, one I know is flattering.

The smile that hooked me. The eyes that felt like home. The jawline that made me stupid.

Then I hit post.

My stomach somersaults.

A minute later, as Ashley, I screenshot the post.

Then, I find Talia. I open the message box and type: Hey cousin, I know we haven't spoken in a while, but I was wondering if you and Leven were still together. A photo of him was just posted in this Facebook group.

I attach the screenshot.

I press send.

My pulse races so fast I can feel it in my teeth.

I barely have time to breathe before she replies.

TALIA: Yes! We are still together, and I am going to kill him. He always tells me he's going to change and he never does. His nickname is so fitting for him. Thank you for telling me.

Nickname? My heart freezes.

Nickname? *My* Leven has a nickname?

He's never mentioned it.

Not once. Not in all our late nights and vulnerable moments. Not in all the stories he told me.

But there it is. Evidence that he has a whole identity I don't know. A whole world I'm not part of. A whole life he lies about. And before I can process that, Leven steps into the room. Fast.

"I have a family emergency," he says, grabbing his wallet, phone, keys in one sweep. "I need to go. I'll probably be there all night."

My heart reacts before my brain does.

Talia called him.

He is lying.

Right here.

In my face.

Looking straight at me.

I stand instantly.

"I'll go too," I say, grabbing my shoes. "I can help."

He freezes for half a second. Just half.

Just long enough for me to see the flicker of panic in his eyes.

Then he pulls himself together, but not fast enough.

I already saw it.

"No," he says, voice too soft. Too quick. "Babe, I can handle it. I don't wanna put any more stress on you."

I can feel the lie in his breath.

He steps toward me, wraps me in a hug that is warm and familiar and soothing. It works on my body. But not my mind.

He kisses my forehead. "The last thing I want is to stress you out about my family problems," he whispers.

And then he leaves.

He leaves without looking back.

Without waiting.

Without breathing.

Like he's running.

"Lock the door behind me," he says.

I stand in the doorway long after the lock clicks. My hands shake.

I go back to Talia's messages as Ashley and type: "Okay, cousin. You know I always have your back. Let me know how it goes."

Then I sit down and wait.

I open Talia's profile again and scroll through the images. I click on one. Leven in a kitchen. Arms crossed. Looking at someone off camera.

I click another. Leven sitting on a couch at some family event. Phone in hand. Expression blank.

I click another. Talia standing close to him, smiling. Her body leaning toward him like it's second nature. But her eyes are void of humanity.

Like she's done it for years.

Like she believes she belongs there.

My finger hovers over his face. Lingers. Strokes the picture like touching him through the screen will calm me.

He is the most handsome man I've ever seen. He is the love of my life. He is everything I've ever wanted.

And even staring at him next to her, even with proof that he is a liar, even knowing he is still hers, I can't stop loving him. I stare into his eyes in the picture.

Eyes that look straight into the camera.

Eyes that look dead and blank and I want to give him all of it. I want to be the reason he smiles like he used to. I want to be the reason he breathes easier. I want to be the person he chooses to confide in.

He lies.

He lies well.

He lies easily.

But I don't want the truth.

Not if it means losing him.

So, I sit there with my fake profile open, holding my breath, waiting for Talia to update me.

Waiting for Leven to come home.

Waiting to confront him about a fake post that I created.

Chapter 12

6 Months And 6 Days After The Phone Call

On the morning of day six, just when I'm convinced he'll never speak to me again, my phone finally buzzes.

My breath stops.

Leven: I needed space.

I sit up so fast the blanket falls to the floor.

Leven: I needed time to think. To figure out if this is really what I want. I hate being questioned. Especially when I'm not doing anything wrong.

My heart twists.

I text back instantly, fingers flying: I'm so sorry. I didn't mean to question you. I didn't mean to upset you. I love you. Please come home.

He doesn't respond for hours.

But the silence is different now. It's warm and thawing and hopeful.

He said he was thinking. He said he needed time. And I can give him that. I *have* given him that.

Around 7 p.m., I hear keys in the lock and I freeze.

The door opens and Leven walks in.

He looks tired, but not angry.

I swallow with relief so strong it feels like I might collapse.

"Hey," he says softly.

Just one word. Soft enough to forgive everything.

I rush to him, throwing my arms around his neck, breathing him in.

He hugs me back, slow, heavy, like he's deciding whether to stay in my arms or pull away.

"I'm so sorry," I whisper against his chest.

He kisses the side of my head.

"It's okay."

And just like that, everything in me lights up because he is home. He came back.

I pull away just enough to look at him. "Can I do anything for you? Dinner? A massage? Whatever you need."

He gives a tiny smile. Small, but real.

"You always want to fix everything."

"Only when it's you," I whisper.

He exhales and rubs his hands over his face. He looks heavy in a way I can't interpret.

And just as I'm about to step closer, DING.

My phone lights up face-up on the counter. A notification banner flashes across the top.

Talia Adams accepted your friend request.

My stomach drops through the floor. Suddenly the room feels too small.

Too hot.

Too close.

I need space.

I need air.

I need to get away from him before he sees the panic in my face.

"I'm gonna, um…run to the store," I say quickly, grabbing my purse.

Leven's brows pull together.

"The store? Now?"

"Yeah," I say, forcing casual. "Just need a couple things so I can make you dinner."

He leans against the counter, arms crossed. Calm. Controlled.

Watching me.

"Why didn't you go grocery shopping while I was gone?"

The question hits like a car door in the dark disguised as curiosity.

I swallow. Hard.

"I…wasn't really thinking about groceries," I say, trying to keep my voice steady.

He nods once.

That quiet, assessing look sweeps over me, the kind that makes me feel seen and exposed at the same time.

"You had six days," he says. "What were you doing?"

My heart slams in my chest. I grip my purse strap tighter. If I stay here another second, he might see the panic on my face. He might ask why my hands are shaking. He might ask what notification just came through.

"I'll be right back," I say, stepping toward the door.

But his voice stops me.

"Reya."

I turn.

He stares at me.

Unblinking.

"You're not running away, right?"

I force a smile. A shaky, pathetic smile.

"No. Of course not. I'm just grabbing a few things."

He watches me for another long, heavy moment. The kind that feels like he's peeling back my skin and looking inside.

Then he nods.

"Don't take long."

I step outside, the cool air hitting my face like freedom and guilt at the same time.

As soon as the door clicks shut behind me…I pull out my phone.

And stare at the words: Talia Adams accepted your friend request.

My entire body shakes because now I can see everything.

And I don't know whether I'm more terrified of what I'm about to find…or of what Leven will do if he ever finds out I befriended his ex-wife on Facebook under false pretenses.

I park outside the store, engine still running, the glow of the streetlights turning everything into a washed-out version of reality.

My hands are shaking.

I open Facebook again.

Ashley Glass: 78 friends, 59 mutuals with Talia.

And then Talia's page opens. Something tightens in my ribs as I scroll through what little is visible.

She doesn't post much, but what she does post tells the story.

A birthday dinner. A family barbecue. A cousin's baby shower.

And Leven is in two of them.

Not close.

Not posed.

Just…there. In the background. In the kitchen doorway. Sitting on a couch scrolling his phone. Wearing a shirt I've washed a dozen times.

A normal man living a normal life. No separation. No divorce. No distance.

Just a marriage he told me was over.

My eyes blur as I scroll faster.

Harder.

A party from five months ago, Talia's arm looped through his. Her cheek pressed to his shoulder.

A picture of their front porch.

A caption from a cousin: "Mr. And Mrs. Hosting again!"

My breathing goes uneven. Panicked.

He was with her, recently.

While he was with me.

My chest starts to cave inward.

I drop the phone onto the passenger seat, pressing my hands to my face.

"What the fuck…" I whisper. "What the fuck, what the fuck, what…"

My phone vibrates and I freeze. Leven is calling.

I stare at the screen, terrified to answer, terrified not to.

I swipe.

"Hello?"

His tone is light.

Too light.

Deceptively light.

"Babe," he says. "Why do I have the feeling you haven't even walked into the store yet?"

"I...I'm about to go in," I lie quickly, wiping my face. "I just pulled up."

A beat.

A soft hummed response.

"I know you, Reya." The words hit like a fingerprint pressed against the back of my neck. "I can tell when something's off."

My throat closes. "I'm fine," I whisper. I know it's crazy, but I look around the parking lot to see if he is watching me.

"Good," he says gently. "Come home soon. I want to cuddle."

And just like that, he hangs up.

And something about me is slipping.

I walk into the store, but the lights feel too bright. Too alive for the dead ache forming in my stomach.

A cart rattles when I push it, the sound echoing louder than it should.

People move around me with purpose. Grabbing cereal, comparing prices, talking to their kids.

Meanwhile, I'm floating. Detached. Barely tethered to the ground. My thoughts are loud, though.

Too loud.

Talia.

I grab a package of chicken without seeing it. Put it in the cart. Stare at it.

I never questioned Leven.

Not once. Not when he came home late. Not when he didn't

come home at all. Not when he said his phone died. Not when he turned it face-down every time it buzzed. I didn't question him because Tim did it all the time.

Tim would disappear for work. For projects. For "the guys." For reasons that made sense.

And I learned not to question men. Because questioning meant conflict. Conflict meant distance. Distance meant losing them.

So with Leven…I didn't ask. I didn't dig. I didn't challenge.

I just trusted.

I walk past the pasta aisle and realize I haven't grabbed pasta.

I backtrack.

I stand there staring at noodles like they hold answers.

For all I know, those tagged pictures could have been taken years ago. People repost old photos all the time. Memories resurface. Family members share throwbacks without saying they're throwbacks.

And Talia. She might be keeping up appearances.

Some people do that.

Some people don't switch their status.

Some people pretend things are normal even when they aren't.

Maybe she isn't ready to let go. Maybe she's trying to save face. Maybe she's delusional. Maybe she's sad. Maybe she's stuck.

I toss a box of rotini into my cart too hard and it bounces out, hitting the floor.

A man walking by glances at me.

I force a laugh, picking it up. "Oops."

But inside, nothing feels funny.

I push the cart again. Turn down another aisle.

My heartbeat is in my throat.

I could confront him.

I could sit him down and say, "I saw pictures. You were there. With her."

I could ask. I could demand answers. I could let the truth destroy the illusion.

But then what? I ruin the happiness? I ruin the softness he gave me? I ruin the nights he held me? I ruin the mornings he whispered he loved me? I ruin the idea of us.

Or, I can keep quiet.

Pretend I didn't see anything.

Pay attention. Be more aware. I can wait for truth to reveal itself. Because it always does.

I grab a salad mix and toss it in the cart.

Maybe I'm spiraling for nothing. Maybe I'm imagining things. Maybe I'm projecting old wounds onto a new man. Maybe Leven is telling the truth. Maybe he left her emotionally long ago. Maybe she's clinging to the relationship status because she's not ready to accept reality.

Maybe…

Maybe…

Maybe.

The cart is half full of items I don't remember selecting.

My hands shake.

And still, I keep pushing.

Because the alternative, confronting him about another woman, challenging him, looking him in the eyes and risking losing what we built is too terrifying.

So I will keep quiet.

For now.

And I will watch.

Because something inside me, something small, scared, but undeniable knows the pictures weren't old.

And knows Talia isn't lying.

The drive home feels longer than it should.

Every thought I have is combative, contradicting itself, arguing inside my head like two people are talking over each other, but neither of them sound like me.

One voice says: You saw what you saw.

The other voice, *his voice*, snaps back: You overthink everything. You twist things. You ruin things with your doubts. You don't trust enough.

By the time I park outside our home, my own thoughts feel foreign, like I'm borrowing someone else's brain.

When I walk into the house, Leven looks up from the couch.

Just looks. Not smiling. Not frowning. Just...observing.

And instantly, my shoulders soften.

My voice lowers.

My steps get lighter, like I'm afraid to disrupt the air he's in.

"Hey," I say gently, carefully, like I'm approaching a wild animal that might spook.

He studies me for three seconds too long. And in those three seconds, I adjust my entire personality. I swallow the questions.

The fears.

The spiral from the store.

The pictures.

The truth.

Because if he sees the panic in me, he'll say I'm dramatic. If he sees suspicion, he'll say I don't trust him. If he sees fear, he'll say I'm self-sabotaging.

So, I give him neutrality.

I give him the version of me he doesn't leave for six days.

I put the groceries away too quickly, making noise as an apology.

He stays on the couch, scrolling, occasionally glancing up like he's checking for…something.

Every time he glances, I correct myself before he can.

If I think, Why didn't he answer for six days?

My mind spits back: You pushed him. You scared him. You're lucky he came home at all.

If I think, Why is Talia still posting pictures like they're married?

My mind scolds: Maybe she's delusional. Maybe she's clinging. Don't be like her. Don't embarrass yourself.

If I think, Why did he flip his phone over?

My mind corrects: Because he hates drama. Don't become drama.

If I think, Why do I feel so alone with him?

My mind quiets me: Because you're too emotional. Breathe. Behave. Don't push.

It's like his voice replaced mine.

I'm not sure when that happened.

At one point, I move too loudly, closing a cabinet faster than he expected.

He glances up. And his glance alone is enough to make my heart sprint.

I smile so fast my face hurts. “Sorry,” I whisper.

He nods once and goes back to scrolling. That nod is my reward. That nod feels like relief.

Like oxygen.

Like I did something right.

God, what happened to me?

Chapter 13

6 Months After The Phone Call

The night is perfect.

We've just finished one of those slow-burn romance shows where everyone whispers and longs and almost kisses for six episodes straight. I'm curled against him, my bracelet catching the light every time he strokes my arm.

The moon charm dangling like a confession: *I love you to the moon and back.* He told me.

I feel relaxed.

Warm.

Floating in that Leven-induced haze I'm always chasing.

So when his phone buzzes on the coffee table, I don't look up at first.

But the screen lights up.

A name.

I see it before I can pretend I didn't.

T. Adams.

I don't say anything. I just glance at him, waiting. Waiting to see what his face does. Waiting to see if he'll make it mean nothing.

Something in his jaw twitches.

Barely.

He reaches for the phone immediately.

Too immediately.

He doesn't answer it. Doesn't swipe it away. Just flips it face down and smiles at me.

The smile looks painted on. Tight around the edges.

"What's wrong?" I ask. My voice is soft. Curious. Not accusing.

"Nothing," he says too quickly. "Just spam."

Spam.

Spam named T. Adams.

His lie is so thin it could snap with breath alone.

I keep my tone light. "Spam has last names now?"

He doesn't laugh. He doesn't soften.

Instead, he sits up straighter. I watch the warmth drain from his eyes in slow, terrifying degrees.

"Why are you questioning me?" He asks.

A cold pinch hits the back of my neck.

"What? I wasn't…"

"You saw a notification and suddenly I'm lying? That's where we're at now?" His voice is calm. The kind of calm that scares you. The kind that means the storm is inside, not outside.

My stomach drops.

"No, baby, I wasn't accusing…"

"You were."

I shake my head, scrambling. "I was just curious."

"You don't get curious about things that don't concern you."

It lands like a clean slice across my ribs. Not terror. Just the crack of something I don't want to name.

He stands and starts pacing in front of the couch. Slow. Measured. Breathing through his nose the way he does when he's holding something back.

Then he stops. He looks at me. Not angry.

Worse.

Disappointed.

"You know how much stress I'm under," he says quietly. "And instead of supporting me, you jump to conclusions? After everything we've been building?"

My heart slams into my throat.

"I didn't mean it like that." My pulse is racing. I didn't mean to ruin our night.

He closes his eyes and nods slowly. "It's fine. I get it. You're scared. People who aren't used to real love always get scared."

Shame floods my face, hot and immediate.

"I'm not scared," I whisper.

He turns back to me and his expression softens.

"It's okay if you are."

The shift makes my eyes water instantly.

He walks back to me, kneels in front of the couch, cups my face in both hands.

"I love you," he says quietly. "You deserve real love, Reya. And I know being loved, truly loved, is hard for you. I know you're not used to it because it feels easy."

My throat tightens into a knot.

He wipes the tear that slips down my cheek.

"I'm yours," he whispers. "Don't let fear ruin what we're building."

The guilt is instant and suffocating.

I nod because his hands are gentle and his eyes are soft and I don't want to lose this version of him.

"I'm sorry," I breathe.

He kisses my forehead. Then my cheek. Then the corner of my mouth.

"Come here," he murmurs, pulling me into his chest.

And just like that, the crack seals itself beneath the weight of his affection.

But the sting. The sting stays. A warning I'm not ready to hear.

***

It happens two nights later.

Leven is cooking, moving around the kitchen with that confident rhythm he gets when he feels in control. Oil sizzling, seasonings shaking, the whole kitchen smelling like something warm and comforting.

I'm sitting on the counter, watching him, loving him, soaking in the domesticity like I've earned it.

My phone lights up beside me.

Ava.

Again.

Before I can grab it, Leven glances over.

"Who's that?"

I answer too casually. "Ava."

He turns back to the stove, but his shoulders tighten. Not dramatically, just enough to change the air.

"You gonna talk to her?" He asks.

"Yeah, I'll just tell her I'll call back."

He nods without looking at me. But the nod lands heavier than it should.

I silence the call, tuck the phone behind me, and hop off the counter, wrapping my arms around him from behind like nothing is wrong.

We move around each other in a rhythm that feels almost normal.

I try to bridge the silence with something harmless. Something safe.

"Tim used to love his fried chicken too," I say, trying to compliment him, to lighten the mood. "He used to say..."

His jaw snaps tight. His fist forms instantly, white-knuckled around the spoon he's holding. He doesn't raise his voice. He doesn't explode. But my stomach dips.

He just sets the spoon down slowly, turns to me, and says with icy precision, "I don't ever want to hear you bring up Tim. If we're moving forward, let's move forward."

"I don't mind if you bring up your ex," I offer softly, gently. "You guys were together for fourteen years. She's part of you. I don't expect you to erase her from your mind."

His nostrils flare.

Subtle.

Dangerous.

It's not angry.

It's final.

But something inside me needs to understand. Needs to make this make sense. A question I have been holding on to for months.

"Have you filed for divorce yet?" I ask. Not accusatory, not emotional.

Just curious. Just trying to learn him. But the second the word leaves my mouth, I know I made a mistake.

A big one.

Leven turns off the burners, one, two. Each click louder than the last. He grabs his keys from the bowl on the counter.

And he walks out.

No goodbye.

No explanation.

Just the soft slam of the door and the echo of his absence. And just like that, I'm on day four of not hearing from the love of my life.

Four days of silence.

Four days of no texts, no calls…nothing.

I don't know where he is.

I don't know if he's okay.

I don't know if he's with someone else, or if I broke him, or if he's punishing me or protecting himself.

I have called dozens of times. Left voicemails that sound increasingly desperate.

Soft apologies.

Long apologies.

Begging, whispering, pleading apologies.

"I'm sorry."

"I love you."

"I didn't mean to make you uncomfortable."

"I shouldn't have asked about your divorce."

"I need you."

"Please come home."

Everything goes straight to voicemail. I check my phone so

much it feels like an extension of my hand. I sleep with it clutched to my chest.

Every ding that isn't him feels like a betrayal. But I have to wait. I have to be patient. I have to let him process.

I can't rush him.

I can't risk losing him forever.

So, I wait.

I wait for him to be okay again.

I wait for him to come back to me.

Because loving Leven means waiting.

And waiting.

And waiting.

Until he decides I'm forgiven.

On day five, the silence stops feeling like punishment and starts feeling like abandonment.

Our home feels wrong without him.

Too quiet.

Too echoing.

Too…empty.

I lie on the couch hugging his hoodie, inhaling a scent that's starting to fade, scrolling through my phone like I'm searching for proof I didn't imagine our entire relationship.

My brain won't stop replaying the moment he walked out.

It loops like a song stuck on repeat. The way he turned off the stove. The way he grabbed his keys. The way he didn't look back.

Every time I blink, I see his jaw tightening.

And then there's the other thing.

The thing I keep trying not to think about.

T. Adams.

The name flashes across my mind like lightning.

Adams.

Adams.

Adams.

And then the puzzle piece clicks and my heart sprints.

Talia Adams?

His ex-*wife*.

I sit up straight so fast I make myself dizzy.

"No," I whisper. "Stop thinking like that. Don't go there."

But it's too late. The thought is alive now.

Breathing.

Whispering.

I open Facebook before I can talk myself out of it.

I type her name.

Talia Adams.

Her page pops up instantly.

Private.

Locked down.

Hidden tight.

But her profile picture is visible. A soft smile, a pretty face, normal clothes.

She looks…real. Ordinary. Human.

Not the villain my mind created to justify Leven.

I scroll. The only public detail is her relationship status.

Married.

My chest goes cold and hot at the same time.

Married.

Married.

Still Married.

I laugh under my breath. A thin, nervous.

"You're being insane," I tell myself. She is using her maiden name 'Adams'. Let it go.

Then I pause. "Would it be crazy if I made a fake page?"

Silence answers me back. "Not as crazy as talking to myself in an empty room," I mutter.

So I do it. Because why not? I have time.

Too much time.

Five days of time.

Five days of silence and paranoia and humiliation.

I make the page. Fake name. Fake pictures. Fake birthday. Fake email account.

Her last name is Adams. Some of her cousins are Adams. Some of them are Glass.

Glass.

Perfect.

My new name becomes Ashley Glass.

A distant cousin. Someone far enough to avoid suspicion, close enough to be believable.

I start small. I find her cousins. I friend-request them.

Then her aunts. Her mom.

Old women with matching last names and profile pictures of plates of food or blurry grandchildren.

I build my friend list slowly, carefully.

And to my shock, people start accepting immediately.

Buzz.

Buzz.

Buzz.

Friend request accepted.

Friend request accepted.

Friend request accepted.

"These people are glued to their phones," I whisper.

My hands tremble as I type her name again.

Talia.

I press Add Friend.

And there it is.

A simple, horrifying pop-up: Friend Request Sent.

My heart beats too fast.

Too loud.

Too hard.

And suddenly, I can't breathe. Not because I'm scared she won't accept...but because I'm scared she will.

Chapter 14

4 Months After The Phone Call

It hits me on a random afternoon. Not a holiday. Not a milestone. Not a moment that should sting.

I'm sitting on Leven's couch, wrapped in his hoodie that smells like his cologne, flipping through my camera roll, half-bored, half-waiting for him to finish a phone call in the other room.

My thumb swipes past a picture of Delilah.

And my heart jolts.

Her gap-tooth smile.

Her hand holding a smoothie and I remember how she reached out for me when I sat on the bathroom floor. When she told me she was proud of me.

I see the pink hoodie she insisted on wearing three days in a row because the hood fit just right.

My Lyla.

I smile at the photo first, the way any mother would. Then I swipe to the next. And the next.

All of them old. Months old.

Months.

I freeze.

I scroll through my messages. The last text I sent her was a video of a sunset.

She'd sent back a single heart emoji.

When was that? Two days ago? Three?

My stomach sinks when I check the date. It was three weeks ago.

I drop my phone on my lap and stare at the wall.

A slow, creeping ache starts behind my ribs.

How did I not notice? I should call her. I should FaceTime. I should check in.

I should…

Just as the panic starts to rise, Leven comes out of the bedroom.

He's smiling.

"Baby," he says, dropping onto the couch beside me. "Come here."

I force a breath in and slide into him.

His arm wraps around my shoulder immediately, pulling me into his side, grounding me, steadying me.

"You okay?" He asks, brushing his fingers down my arm.

I open my mouth to say I miss my daughter. To say I feel guilty. To say it's been too long.

But when I turn toward him, his face is so gentle. His eyes so affectionate. His presence so soothing that the words dissolve.

Instead, I say, "Yeah. I'm okay."

He leans in and kisses the corner of my mouth, slow, warm, addictive.

"You look tense. Don't be tense."

"I'm just thinking about my daughter," I admit softly. "I feel like I haven't talked to her enough."

He nods. He always understands me.

"Baby, she's good. She's with her dad. She's surrounded by love. And you needed this time." His hand runs through my braids. "You needed space to grow. To figure out who you are again."

"I know," I whisper. But something inside me curls in on itself.

He kisses my forehead.

"Don't punish yourself for healing."

He pulls a small box from behind the couch cushion, like he'd been hiding it until the perfect moment.

"I got you something."

I take a deep inhale.

"Why?" I ask.

"Because you canceled that girls trip," he says, kissing my cheek. "Because you chose us. Because you've been so present. So focused. So…mine."

His words melt me instantly.

My guilt evaporates beneath the warmth of being appreciated.

I open the box.

Inside is a delicate gold bracelet. Thin, simple, with a tiny charm shaped like a crescent moon.

My throat goes dry.

"It's beautiful…"

"It reminded me of you."

He fastens it onto my wrist himself, his fingers brushing my skin lightly.

"A constant. Something I can look at and know you're here with me. Even when you're in another room."

God.

My heart swells so big, it fills the whole apartment.

He brings my wrist to his lips and kisses it. "Thank you for loving me," he murmurs.

And that's all it takes.

The ache for Delilah fades to a dull hum.

Not gone. Never gone. But quiet enough to ignore.

Quiet enough to replace with the feeling of being wanted.

I curl into him, bracelet glinting under the lamplight.

He holds me tighter.

And for a moment, for one small, shameful moment, being Leven's moon feels easier than being Lyla's mother.

Chapter 15

3 Months After The Phone Call

Ava is already seated when I walk in.

She stands when she sees me, arms open, smile easy. Effortless.

She didn't get my height, not even close. I hover over her by a few inches, but she's never felt small a day in her life. What she lacks vertically, she makes up for everywhere else. Curves that settle into every outfit like they were designed for her specifically.

Her skin is radiant.

Not just smooth, but alive. Glowing in a way that makes you look twice. The kind of skin people spend hundreds trying to replicate with serums and filters and good lighting.

And her hair.

My God.

Her curls fall wild around her face, but not messy. Intentional chaos. The kind of "I woke up like this" people pay stylists to fake. They frame her perfectly, softening her features, pulling your attention exactly where she wants it.

We used to joke that the only thing she ever gave me was my birthmark.

"Look," she used to say, pressing her arm next to my face, "we're the same color."

She's the shade of the mark under my eye that is lighter than the rest of my skin, soft and warm.

"About time," she says, pulling me into a hug. "I thought you stood me up for your new man."

I laugh, sliding into the seat across from her. "Relax."

Menus come. Mimosas. Small talk.

Then she leans forward, elbows on the table, studying me.

"So," she says casually, "you ever gonna answer my question from last month?"

I already know what she is referring to.

The girls trip.

"I told you," I say, picking at the edge of my napkin. "I just…I needed to talk to him first."

Ava blinks. Slow. Then she leans back and laughs.

"Reya," she says, shaking her head, "you know this is how cults start."

I roll my eyes. "Oh my God."

"I'm serious," she continues, grinning. "First, it's 'let me ask him,' next thing you know you're drinking Kool-Aid and cutting off your whole family."

I laugh, but it's tight. "It's not like that."

"Mm," she hums, lifting her glass. "That's what they all say before they wake up dead."

I lean forward now, defensive before I even realize it.

"He's not controlling, Ava."

"I didn't say he was."

"You implied it."

"I *joked*," she says, softening. "There's a difference."

I shake my head. "You don't understand him."

Her expression shifts, just slightly. Careful now.

"Okay," she says gently. "Help me understand."

I sit up straighter. Because I *can* help her understand. Because I know him.

"He's...protective," I say. "Attentive. He pays attention to everything. The way I feel, the way I think. The way I respond. He challenges me." I smile at the thought of it. At the thought of him.

Ava tilts her head. Listening.

"He doesn't just let me...float through life," I continue. "He makes me better."

"By what?" She asks softly.

"By...pushing me," I say. "By holding me accountable."

She nods slowly. "And you like that?"

I smile before I can stop myself.

"I've always liked tests," I admit. "Quizzes. Proving I can get it right."

Ava watches me carefully. "And he's a test for you?" She asks.

I shrug, but I'm already nodding.

"Yeah," I say quietly. "A test I want to pass."

There's a pause.

Not awkward.

Just...full.

Ava exhales through her nose, tapping her fingers lightly against the table.

"Reya," she says, softer now, "you don't have to earn love."

I shake my head immediately.

"It's not like that."

"Then what is it?"

I hesitate because I don't have a clean answer. Because it does feel like that sometimes.

"He just..." I start, then stop. "He cares. A lot. More than anyone ever has. He is passionate, and brilliant. And he uses his brains for good, not for evil, Ava."

Ava nods. "I believe that," she says.

And she does.

That's what makes her dangerous.

Because she doesn't attack him. She just...keeps looking at me.

"And you feel safe?" She asks.

I answer too fast. "Yes."

She holds my gaze a second longer than I want her to.

Then she smiles. "Okay," she says lightly, lifting her glass again. "No Kool-Aid for you. Yet."

I laugh, relieved. And the tension dissolves just enough while we eat. We talk about nothing. Old memories. Work. Her kids. My writing.

When the check comes, I grab it before she can.

"Reya..."

"I got it," I say, already sliding my card in.

She rolls her eyes. "You always do this."

"I know."

The server walks away.

Ava smirks at me. "So this is what Leven's money feels like?"

I snort. "Girl, please."

Then I point at her. "But don't forget to send me your half."

She gasps, clutching her chest. "Wow."

"I'm serious," I say, smiling. "There are no freebies over here just because you're light-skinned."

She bursts out laughing.

"Rude."

"Accurate."

She shakes her head, still smiling.

"I'm definitely not sending it now."

"You are," I say.

We both know she will.

We both know I'll remind her if she doesn't.

Chapter 16

2 Months 2 Weeks After The Phone Call

They say dancing shows you who a person really is.

If that's true, then tonight is the most honest Leven has ever been.

We're standing in the middle of a small studio that smells like polished bad decisions and wood floors. The lights are low and golden, soft enough to make everything feel romantic. Even the giant wall of mirrors that is currently reflecting my lack of coordination back at me in high definition feels like love.

"I can't believe you talked me into this," he mutters, adjusting the cuffs of his black button-down like we're about to negotiate a contract instead of trying a salsa basic.

I grin. "You went to Memphis with me and survived. You can survive this."

He huffs, but the corner of his mouth betrays him. In Memphis, I saw a different version of him. A looser, nostalgic, almost boyish version of him. Tonight he feels like that again. No armor. No strategy.

Just us.

The instructor claps her hands. "Okay, leaders on the left, followers on the right!"

Leven hesitates for half a second before stepping into place like he's committing to a business merger.

I smile because it's just so…Leven. Careful. Like even this. This tiny ridiculous dance class matters more than it should.

I bounce on the balls of my feet.

"I should warn you," I whisper, "I dance like I'm allergic to rhythm."

He leans closer. "And I have two left feet."

"Perfect. We'll cancel each other out."

The music starts fast and my hips immediately do something that has nothing to do with the beat. I step forward when I'm supposed to step back and nearly collide into his chest.

He catches me automatically; hands firm on my waist. He pulls me in closer and I melt into him.

"Wrong direction," he says.

"I'm improvising." I say. The way he reaches for me makes my heart skip a beat.

"That's not what this is."

I look up at him, eyes wide and innocent. "Says who?"

He tries to stay serious. He really does. His jaw tightens like it always does when he's concentrating, like he's solving a complex equation instead of just being here with me.

"One-two-three. Five-six-seven." He counts under his breath.

I deliberately spin the wrong way.

He sighs.

Then I laugh.

And something in him cracks.

It starts small, a breath through his nose. Then his shoulders shake. And suddenly he's laughing. Not polite. Not controlled.

Full, unfiltered laughter that makes his eyes disappear at the edges.

There is a break in the version of him he shows everyone and something in my chest opens so wide it almost scares me. If I can make him laugh like this forever, I will be happy forever.

"You're impossible," he says.

"And yet," I reply, stepping on his foot, "you're still here.

He looks down at our feet tangled together and then back at me. "Because I like it."

"Like what?"

"You," he says simply as he kisses my nose.

No performance. No grand speech.

Just me. And for a second, everything goes quiet. It's only me and him in the entire world. Me looking at him like he is perfect just because he exists, him looking at me like I'm enough.

The instructor walks past and gently repositions his hand higher on my back. "Relax your shoulders," she tells him, breaking the Leven-induced fog I was in.

I reach up and physically shake his shoulders. "Relax, sir. Like this." I do a little shimmy with my arms that makes him laugh again, then immediately serious.

He swats my hands away, but he's smiling now. Actually smiling. The kind that reaches his eyes. The kind he doesn't give away easily and I hold onto it longer than I should.

We try again.

One-two-three.

Five-six-seven.

This time we almost get it right.

I focus on his chest instead of my feet. He focuses on guiding instead of controlling. There's a difference, I realize. Guiding feels softer. It feels like being invited instead of directed.

When he spins me, I actually complete the turn. I gasp like I've just won an Olympic medal.

"Did you see that?!" I shout.

"I did," he says, and the look on his face makes my chest do something I don't even try to understand. "Don't let it go to your head."

Too late.

The song shifts to something slower. The lights dim slightly, and couples move closer together. Leven's hands settle more naturally at my waist now, less rigid.

"You're not counting," I notice.

"I gave up," he admits.

"Good." I rest my forehead lightly against his chest. His heartbeat is steady. So is mine.

No tension.

No silent calculations.

No scanning the room.

No wondering who's watching.

Just him.

Just us.

Just warmth.

"Are you embarrassed?" He asks quietly.

"Never," I say immediately.

He studies me like I've said something profound instead of reckless.

"You don't care what people think," he says.

"I do," I correct gently. "I just don't let it stop me anymore."

He exhales slowly, like that concept alone is foreign.

The song ends. We're both slightly out of breath, slightly sweaty, completely off-beat.

And completely happy.

On the drive home, the windows are down. The night air is cool against my face. The radio plays something old-school and dramatic, and I sing at the top of my lungs.

He joins in.

Off-key.

Unapologetic.

And I laugh in the middle of the lyrics because he doesn't even try to fix it.

At a red light, he looks over at me and shakes his head.

"What?" I ask.

"You're going to be the reason I loosen up, huh?"

There's something in the way he says it. Not joking. Not annoyed.

Almost surprised.

I smile, leaning back in my seat. "That's the plan."

He watches me a second longer than he needs to then he reaches over, laces his fingers through mine, and squeezes.

I look down at our hands, then back out the window, smiling to myself. Because it feels like I'm getting the pieces of him no one else gets.

Loving him feels like a dance I'm allowed to learn as I go.

Chapter 17

2 Months After The Phone Call

These months with Leven blurs into something that doesn't feel like real life.

It feels like a dream.

A fever dream.

A beautiful, chaotic, intoxicating fever dream I don't ever want to wake up from.

Some nights we stay up until 3 AM talking about life and fate and if souls can recognize each other across universes.

Other nights we fall asleep on the couch halfway through a movie, my head on his lap, his fingers tangled in my hair, the TV glow painting us in soft blues.

We dance in the kitchen at midnight to songs neither of us even likes. We race to the car in the rain. We sit on the floor eating cereal straight out of the box because we forgot bowls exist. We laughed so hard once that he had to hold his stomach and beg me to stop talking.

And God, those moments feel like magic.

Like fate.

Like a second life I get to live.

And I fall deeper.

Willingly.

Gratefully.

Because loving him feels like being chosen by the universe.

And then, my phone rings.

Ava.

The name alone is grounding and jarring at the same time.

I answer with a smile in my voice. "Avaaa!"

"You sound…high," she says. "Not literally high. Love-high. Or…something-high."

I laugh. "Is that a problem?"

"It is if you're ignoring your sister," she teases. "ANYWAY. I'm calling because I need a break. And you need a break. Sooo…girls trip?"

My heart skips a beat. Not with dread, but with the immediate impulse to check with Leven.

"Where?" I ask, stalling.

"Anywhere. Beach, mountains, I don't care. Just us. No men. No drama. No phones. A reset."

I hesitate.

Ava hears it instantly.

"Oh God," she groans. "Don't tell me you have to ask him."

"I don't *have* to ask," I say too quickly. "I mean…I should run it by him."

"Run it by him?" Ava repeats. "Reya, you've been with him like five minutes."

"And?" I ask, irritation prickling my voice. "Couples talk about things."

"Yeah, but you don't need permission," Ava says slowly, carefully. "Right?"

I roll onto my back on Leven's couch, heart thudding. "It's not permission, Ava. I just…I like talking to him. He's my voice of reason."

There's a long beat of silence.

Like Ava is choosing between telling me what she really thinks and keeping the peace.

"Voice of reason," she repeats softly. "Girlllll. Okay. If you say so."

Her tone is wrong.

Off.

I sit up a little straighter. "Ava, don't do that."

"Do what?"

"That tone. That…'I'm worried about you' thing. You barely know him."

"*You* barely know him. And I know you," she says gently. "And I know what it looks like when you disappear into someone."

My stomach pulls tight.

"It's not like that," I say firmly. "Leven is…he's different."

"Different how?"

I open my mouth, then close it. Because I don't have the words. Or maybe I do, but they sound crazy out loud.

Finally I say, "He just…makes sense. He gets me."

Ava exhales. "Okay. Fine. Ask him then. But Reya…if he tells you no, that's a problem."

I swallow. Hard.

"He won't say no," I whisper.

Ava softens her voice. "Call me later, okay? And…I'm here. If you need me."

I nod, though she can't see me. "I know."

We hang up, and the room feels different.

Like Ava opened a window I wasn't ready to look out of.

I pull my knees to my chest and breathe slowly.

I try to push her words away.

I wait until later that evening, after we've eaten and the lights are low and his mood is soft.

He's lying on the couch, head in my lap, scrolling something on his phone while I run my fingers along the curve of his shoulder.

"Hey," I say lightly, playing with the collar of his shirt. "Ava called today."

He doesn't look up from the phone. "Yeah? How's she doing?"

"She's good," I say, smoothing a wrinkle in his shirt. "She, uh…she mentioned maybe taking a girls trip."

He pauses his scrolling.

Not a full stop. Just a half-second freeze.

He turns the phone over in his hand and rests it against his chest, looking up at me with warm eyes.

"A girls trip," he repeats, like he's tasting the words.

"Yeah," I say, smiling a little. "It could be fun. Me and her haven't done anything together in forever."

"And you want to go?" He asks. Not sharp, not accusatory.

"I mean…yeah," I say. "I think I do."

He nods slowly, like he's processing something deep.

Then he shifts, turning onto his side so his head rests on my stomach, his arms wrapping around my waist.

"Babe," he says softly, almost a whisper. "You can do anything you want."

The relief is instant. Warm. Melting.

"But..." he adds. Softly, carefully, like he's holding something fragile. "There's just something I need you to think about."

My breathing changes, but his tone is so tender I don't brace myself.

"You've been doing so well," he says. "You've been grounded. Present. Calm. I've seen so much growth in you."

Warmth floods me.

"And I just don't want you to lose that," he continues, rubbing small circles into my back. "You know how you get around certain people. Certain energies. They...pull you off your path."

I bite my lip.

"Ava doesn't pull me off anything."

He smiles a soft, patient smile.

"I know you don't see it. And that's okay. That's why I'm here. To help you see the angles you don't always catch."

I nod slowly.

Because he does help me. He does catch things. He does understand me.

"So, if you really want to go," he says, tucking a strand of hair behind my ear, "I won't stop you. I would never stop you. But babe...I would miss you. And I love the space we're in right now. Just you and me. Just us building something solid."

He looks into my eyes like he's studying my soul. I look at the hairs coming out of his ears. God, I love those hairs.

"Trips can wait," he whispers. "We can do one together. Just us. Something romantic. Something real."

My heart flips.

Hard.

A girls trip suddenly feels small.

Immature.

Unnecessary.

A trip with Leven feels…right.

"I just want us focused," he murmurs against my stomach. "I want you grounded. And I can't protect you when you're far away."

He says it with so much love, so much sincerity, that I nod without thinking.

He kisses my hip.

My stomach.

My ribs.

"You're my peace," he whispers. "I want to keep you close."

My chest fills with warmth and purpose and devotion.

"So…you think I shouldn't go?" I ask gently.

He smiles and shakes his head, lifting himself up just enough to kiss me.

"I think," he says softly, "that you already know what's best for you. I think your heart is here. With me. And I think you don't need to run away to find clarity when you've already found it."

I exhale shakily.

He kisses me again. "I'm not telling you no," he says. "I'm telling you I love you."

And it feels—God, it feels—so loving.

I nod. And say, "Okay."

And Leven smiles like I gave him the world.

Chapter 18

31 Days After The Phone Call

The night after the chocolate incident has settled into the cracks of my chest when Leven comes out of the bedroom.

His face is softer now.

Eyes warmer.

"You've been amazing," he murmurs. "Going to the store for me. Trying to take care of me. You're so thoughtful, babe. Most women wouldn't do half the things you do."

My chest warms.

Blooms.

Glows.

He keeps rubbing my legs, eyes tracing every movement my body makes. "I'm really lucky," he says, quieter this time. "You know that?"

I swallow hard. "I just want to make you happy."

"And you do," he whispers, leaning in to kiss my knee, my thigh, slow and thankful. "You make me so happy."

I feel tears sting the backs of my eyes. Not sad tears, but the kind that come from finally being enough.

He pulls me into his chest, his chin resting on top of my head, his arms wrapped around me with a tenderness that washes away every tense second from yesterday.

"Come here," he says, voice low. "Let me hold you."

I bury myself in him, inhaling the scent of his neck, feeling his hands rub slow circles on my back, feeling every inch of me relax.

"Tell me a story," I whisper, laying my head on his chest.

His skin is warm beneath my cheek.

His breath brushes the top of my head, steady, slow, safe.

I study the pattern of hair across his chest like it's scripture. Like it is something sacred I'm meant to memorize.

He exhales through his nose, amused.

"You always want someone to tell you a story," he says. Not annoyed. Just...Leven.

A little teasing. A little guarded.

"Why don't you tell me one?" He adds.

I smile against his skin. "No, I asked first."

He shakes his head softly, but I feel the laugh in his chest and that's enough for me. I swear I'd chase that sound for miles.

"Fine," he murmurs.

I get comfortable, pressing closer, letting my fingers lightly run down his ribs. I close my eyes. I want him to tell me something honest. Something that proves I'm inside the walls he keeps up for everyone else.

He inhales, slow and thoughtful, then he begins.

"There once was a man," he says, his voice smoothing into a low, rhythmic pace. "A man who lived a very long time believing that nobody could truly know him."

I feel my chest flutter.

Already, I'm imagining him as the man.

Already, I'm romanticizing the ache.

"He had everything," Leven continues. "Women. Attention. People who adored him. People who thought he was strong and in control."

His hand traces my shoulder lazily.

"But none of them made him feel anything real."

I breathe deeper, letting the words soak into me.

"One day, he met someone different," he says. "Someone who made him think maybe he wasn't so empty after all."

My heart squeezes itself.

He means me.

He has to mean me.

"He liked her laugh. He liked her flaws. He liked how much she needed him. How much she trusted him. It made him feel important."

Another pause.

"But he wasn't used to feeling…exposed."

My eyes open slowly.

Exposed.

Such a strange word.

I lift my head slightly, opening my mouth to ask, but he keeps talking.

"He didn't tell her everything," he says softly. "Not because he didn't care. But because some truths…some truths would ruin things if they came out too soon."

A tiny chill runs across my scalp.

"What kind of truths?" I ask quietly.

He shrugs beneath me, fingers idly combing through my hair. "Things from before. Things he didn't have the heart to say. Things he hoped wouldn't matter if he loved her right."

My pulse quickens.

"So, he lies?" I ask, trying to keep my tone light.

"Not lies," he says, too fast. "Just…timing."

The chill deepens.

Just one degree.

Barely noticeable.

He keeps going.

"And this woman, she loved him so much she didn't want to question him. She didn't want to lose the feeling he gave her. She didn't want to break the magic."

He says it like a warning.

Like a promise.

Like instruction.

"So, she didn't," he finishes. "She let him be who he was. And because of that…he loved her even more."

Silence washes over us.

He strokes my hair, slow and soothing, as if the story is nothing more than a bedtime tale.

I nestle back onto his chest.

"I like your story," I whisper.

And it's true.

I like the version where love doesn't ask questions. Where timing explains everything. Where I don't have to look too closely because I trust him.

I lay in his embrace, molded into him, like if I don't move…nothing about this moment will change.

Chapter 19

1 Day After The Phone Call

I slip back into the house just after sunrise, shoes in my hand, trying to make my breathing sound normal while my fiancé, Tim, is still asleep in the bedroom. The house is quiet. The kind of quiet that makes guilt echo.

I pause at Delilah's door.

I told myself I wouldn't wake her.

That I'd make coffee and sit on the couch and pretend I'd been here all night.

But one peek won't hurt.

I push the door open.

She's curled sideways across the bed, hair a wild halo, mouth open, blanket half off her still body. She looks younger when she sleeps. Softer. Not a teenager, but a child. Something in my chest releases at the sight of her. This tiny human who doesn't even know what her mother did last night.

I step inside and kneel beside her.

My throat thickens.

"Lyla," I whisper.

Her eyes flutter open, confused and sleepy, but God…she smiles when she sees me.

"Mommy…?"

The nickname sits warm on my tongue.

Lyla.

It makes me feel like a good mom. Like I've finally unlocked something. Like I'm close enough to her now to deserve a nickname.

I stroke her frizzy hair. "Hi, baby. Get dressed, okay? I have a surprise for you."

She lights up instantly. Kids don't need much, just presence. Attention. A parent who shows up.

I can do that.

I can be that.

We spend the morning in the kitchen, making pancakes from scratch. I let her stir the batter even when she spills flour everywhere. I let her sing whatever nonsense song she wants. I let her talk for thirty minutes straight about a craft project she wants to make and nod like it's the most important conversation in the world.

Maybe it is.

"Can we go to the mall?" She asks once breakfast is done, bouncing on her toes.

"Of course, Lyla," I say, and it feels good. Too good.

We spend hours there.

Hours I don't usually give her.

I walk into stores I don't usually look at twice.

I give her a thumbs down on a blouse that is too revealing.

I say "Yes" to almost everything: ice cream, one more store, another swimsuit, another story, another hug.

And every time I say "Yes," the guilt loosens a little.

This is who I'm supposed to be.

When we sit on the grass to eat the ice cream sandwiches I bought "just because," she leans against me, her sticky fingers brushing my arm.

"I like when you're like this," she says softly.

The words go straight through me.

I swallow hard. "Like what?"

"Hmmm..." she thinks for a second, face scrunched. "Happy."

Happy.

God.

My eyes burn, but I force the tears back. I'm not crying today. Not when I've finally done something right. Not when she's calling me "Mommy" and looking at me like I'm her whole world.

I kiss the top of her head. "I like being like this too."

But the truth?

It's not motherhood that made me smile today.

It's the afterglow of Leven.

The warmth of being wanted.

The feeling of belonging somewhere, even if it's the wrong somewhere.

I look at my daughter and tell myself that loving him and loving her don't have to conflict.

That I can balance both worlds.

That I can give him my nights and her my days.

That I can be everything to everyone.

***

Delilah is in her room packing her pink and brown suitcase. Her flight is tomorrow. I can hear her humming, bouncing around, completely unaware that her mother is about to detonate the entire house.

I stand in the living room with my hands clasped in front of me, staring at the hallway, waiting for Tim to come out. My stomach feels like a fist. My pulse feels like it's trying to outrun me.

He steps out of the bedroom, halfway through folding laundry.

"Hey," he says casually. "You okay? You've been quiet all afternoon."

Quiet.

Because I've been rehearsing this conversation in my head a hundred different ways.

None of them feel right.

All of them feel cruel.

I take a breath so deep it shakes on the way in.

"Tim…can you sit down? I need to talk to you."

He gives me a slow, confused look. But he sits.

His knee bounces once. A habit of his when something feels off.

"What's going on?" He asks.

I sit across from him with just enough space that the truth can't be softened.

"I'm leaving," I say.

His knee stops bouncing.

His breath uneasy.

He blinks. Once. Twice. Then tries to keep his face calm, neutral, readable.

He fails.

"Leaving..." he repeats, his voice thin. "Leaving...what? Like, you're going to your mom's? Or you need space? Or..."

"No," I cut him off softly. "Leaving. Like...leaving you."

The air thickens between us.

The room feels too small.

The walls feel too close.

Tim sits very still.

I force the words out before I lose my nerve. "Once Delilah leaves tomorrow...I'm moving out."

He inhales sharply through his nose, his jaw locking like he's clenching a scream.

There's this horrible, fragile silence where I can see his brain trying to build a wall fast enough to protect him.

Finally he asks, "Is there someone else?"

The question slices clean through me.

I don't answer because he isn't stupid. His eyes close. His shoulders drop like I just took something out of him he needed to stand upright.

He nods once, slow and painful. "Okay. Okay."

He keeps saying "okay" like if he repeats it enough times he'll actually believe it.

But his hands are shaking.

"I don't want to fight," I whisper. "I don't want this to get ugly. I just...I need to go, Tim. I need to choose what's best for me."

He lets out a broken breath. "And I'm not that."

I swallow. "I'm sorry."

He laughs. Sharp, desperate, disbelieving. "You're sorry."

"Tim…"

"No, it's fine," he says too quickly. Too brightly. "It's okay. If this is what you need."

He looks up at the ceiling like he can hold the tears in by sheer force of will.

And then it happens.

His face caves.

His lip trembles.

His shoulders shake.

He breaks.

Not loud.

Not dramatic.

Not angry.

Just…breaks.

Tears spill down his cheeks, and he tries to wipe them away fast, as if crying is a crime he doesn't have permission to commit.

"Reya," he whispers, voice shattered. "I love you. I've been trying so hard. I thought we were okay. I thought we were working on it. I thought…"

He can't finish.

Guilt presses down on my lungs.

"Please don't cry," I say, uselessly.

He laughs again, choked, disbelieving. "What do you expect me to do? You're…you're ripping my heart out while your daughter is in the next room packing for her flight."

His hands cover his face. His shoulders shake harder.

"I finally got to meet such a precious little girl and…" He starts but can't finish. Emotions overwhelm him.

I look down at my palms, small and trembling in my lap.

I caused this.

I knew I would cause this.

But Leven's voice last night: *Come back. Stay with me. The way it's supposed to be.* Pulls at me like gravity.

"I'm sorry," I whisper again.

Tim lets out a long, trembling breath. "Just…please don't do this in front of her. Let her leave without thinking the reality she's in is falling apart."

"I won't," I say.

He nods, wiping his face, trying to pull himself back together.

Trying to be strong.

Trying to be the version of himself I always said I wanted.

"After she leaves," he says, voice barely steady, "just tell me what you need me to do."

I stand and walk past him to Delilah's door. I press my fingers to the wood. Listening to her shuffling around packing her suitcase while singing to the beat.

Tim wipes his face with both hands, slow and shaky, like he's trying to wash the grief off. But grief never washes off. It settles. It stains. It becomes part of your expression.

He sits there for a long moment, breathing unevenly, eyes red, chest still hiccuping with the tail end of a sob. And then, he inhales sharply and forces himself to get up.

"I should…go help her," he says quietly, voice paper-thin.

He walks down the hallway with the stiff posture of a man holding his own ribs in place. He knocks softly on her door before opening it.

"Hey, D," he says with a voice so soft it almost breaks him again. "Need help packing?"

Delilah looks up from the pile of clothes she's been sorting on her bed. She beams. "Tim! Yes, I need help. What dress should I wear for airport day?"

Her innocence slices me right down the middle.

Tim must feel it too, but he kneels beside her, making sure his face is turned slightly away from her and toward the pile of clothes so she can't see what's left of the crying.

"I think you should wear the yellow one," he says, smoothing the dress before folding it. "You'll look like a superstar."

Delilah giggles. "I am a superstar."

"Yeah," he whispers, swallowing hard, "you really are."

She keeps talking, rambling about snacks and airport food and how she hopes her dad bought the cereal she likes. Tim keeps nodding, smiling, answering every question with warmth he barely has the strength to fake.

But he does it anyway.

For her.

He wipes his eyes once while she isn't looking.

At one point she drops a bundle of shirts on the floor and sighs dramatically. "Ugh, packing is so hard. I'm over it." She says as she rolls her eyes.

Tim laughs, a genuine little laugh that cracks at the end. "I know, baby. I'm struggling too."

He helps her fold everything.

He tells her to sit on the suitcase so he can zip it.

He picks up the socks she keeps throwing because she can't find the match.

Then she notices something. She grabs his face with her hands, squishing his cheeks.

"Tim," she says. "Your eyes look sad."

Tim freezes.

I feel my heart stop.

He swallows. "Oh, no. I'm okay. Just tired."

She's still studying him. "You gonna be okay while I'm gone?"

He nods quickly. Too quickly.

"Of course. I'm…I'm gonna miss you like crazy. I just got to know you and you're leaving so soon. But I'll be good. Don't you worry about me."

She smiles, satisfied with his answer, and goes back to her suitcase to shove her new purse inside.

He sees me standing in the doorway.

For a second, neither of us speaks.

And then he clears his throat, trying to pull himself together one more time.

"I'll finish helping her," he says quietly. "Just…can you give me a little space?"

I nod. And even though I want to help her pack, I give them this moment. He deserves this moment.

He's just trying to stay intact long enough not to ruin Delilah's last night here. He's trying to be the parent I'm pretending to be.

I step away from the door, leaning against the hallway wall, listening to Delilah's laughter spill out of the room like everything is normal.

And Tim…Tim is in there stitching himself together with threads that keep snapping.

Chapter 20

6 Hours After The Phone Call

I show up at Leven's apartment that night.

The blue door, the one that always gives me anxiety and somehow calms my weary spirit, feels different now.

Almost…judging.

Like it knows something I don't.

Like it's warning me.

Or disappointed.

But I don't cry.

This is what I want.

What I have always wanted since the day I met him.

Since the night we sat on his couch and watched Woman King, when he held my ankle absentmindedly and I swore I felt fate tugging on me.

But that feels like a lifetime ago. And I don't even think Leven is the same person I met.

But I also know that's mostly my fault. Because I hurt him. Because I accepted Tim's proposal.

I doubted.

But right now, I choose him.

And I will always choose him.

When he opens the door, he doesn't look like himself.

He's still got the clenched fists. Still the ticking jaw. Still the intensity in his eyes that makes me feel small and chosen at the same time.

But tonight…he looks different.

Like there's something behind his eyes that wasn't there before.

A shadow. A bruise that hasn't surfaced yet.

He doesn't step aside to let me in. So we just stand there, staring at each other.

The background humming. My palms sweating. His breathing uneven.

It's almost as if he's shocked to see me.

As if part of him didn't think I would really choose him.

Didn't think I'd leave my daughter sleeping in her bed to come here.

I don't know who should move first. If I should wrap my arms around him like in the movies. If I should thank him for choosing me over his wife. If I should ask about the wife at all or pretend she never existed.

If I should apologize or wait for him to apologize or just stand here and let him decide what happens next.

We stay like that one second too long.

Long enough for doubt to flicker in my chest.

Then he reaches for me.

He yanks me forward, pulls me into a sloppy hug, and starts kissing me. Hard, hungry, frantic. Like he needed me to finally breathe again, like he's trying to devour every part of me that dared to leave him.

Our hands race against each other, grabbing, dragging, claiming.

His mouth is everywhere. My body is shaking. My thoughts dissolve.

Because in this moment, he wants me.

In this moment, he chooses me.

In this moment, everything else—Tim, Delilah, his wife, reality—vanishes.

In this moment, I finally feel like I belong to someone.

He pulls me inside without breaking the kiss, the door slamming shut behind us, loud enough to make my heart jolt. His hands are already on my hips, sliding under my shirt like he's angry I still have clothes on.

Everything is rushed.

Desperate in a way that doesn't feel flattering, it feels like I'm a lifeline he's drowning against.

We barely make it to the couch before he pushes me down onto it, his breath hot against my neck, his weight settling over me like he's trying to pin the whole world in place.

"Don't leave me again," he murmurs against my skin.

I whisper, "Never," even though I'm not sure he hears it.

He moves like he's been starving. Like he's punishing me. Like this is the only language we have left.

I don't say a word.

I don't slow him down.

I don't ask if he's okay or if he needs a minute.

I let him take whatever he needs from me, because I believe I owe him that much.

Our bodies find a rhythm that we've built over months. Fast, rough, needy, familiar in ways that make my chest ache. His fingers dig into my thighs like he's trying to anchor himself to something real. I grab onto his shoulders like if I hold tight enough, maybe he'll soften, maybe he'll love me the way he used to.

When he finally collapses onto me, his breath ragged, something in him loosens.

Not warmth.

Not love.

Just…relief.

Like anxiety draining from a wound.

I turn onto my side, watching him for any sign that he's still mine.

"Leven?" I whisper.

He doesn't look at me.

For a moment, I don't know if I should reach for him or pretend I'm fine or ask him if he's okay. I'm terrified the wrong choice will push him away again.

Finally, he says quiet, cold, almost distracted. "You did the right thing."

I must fall asleep at some point, wrapped around him like he's the answer to every question I should have asked myself, because when I open my eyes, the room is soft with early morning light.

I expect distance.

Coldness.

Regret.

I expect him to be turned away from me, already dressed, already on his phone, already somewhere else in his mind.

But instead, he's watching me.

Watching me like he never slept.

Watching me like I'm the only thing in the room worth looking at.

His hand moves slowly up my arm, fingertips tracing my skin like he's mapping it. Like he's relearning me. Like he's memorizing me.

"There she is," he whispers.

I fall in love with him again.

"I missed you," he says, the words spilling out like he couldn't hold them anymore. "God, Reya…I missed you so much."

Something inside me melts.

Dissolves.

Becomes liquid and warm and stupid.

He kisses my forehead, then my cheek, then my jaw, slow and affectionate, like we've been together for years.

Like last night wasn't frantic and angry.

"You don't understand what you do to me," he murmurs. "The way I feel when you're here…it's like everything makes sense again."

My chest desperately reaches for him.

A deep, embarrassing ache.

He lifts my chin so I'm looking right at him.

His eyes are soft, open, vulnerable in a way I've never seen. Not even in the early days.

"You're my peace, Reya." He says. "I love you to the moon and back." He nestles his nose into my neck, but the words are what steal my breath. Steal my logic. Steal every question I planned to ask.

He pulls me into another kiss. Slow this time, tender, purposeful. The kind of kiss that fools you into thinking everything is okay. Everything is meant. Everything is destiny.

When he pulls back, he brushes his thumb across my bottom lip like he's savoring it.

"I don't want you leaving today," he says. "Not after last night."

My voice comes out small. "I have to get back to Delilah."

He nods, but he doesn't let me go.

Instead, he tightens his arm around me, pulling me back into his chest like he's afraid I'll evaporate.

"Okay. But come back tonight."

A beat.

"Stay with me. The way it's supposed to be."

My heart flips.

Literally flips.

And in that moment, his wife becomes a ghost.

A flicker in my peripheral vision I don't dare turn toward.

Because if I say her name…if I even breathe the question…

If I ask, Who is she?

Why didn't you tell me?

What does she mean to you?

This moment will evaporate.

This softness will harden.

This rare version of him will vanish.

So, I don't ask. I just love him through it.

Chapter 21

1 Hour After The Phone Call

I text him with trembling thumbs.

"Delilah leaves on Thursday. Can you wait until then? I promise I will be yours."

The dots appear instantly.

Disappear.

Reappear.

Then one word comes through: No.

My breathing stops for a second.

Then becomes sharp. Weak. Hollow.

I inhale, long enough that it hurts. I am being pulled in two directions. In two realities I desperately want but can never have at the same time.

I could bring Delilah with me.

Sit her down and explain that her mother has been cheating on her fiancé and now we're going to go live with Leven, a man she's never met or heard about. Tell her this is "love." Tell her this is normal. Tell her this is the life her mother chose.

But she just got here.

She's a kid.

And dragging her into my chaos feels like dragging her into a fire and calling it warmth.

I could lie to Tim.

Tell him I'm overwhelmed.

Tell him I need a little air, a little space, a little night drive to clear my head. I could sneak out, meet Leven, let him hold me, breathe him in, remind myself who I am when I'm with him.

Or I could walk away from Leven.

I could wipe my hands of him.

Block him.

Delete him.

Pretend none of this ever existed.

But that last one isn't an option.

When I'm with Leven it's the only time I feel like I can truly breathe.

Like my lungs remember how to expand.

Like my heart remembers how to beat.

And *I* hurt *him*.

I broke us.

And he still wants me so badly that he can't go one more night without me.

My only two options are: take Delilah…or leave Delilah.

And both options feel like choosing which part of myself to sacrifice.

Chapter 22

45 Minutes After The Phone Call

I'm wiping down the counter when my phone buzzes again, his name lighting up the screen like it has the right to still be there.

Leven.

Calling.

Calling again.

My hands shake so hard I have to grab the edge of the sink just to steady myself. Delilah is in the living room humming at the TV, wrapped in the blanket she still drags around like a security badge, and I swear to God the sound of her small voice is the only thing keeping me from falling apart on the tile.

Married.

He is married.

Married.

I keep repeating it in my head like maybe the word will change. Like maybe I misheard. Like maybe the woman, *his wife*, got something wrong.

But his voice in the voicemail said, "Please answer. I can explain."

Explain what?

Explain who I've been sleeping with?

Explain why a whole wife is calling me asking if I know she exists?

My phone buzzes again. This time it's a text.

Leven: Babe please. I'm begging you. Don't do this. Don't shut down. It's not what you think.

My stomach pulls tight, the way it always does right before I fold. I hate that my body responds to him even now, after this, like it forgot how to protect me.

I force myself to turn the screen face down on the counter. I try to breathe. I try to be a mother. The good version of myself. The one who doesn't break in front of her daughter.

But the phone goes off again.

And again.

Delilah looks up.

"Mommy, your phone's loud."

I swallow. "I know baby. Just ignore it."

Except I can't.

I grab the phone and step into the hallway, pressing it to my ear before I can think better of it. "What?"

His voice comes in rushed, frantic, as if I betrayed him.

"Reya…I swear to you, this is not what you think. She's lying. She always lies. You know how many times she's tried to ruin my life? How many times she's tried to destroy what we have?"

My forehead presses against the wall, cold drywall grounding me. "She's your wife."

There's a sharp inhale on his end. "I told you it was complicated."

"Complicated?" A laugh slips out. Ugly, sharp, hysterical. "A whole marriage is not complicated, Leven."

But then his voice softens, and that softness always does something to me.

"Baby…babe, listen. I'm not the one who did something wrong here. You are the one who walked away from me. You left me for Tim. That…what you did, that's what put us in this position."

The guilt hits fast and hard, even though I know it shouldn't.

Even though it's backwards.

Even though he should be the one drowning in it.

But that's the thing about Leven, he never has to prove anything. He just has to say it with enough conviction, and suddenly my shame belongs to him.

"Reya," he says quietly, "if you want me to forgive you…if you want any chance of us getting past this…you need to leave Tim. Now. Today. And come home."

Home.

He says it like it's a place I've actually been allowed to belong.

My throat thickens. "I can't just…leave. I have Delilah. And I told myself I'd never…"

"Don't start that," he snaps, then steadies his tone. "If you loved me the way you say you do, you'd show me. Actions, Reya. Not words. You say you're all in? Prove it."

I close my eyes.

Because part of me wants to.

God help me, part of me wants to run to him, to cling to the fantasy I built out of scraps. The version of him that only exists in my head.

But then I hear Delilah's laugh from the living room, light and soft and real.

"Leven…I can't leave her."

"I'm not asking you to leave her," he says, but there's an edge in his voice that says he absolutely is. "I'm asking you to stop choosing Tim over me. I'm asking you to fix the damage *you* caused. If you don't come here, Reya…if you don't show me that you choose me…I'm done with you."

The words linger like a bruise beneath the surface.

Because I'm terrified he means it.

Because some horrible, broken part of me believes this is my last chance at being loved by him. The wrong man. The right man. The man who has never actually loved me the way I loved him.

"I can't just pack up and leave," I whisper.

"You can," he says. "You just don't want to."

Silence.

His voice softens again, velvet and poison. "Babe, don't make me walk away. You know I won't stay where I'm not chosen."

I don't answer.

"You think. You decide. But if you want me, Reya…you come tonight."

The line clicks.

I stand there, phone in hand, heart splitting into the version of me I promised I'd be and the version of me he built out of weakness.

Delilah calls from the living room.

"Mommy? Can we have pizza for lunch?"

My voice cracks. "Yeah, baby. I'm coming."

I wipe my face.

Straighten my shoulders.

Try to breathe around the fracture.
Tonight.
He wants me tonight.
And I don't know which version of myself is going to win.

Chapter 23

10 Minutes After The Phone Call

He was the perfect man for me…the only man for me. My safe place. My secret.

"Mommy, can we do something together?" Delilah's voice floats through the bedroom door, light and hopeful.

I snap back into reality, realizing my cheeks are wet. I swipe at them, but the tears just smear. "Uh…yeah, baby. Let me umm, take a shower first."

"Okay!" She calls back, her footsteps skipping away.

I close the door to the bathroom and twist the shower knob until the water roars. Steam climbs the walls. I crank the music as loud as my phone will go, the bass thudding in my chest like a second heartbeat.

I don't even make it into the shower before it breaks out of me. Loud, ugly sobs that tear from my throat. It's the sound you make when you've been burned, when the pain is so sharp your body doesn't know how to contain it. Like I just lost my closest friend.

I sink to the floor; knees tucked under me. The tile is cold through my skin, but I can't stop shaking. My chest heaves. My breathing is ragged, uneven.

He's married.

The words slam around in my skull, over and over, until they feel like a chant.

He's married.

He's married.

He's married.

I knew something was off. I felt it in my bones. But I made myself believe him. I let him make me believe him.

I go through my mental Rolodex:

The extra loofahs he swore belonged to his daughter. The women's clothes he explained away without blinking. The toothbrushes lined up like soldiers in a cup.

The book he told me I wasn't allowed to talk about.

All of it. Right there. I just didn't want to see it.

"How could I be so stupid?" I whisper to the empty room.

I stretch out on the cool floor, the steam curling around me until the air feels heavy. My hair sticks to my damp face. My body feels hollow.

And it's the worst possible timing. I don't get to shatter. I don't get to process. My daughter is waiting for me to fry eggs and pour juice. Tim is somewhere in this house, probably already suspicious.

How do I mourn a relationship I was never allowed to have?

How do I grieve someone who, by his own lies, never belonged to me in the first place?

The water is still running, pounding against porcelain. I haven't stepped under it once.

How can he hide an entire marriage? Where does she live? Why don't they live together? How is he able to live two completely separate lives?

So many questions that I need answers to.

My phone sits on the counter, screen dark. No new messages.

I force myself to stand, splashing cold water from the sink over my face until my skin tingles. The steam has loosened my curls, and I twist it into a messy bun just to get it out of my way. I study my reflection in the mirror, red eyes, damp cheeks.

Smile.

Smile for the sake of the little girl outside that door.

It feels foreign on my face, but it's enough to pass at a glance.

By the time I step into the kitchen, Delilah's already at the table.

"Can we make bacon too?" She asks, her voice bubbling with excitement.

"Bacon it is," I say, my voice cracking but forcing lightness into my tone. I pull the pack out of the freezer and put it in the sink with trembling hands.

Tim wanders in a minute later, rubbing his eyes, the faint smell of beer clinging to his T-shirt. He leans against the counter, watching me over the rim of his coffee mug.

"You're up early," he says. It's casual, but there's a flicker in his eyes, the kind that makes me feel like I'm under a microscope.

"Delilah wanted breakfast," I answer, flipping a pancake before it can burn.

He nods slowly, his gaze lingering a beat too long before he looks at my daughter. "Smells good, kiddo."

Delilah beams. "I helped."

I keep my focus on the pan, hiding the way my fingers tremble when I reach for the spatula. My phone sits face-down on the counter, inches from Tim's elbow. I can feel it there, heavy as a stone.

One part of me wants to grab it, call again, demand answers. The other part knows I have to wait. Wait until I can breathe without my voice shaking.

Wait until I'm alone.

Wait until he's ready to talk to me.

Leven has my heart in his hand, and now he's squeezing.

I smile again, plating pancakes, sliding one in front of Delilah with extra syrup.

"You're the best," she says between bites.

Inside, though, the words echo in my head like a drumbeat: He's married. He's married. He's married.

Chapter 24

The Phone Call
The Day I Chose Him

"I'm sorry to bother you," the woman on the phone begins, her voice tight, almost trembling. A pause stretches on the line, thick with tension, and my grip on the phone tightens. "But I think you're sleeping with my husband."

Her words hang in the air, detonating like a bomb.

A cold, icy dread slithers down my spine. My breathing changes, and my mind races, trying to process what she's just said. "What?" I croak out, my voice barely above a whisper.

***

I'm pacing the room, ready to hurl the phone at the wall, when it finally rings. His name, Leven, lights up the screen. My stomach flips, relief surging so hard it almost hurts. I swipe to answer.

"What the hell, Leven! You're fucking married?" The words burst out before I can think. I press the phone harder against my ear, like pressure might change what I'm about to hear.

My heart is breaking.

His voice is steady.

"First of all, calm your tone. Who are you cussing at?"

I freeze. "Sorry, I was just…"

"I don't care if you're mad or not. You know how to talk to me."

"Sorry," I say again, my voice smaller now. "You're married? And you failed to mention it?" The way he talks to me, he knows how to handle me. I love how he is able to command respect, even now. Even now when I am falling apart, I can't help but smile.

There's a sigh on the line, one I can picture: head tilted back, eyes closed, his fingers on the bridge of his nose, gathering patience. "I didn't think I had to mention it because me and Talia are through."

I don't say anything. My mind is too loud, the extra toothbrush, the women's clothes, the nights he didn't answer. All of it crashing together.

"I know I should have told you," he continues, "but I didn't think it was necessary since me and her haven't been a thing in years."

"But…"

"I have no reason to lie to you, Reya."

The certainty in his voice is a drug. My chest loosens; my pulse slows. "True," I whisper. And I believe him.

He exhales like he's been waiting for me to say that. "Talia got into my phone earlier. She blocked your number. That's why you couldn't reach me."

I swallow. "Oh." My mind wants to argue, but my heart clings to the explanation like a lifeline.

Then his tone shifts, sharper. "I've already filed for divorce. I've just been waiting on her to sign the papers." His voice is soothing. "You know the only reason I even went back to her was because you were wearing Tim's ring. You flaunted that ring in my face like it wouldn't hurt me. But it did, Reya."

The accusation stings, but I take it in. "I…I didn't mean…"

"You knew how that would look and you made a choice. Don't act like I wanted this."

I close my eyes because part of me wants to argue.

To say this isn't the same. That this is a whole life that he didn't tell me about.

"I'm sorry," I say, the words tasting bitter on my tongue. "I didn't mean to push you away."

He lets the silence stretch before speaking again, his voice softer now, almost tender. "I know you didn't. That's why I'm here. I just need you to understand my side."

"I do," I say quickly. And I mean it. Or maybe I just need to mean it.

"Good," he says, and my whole body reacts, the tension in my shoulders easing, the corners of my mouth twitching like I've been given something precious instead of something poisonous.

We hang up, and I just sit there, trying to trace the moment. Trying to find the exact second everything flipped. How I went from furious to apologizing…in less than ten minutes.

Wondering if this is the only lie. Because if this is the only lie he has ever told me, then I can handle this. We can get through this.

I press my thumb against the screen like it might give me answers.

But all I feel is him.

And I sit there wondering…will I make the right decision.

Part 3

Reya

What's Left

I tell myself I'm moving forward.
Some days I believe it.
Some days…I don't.

Chapter 1

10 Minutes Free

Fuck.

Fuck.

Fuck.

My knuckles slam into the steering wheel, the hollow thud vibrating up my forearm. The leather under my fingertips feels too smooth, too cold, too wrong against the heat rushing through me. Tears spill fast, hot, blurring the road into a watercolor wash of blue and beige and sunlight.

My foot sinks like dead weight against the gas. I peel away from the beach, the salt air still clinging to my skin, still burning my eyes. If I smell the ocean for one second longer, I'll turn the wheel around and go back.

This is the only way I can leave him, by making him angry enough to let me go.

Because I'm not strong enough to walk away from his softness. Not strong enough to walk away from the way he says my name.

My phone lights up.

His name glows on the screen like a warning.

Fuck.

Breathe.

Steady.

Steady.

I swipe.

"Hello?"

"Hey," he says. His voice, God his voice, it comes through warm, smooth, familiar. Like honey poured over a bruise. "What's taking so long?"

My chest hurts. I grip the wheel so hard my fingers ache.

"Leven…" I inhale deeply. I picture him standing on the beach, looking toward the parking lot. "I'm not coming back."

Silence. Not the peaceful kind. The kind that stands in front of you with its fists clenched.

"What do you mean, Reya?" His voice lowers.

I can practically hear his jaw tightening.

"I love you, Leven." The words scrape on the way out. A piece of me is still clinging to them, clawing at them. "I love you so fucking much." My eyes moisten because I know that is the last time I will say those words to him.

"But I can't do this anymore."

He exhales hard through his nose. I imagine the flare of his nostrils, the disappointment settling on his face.

"So, you're just gonna leave me in San Diego?" His tone shifts. Blame, then pity, then something darker. "I don't think you thought this through."

My throat goes dry.

Tears leak again, slow and steady.

"I did think this through," I whisper. My voice is thinner now. Smaller.

"Reya, you know if you don't come back, we're done. Right?"

"I know," I breathe. "That's what I'm hoping for."

I hang up before I lose my nerve.

My hands are trembling against the wheel. The tremble climbs up my arms and into my shoulders like electricity. As I get on the freeway, the world tilts. Like the asphalt isn't flat, like the sun is too bright, like everything around me is spinning a half-second faster than I can think.

I inhale.

I exhale.

I fail at both.

What do I do now?

What the fuck do I do now?

I call Ava.

She picks up on the second ring. "I can't believe I'm talking to you twice in one week," she says lightly.

Doesn't she hear the storm tearing through my chest?

I don't respond.

"Reya? Hello?"

"I want to go back." My voice cracks. "What if he hates me?"

"He will hate you," she says. "But you have to be brave."

Be brave.

Be brave.

Our childhood mantra echoes in my skull. The one Mom made us whisper after my dad, Luther, took the first creature that ever loved me. "Be brave girls, be brave." The memory comes back metallic and sharp, like tasting blood.

Ava feels it too. "You are Luma," she says softly.

I scoff. "That was just a stupid story we made up."

"Why did we make it up, Reya?"

Because we needed light in a house full of shadows.

"Because we were living with a monster," I answer.

"Because we had a giant," she corrects. "And we needed to survive him."

Leven is not a monster like Luther.

Leven was gentle.

He…was gentle.

I swallow hard.

The past tense slices through me.

Like part of me already knows I'm not going back.

"My light is gone," I say. Everything blurs. Billboards, mountains, sky. My mind is spinning faster than the wheels on the asphalt.

"No," Ava says. "Your light is dim because you keep giving it to giants."

"Leven is nothing like Luther." I try to believe it. I try to anchor myself to that truth. I never woke up with bruises on my face, only on my heart.

"Sometimes emotional abuse is worse," she says. "Because it steals your reflection. It steals your certainty."

My phone buzzes.

A text from him: Please don't walk away from me, Reya. You're the only woman who ever understood me.

My chest caves in.

"What if he was genuine?" I whisper. "What if I mistook everything? What if he just wanted to be understood?"

"Okay," she says. "What if he was genuine?"

A beat.

"Were you happy?"

The silence that follows is thick enough to choke on.

"Did he ever make you feel important? Or did you spend every minute trying to earn a place in his life?"

My lips part to respond but… "You don't understand," I choke. "I killed my baby."

The dam explodes.

The sob tears out of me like a scream swallowed by my own body. My chest constricts so tightly I can't breathe. I swerve, crossing two lanes before my brain catches up. Horns blare. Someone yells. I pull over and slam the car in park.

My forehead hits the steering wheel. The horn honks under me until it doesn't. I'm shaking so hard the car feels like it's vibrating.

"I killed my baby," I repeat. It comes out like a confession and a punishment. Drool spills from my mouth onto my shirt. I can't inhale. I sound like I'm choking on my own heart.

"Oh my God," Ava gasps. "Reya…I'm so sorry. I didn't know."

I sob harder. My lungs seize. The air in the car feels too thick to swallow.

Clarabelle.

Or Brandon.

Or the maybe that never became anything else.

My baby is gone and I am driving into a future that terrifies me.

"Can I call you back?" I whisper.

"No."

"Ava, please. I can't…"

She exhales. "Okay."

I hang up.

I press my forehead to the steering wheel again. My breathing is ragged, uneven, like each inhale is a punishment. I close my eyes. The darkness feels safer than the world outside.

Then, from somewhere deep in my memory…Luma.

Her story rises in me like something ancient. Something I buried to survive.

Chapter 2

Luma

Once, before the sky remembered how to be blue, there lived a tiny creature named Luma.

She was no bigger than a pinecone, with soft moss-green fur and a belly that glowed like a firefly trapped behind glass. Inside her chest hung a lantern, small as a teardrop, warm as a bedtime story whispered under blankets. It pulsed whenever she felt safe. Whenever someone loved her. Whenever the world was gentle.

The forest she lived in was old. Older than names. Older than promises. Trees curled like dancers frozen mid-spin, mushrooms glowed a soft blue near the roots, and the river shimmered like melted moonlight. Every sound…every chirp, rustle, breeze, felt like the world humming her name.

Luma's lantern glowed brightest when she loved the world.

And then, one day, the world shook.

Birds fell silent.

The river stilled mid-whisper.
Even the sun dimmed in confusion.

The giant had entered the forest.

He towered above the treetops. His shadow swallowed the ground. His footsteps cracked branches like bones. His eyes were storms. Grey and roaming and searching for something else to break.

He noticed Luma almost instantly.
Her innocent little glow flickered in the darkness, calling attention like a spark in a cave.

He crouched. The trees groaning under his weight and narrowed his eyes.

"That," he growled, "is too bright."

Before she could hide her glow, before she could dim herself, before she could even run…he wrapped his massive hand around her and squeezed.

The lantern inside her tiny chest shattered with a sound soft as a sob.

Fragments burst into the air like dying stars. The light scattered, the glow extinguished, and the giant dropped her to the forest floor without a second thought. Her small body stilled. Her glow went out.

He left the forest darker than he found it.

But as the shattered fragments drifted through roots and shadows, something happened the giant didn't see:

One shard hadn't flown far.

It was small, no bigger than a grain of rice, nestled against Luma's rib where the lantern had once been. A secret scrap of light.

It didn't shine brightly.
Not anymore.
It glowed faintly, timidly, like a heartbeat afraid to hope again.

And every time Luma found the strength to create even the slightest warmth within herself: a thought, a memory, a tiny moment of gentleness...that little shard glowed.

Barely.
Softly.
But enough.

Enough to remind her she was still here.
Enough to whisper: You are not gone.

Meanwhile, the other lantern shards scattered.
They crawled beneath roots, slipped under stones, hid inside moss beds, and curled like small, frightened animals. And every night they whispered:

Stay small. Stay quiet. Stay safe.
The giant can't crush what he can't find.

Years passed.

Trees thickened.
The river found its voice.
The sky learned blue again.

And one night, a warm breeze swept through the forest. A lullaby-breeze. The kind that arrives only when the world decides something is ready to change.

It touched every hidden shard and whispered: You can stop hiding now.

The shards stirred.
Some flickered. Some trembled. Some glowed angrily red. Some glowed sleepily blue.
But they all began to crawl back to the old oak, the place where Luma once danced in puddles and chased the wind.

Luma felt the breeze too.
The little shard inside her chest quivered.
It glowed just a little brighter.

She placed her hand over her small heart, surprised by the warmth rising from inside her instead of around her.

For the first time in years, she stood.
She followed the trembling in her chest.
She walked toward the oak.

The scattered shards gathered. Touched. Fused.
And when Luma stepped into the clearing, the lantern re-formed: crooked, cracked, beautiful.

The shard inside her chest leapt toward its place, sliding into the lantern like it had been waiting for home.

Her light rose.

Not perfect.
Not smooth.
Not the innocent glow she once had.

But stronger. Deeper. Braver.

And the forest bloomed with light again. Not because everything healed, not because the giant vanished, but because Luma's tiny shard of self-made warmth refused to die.

Lanterns don't stay broken.
Not forever.
Not when even a single piece keeps glowing.

My breathing slows eventually. Not because I calm down, but because my body runs out of places to fall apart.

The forest inside my head fades. The giant. The shards. The light. All fade into nothingness.

All I'm left with is the sound of passing cars and my own heartbeat pounding against my ribs like it's trying to escape too.

The steering wheel is warm beneath my forehead.

My cheeks are wet.

My shirt is soaked with tears and the kind of drool that belongs to grief, not shame.

I press my palm against my stomach.

There is no flutter.

No heartbeat.

No life.

But there is a memory.

A warmth so faint I don't know if it's real or if I'm begging it to be.

A single shard. A single piece of me that might still glow if I can just believe in it long enough.

My voice is barely a whisper.

Barely breath.

"I am Luma."

The words tremble out of me like a spark trying to decide if it wants to live. I close my eyes and press my hand harder against my belly.

"I am Luma," I say again, quieter this time, but steadier.

I sit in the car, broken and cracked and trying to breathe, hoping there is still some tiny warmth left inside me.

Hoping one shattered piece is enough to begin again.

Chapter 3

I Don't Turn Around

Wednesday is a great day when it's not day six of the silent treatment.

My nervous system can't decide whether to stretch or flinch.

It keeps waiting for noise. For impact. For *him*.

The quiet in Ava's apartment feels wrong. Too gentle. Too safe. Like my body doesn't know what to do without the steady chaos Leven used to pump into my bloodstream. The ache of pleasing someone. The rush of anticipating his needs.

It's embarrassing how much my muscles miss it.

How much my mind keeps reaching for the pattern.

When I was with Tim, I morphed into the prettiest, softest, most deserving version of myself so he wouldn't see the cracks.

With Leven, I didn't morph.

I disappeared.

I shape-shifted into the woman he needed. A woman that was loyal, eager, devoted to his moods and his rhythms. I made myself proof. Proof that I loved him. Proof that I was worth choosing. Proof that he was my soul mate, even when he wasn't choosing me back.

Now the silence stretches around me like a hallway with no exit.

I'm sitting on my sister's couch, wrapped in her oversized throw blanket, a mug of coffee warming my palms. The sun through her blinds cuts the room into stripes, and the morning air smells like vanilla creamer and the detergent she loves too much.

And for the first time in days, no one is calling me.

No one is waiting for me.

No one is angry at me.

And I don't know what to do with that.

I take a sip, swallow, and stare into the rippling surface of my coffee.

What happens now?

What happens to a woman after she leaves her giant?

The coffee in my hands goes lukewarm, but I keep sipping it anyway. It gives me something to hold, something to do, something to pretend is grounding me.

It's been almost a week since I left San Diego.

Six full days.

One hundred and forty-four hours.

Long enough, I tell myself.

Long enough to prove I'm strong.

Long enough to text him without falling straight back into his orbit.

Right?

I pull my knees to my chest, tightening the blanket around me. My brain starts the soft manipulation I always fall for: You're okay now. You're different now. You can handle a message. You can handle him.

My gaze drifts toward my phone, hovering above the screen like it's hovering over a detonator.

I imagine the text I'd send: Hey. Just checking on you.

Or maybe something lighter.

Something harmless.

Something that doesn't scream "I'm drowning without you".

My pulse quickens and hope curls in my belly like smoke.

I'm ready.

I'm strong enough.

I can do this.

My phone buzzes.

The sound slices through the room.

Before my brain even forms a thought, my entire body reacts. I grab the phone faster than the speed of light. My heart leaps. My breath stops. My fingers tremble around the screen.

It has to be him.

It has to be.

He felt me thinking about him. He knows. He always knows.

I flip the screen over.

Scam Likely.

The name stares at me like a joke.

My chest collapses in on itself. My hands shake because I can feel it. In the way my heart crashed, in the way my breath hitched, in the way my mind reached for him like a starving animal.

I'm not ready.

Not even close.

And maybe...maybe I will never be ready.

"Please don't tell me you're about to call him."

Ava's voice floats in from the hallway.

I jump.

I wipe my face even though I wasn't crying.

And I pretend I wasn't just bargaining with the universe for a ghost of him.

Ava steps into the room, hair tied up, wearing her giant college hoodie, studying me the way only an older sister can.

She raises an eyebrow.

"Well?" She says.

And I know she already knows the answer.

Ava folds her arms, leaning against the doorway with that look, the one that says she's about to snatch the fantasy right out of my hands before I can glue it back together.

"Reya," she says carefully, "you jumping at your phone like that? That's not strength. That's addiction."

I roll my eyes, but it's weak. My throat is already tightening.

She walks closer, sits on the arm of the couch, studying me like she's trying to measure the distance between the story I'm telling myself and the one she sees.

"You miss him," she says. "I get it. Withdrawal feels like grief when the person was your whole world. But missing someone does not mean you were meant for them."

I clench my jaw.

Ava continues, gentle but relentless. "He hurt you, Reya. He made you shrink to fit his moods. And now your brain is trying to rewrite the whole damn relationship so you can go back to something familiar instead of facing the unknown."

I fidget with the bracelet around my wrist. The one with the small moon that was once filled with love and promises.

The words hit hard and I don't want to hear them.

Not from her.

Not from the sister who left.

My fingers tighten around the blanket I wrapped myself in. "You don't understand."

Ava sighs. "I understand more than you think."

"No, you don't." The heat builds in my chest. "You weren't there. Not really. You never stayed long enough to see what it was like after you walked out the door."

Ava blinks, surprise flickering across her face.

I keep going, because the truth is rising in me like a storm I can't stop.

"You get to sit here and talk about what's best for me, what I need to do, how I should heal." My voice cracks. "But where were you when we were kids?"

Ava's jaw ticks.

She takes a deep inhale.

Her eyes drop for half a second, and that's all it takes for the fury in me to find oxygen.

"Now you want to be a sister?" I spit the words. "Now you want to show up? Where were you, Ava? Where were you when I needed you…"

I cry. "I needed you…"

My voice breaks.

She doesn't defend.

She doesn't look away.

She swallows, then says softly, "I'm sorry I left you there with him."

My breath stops.

She continues, voice low and shaking, "I'm sorry I ran. I'm sorry you were alone with a monster. I'm sorry you had to face things you were too young to understand." Her eyes shine, but she keeps them steady on mine. "But Reya…I was a kid too."

My throat goes dry.

She presses her hand against her chest. "I had to get out. I had to. If I didn't leave, I don't know who I would've become. And yes, it was selfish. Painfully selfish." Her voice cracks. "And I have hated myself for it every day."

Silence stretches between us.

Heavy and human and old.

Ava leans forward, her voice barely above a whisper. "Some days I was so sad, I was mad at the world. I didn't know how to be your sister when my world had no walls. No structure. I was dying too, Reya." She looks at me. Really looks at me.

"But I'm here now." Her eyes soften. "And I'm not leaving this time."

My chin trembles. "You promise?"

She nods. "Yeah. I promise."

I exhale a shaky, uneven, childlike breath.

The kind you take when someone finally says the words you needed thirty years ago.

Ava inches forward, like she's approaching a wounded animal. Slow, careful, giving me every chance to pull away.

I don't. I can't.

She reaches for me and pulls me into her chest.

My forehead drops into her shoulder.

Her arms wrap around me tight. Tighter than she ever held me as a kid, and something inside me cracks open so violently I grip the back of her hoodie just to stay upright.

I crumble.

Right there on her couch.

Right there in her arms.

Right there in the place I never thought I'd feel safe enough to break.

Ava presses her cheek against the top of my head, breathing shakily. "I've got you," she whispers. "I've got you now."

The words hit me harder than any memory ever has.

I shake.

I sob without making sounds.

I let everything inside me tremble and fall and scatter like shards on the floor because the love she is offering me is pure.

And then little footsteps thunder down the hallway.

Ava barely has time to loosen her grip before her kids launch themselves onto the couch. One on my lap, one climbing over her shoulder, both giggling with the kind of joy that doesn't ask permission to exist.

"Mom! Auntie Reya's crying!"

"I wanna sit on her! Let me sit!"

Ava bursts into a wet laugh, wiping her eyes. "Okay, okay but gentle you two. Gentle. Your Auntie is fragile." She says as she looks at me.

They pile onto us anyway, all elbows and tiny knees and warm little bodies pressing against mine. I'm swallowed in the chaos of it. The weight of it. The innocence of it.

And it does something.

Something small.

Something warm.

Something I didn't expect.

Deep inside me, right beneath the ache and the fear and the

bruised places I don't talk about, a faint glow stirs.

A tiny shard.

A broken piece of me I thought was dead lifts its head, crawls forward, and settles into the hollow space behind my ribs.

It glows.

Barely.

Softly.

But enough.

A warmth rises in my chest. Thin at first, then steadier as two little humans squish themselves against me like I'm some kind of safe place.

I close my eyes.

I inhale.

I hold onto the warmth like it's the last light in the forest.

Because maybe, just maybe…I am Luma.

And maybe this tiny piece of new warmth is enough to keep me alive until the rest of me finds its way home.

Chapter 4

Still Here

When I was in jail, I learned about addictions and triggers and the stupid, simple ways people fall apart.

They drilled the HALT theory into us like it was scripture:

Never get too Hungry.

Never too Angry.

Never too Lonely.

Never too Tired.

That's when you slip.

That's when you relapse.

That's when you crawl back to the thing that ruined you because it feels safer than facing yourself.

And today…

I'm not hungry.

I'm not angry.

I slept a full eight hours, so I'm not tired.

I guess that means I'm lonely. Or maybe I'm just alone.

I don't know the difference yet. I don't even know if there is one.

But I know I need to figure it out.

I need to figure me out. Reya Carter. The actual person, not the reflection of the people I attached myself to.

What makes me happy?

What fills me up?

What makes me feel whole without needing attention, affection, or someone else's validation buzzing through my phone?

I don't know. I never had room to know.

Everyone has something that lights them up on the inside except me.

The only thing I have ever loved. Truly, recklessly, painfully loved, was Leven Mercer.

And that realization is as pathetic as it is freeing.

I inhale deeply and pull out my phone.

My first instinct is to shop.

Retail therapy. Instant gratification. The easiest way to pretend I'm taking care of myself.

But if I start buying things every time I feel lonely, I'll end up broke, numb, and still missing him.

No. Not this time.

I deserve better habits. I deserve a better life. I deserve to choose something other than pain. I set the phone down and stare at it like it's a test I've failed before.

This time, I want to pass.

I slip on my sneakers and head out the door before I change my mind. The air outside hits my face like a reset button. It's dry, warm, and full of the strange chaos that only Las Vegas mornings have.

Cars hum down Maryland. Someone is yelling across a parking lot. A bus whooshes past in a cloud of dust. A group of hotel workers in uniforms power-walk to their shifts, balancing iced coffees and half-opened energy drinks. The city is alive in that impatient way that always makes me feel like I'm late for something.

I breathe it in anyway.

I start walking.

One block.

Then two.

The desert is loud today: bugs hum in the trees, wind brushing sand across the sidewalk like tiny whispers. The mountains in the distance glow pink and lavender under the early sun, like they're trying to seduce the city into slowing down.

For a moment, it works.

My body loosens.

My shoulders drop.

My thoughts stop sprinting.

Walking has always done that to me.

Even when I was locked up, pacing tiny sections of concrete was the closest thing to freedom I had.

A breeze sweeps past me, hot and dry, carrying the faint smell of dust and sage. It reminds me of that hike, the one where I reached the river and felt my lungs open for the first time in years. Where the world felt too big for my pain, and I felt too small to ruin anything.

Where I felt free.

My feet slow. A strange, quiet certainty settles into my chest.

If I'm Luma…if I'm supposed to put myself back together. If I'm supposed to gather my shards and rediscover my glow, then I need the forest.

Not the metaphorical one.

A real one.

Something green. Something alive. Something untouched by *him*.

I pull out my phone, not to text Leven, but to open a new tab for the first time in days.

"Best places to travel alone," I type. My thumb hesitates.

This would be the first trip I've ever taken by myself.

Just me.

I inhale.

I scroll.

I choose and this feels like the beginning of a new kind of light.

Chapter 5

The First Exhale

By the time I finish the walk and climb the stairs back into Ava's apartment, my cheeks are flushed, my shoulders loose, and my breath feels just a little lighter than it did this morning.

I push the door open, and stop.

Ava and Clara are standing in the kitchen, shoulder to shoulder, both staring at me over mismatched coffee mugs like two moms waiting to lecture their teenager.

I look between them.

"Oh my God," I deadpan. "Is this an intervention? Because I swear I didn't call him."

They both burst into laughter at the same time, loud and overlapping and so familiar it makes my chest ache.

Ava rolls her eyes. "Girl, nobody is thinking about him except you."

Clara sets her mug down and opens her arms. "Come here, baby."

I walk into the hug. Hers is always warm and soft and smells faintly like cocoa butter and laundry detergent. Ava joins from the other side, squeezing me until I squeak.

"I missed you." Clara says into my hair, voice thick with

honesty. “You get taller every time I see you.”

“I literally saw you a few months ago,” I mumble, trying to hide the way her words soften something in me. But was it 8 months ago? Or 9? A guilt flushes over me.

“A lot can happen in a month,” Clara shrugs, pulling back to look at me. “You left a man, cried on my voicemail, had a mental breakdown, and almost let Scam Likely ruin your day. That’s like…six months of content in Reya time.”

Ava snorts into her coffee. “‘Reya time’ is wild.”

I shove them both lightly. “Okay, can we stop acting like I’m some walking reality show?”

Clara smirks. “Are you kidding? You’ve always been our entertainment. Remember when you tried to run away from home at twelve but only made it to the next street over because you got tired?”

Ava laughs so hard she nearly spills her drink. “She took a BAG OF JOLLY RANCHERS as a survival kit.”

Clara claps her hands. “And a hair straightener! Like she was gonna find electricity in the wild.”

I groan, covering my face. “Y’all are so disrespectful.”

Clara puts a hand on her hip. “Oh, please. Remember that time Ava stole my car and you were her lookout, but you fell asleep on the porch?”

Ava gasps. “YES! And she snitched when she woke up because she thought I’d been kidnapped!”

“I WAS TWELVE!” I protest.

“TwELve,” Clara mimics my voice.

We dissolve into messy, stupid laughter, the kind that hurts your stomach and makes you lean on whoever’s closest.

For a moment, it feels like time folded in on itself and gave us our younger selves back, crowded in our old living room, passing cheap snacks back and forth, whispering secrets we were scared to say out loud anywhere else.

Ava bumps her shoulder against mine. "Seriously though," she says, voice softening, "I'm proud of you."

Clara nods. "Me too. You're doing the hard thing."

I look at both of them, two women who lived in the same broken house, who survived in their own ways, who somehow made it back to me. To each other.

For the first time in a long time, the kitchen feels full.

Full of warmth.

Full of laughter.

Full of something like home.

And inside my chest, the tiny Luma-shard glows again, just a little brighter this time.

"But seriously though, the dick must have been good," Ava says into her mug.

I nearly drop my coffee, mouth ajar as I stare at her. "AVA!"

"What?" She says in her most innocent voice.

"Had to have been," Mom agrees. "I told her orgasm and happiness has to come in the same package, but all she heard was orgasm."

"This is completely inappropriate." I say as I get out of the chair.

"Girl, we are just talking." Ava says. She stands up along with me. "No one is making fun of you, this is just how we communicate with each other." She looks at me like she is sorry.

And I realize I get defensive when it comes to Leven. Because

I should have known better. Because I should have never left Tim. Because I should have chosen better.

I sit back down. "I'm sorry. I don't know why I snap when it comes to him."

"Because you love him." Mom says. And she puts her hand on mine. "Trust me, I get it. Couldn't nobody tell me anything about Luther. Not now, and definitely not then."

She looks from me to Ava. Then settles back on me. "But baby, you made a decision to leave Tim. To pursue Leven, and that's okay. Don't be ashamed of that decision."

Her voice is soft.

"Yea, trust me, I made some bad ones myself," Ava says looking at me. "When I left home, you wouldn't believe the trouble I got myself into. I wanted to come back home every day. But I felt embarrassed because I told everyone I was better off on my own."

No one is looking at each other now, we are all looking into our own decisions. Thinking about how we failed ourselves, and how we failed each other.

"All we have is each other," Mom says to the two of us. "We are a triangle."

"I agree, and we have to make it a point to do better. We keep failing, but there is always a new day." Ava says.

I relax a little and let the comfort of my family be the anchor I need right now.

"The dick was fucking amazing," I say. Laughing a little.

"I knew it!" Ava says. And we all laugh at the beauty of it.

At the audacity of it.

At the love of it.

"I'm glad y'all are here and so understanding, because I need to borrow some money."

"Daaamn, why can't we just be here for you emotionally, why you always need some money?" She laughs.

"I want to go on a trip. To get my mind off things. And I will pay you back, geesh."

"Finally, the girls trip I been trying to get you to go on?"

"No, I think this is something I need to do on my own." I say. And as scary as it sounds, I am fully confident that this is what I need.

Chapter 6

The Dream

That night, Ava falls asleep with the television still whispering in the background.

I lie on her couch staring at the ceiling fan watching it turn slow.

My body is exhausted. My mind is not. When I finally fall asleep, I don't fall gently.

I am standing in a hospital room washed in pale gold light. Not harsh. Not fluorescent.

But soft.

The kind of light that makes everything look sacred. There is no panic here. No rushing nurses. No machines screaming. Just the steady hum of something distant and rhythmic, like a heartbeat underwater.

My body feels heavy and weightless at the same time.

I look down and my hands are trembling.

And then I hear it.

A cry. A thin fragile, brand-new cry.

The sound slices straight through me. And then they place her in my arms.

She is warm. She is so warm.

Her skin is brown and damp and perfect. Her tiny fingers curl instinctively around mine, impossibly small and impossibly strong. Her eyelashes are barely there, just soft shadows against her cheeks.

I bring her innocent body up to my face and plant my nose in the wrinkles of her neck. She smells like something I don't have words for. Milk. Warmth. Beginning.

"Clarabelle," I whisper.

The name feels like a confession and a prayer at the same time.

Her cry quiets when she rests against my chest. I feel the weight of her. Real weight. Not imagined. Not hypothetical. Solid.

Her head fits into the curve beneath my chin. Her breath flutters against my collarbone, fast and delicate. My body knows what to do.

It rocks.

It hums.

It curls around her instinctively.

Tears slide down my face without permission. "I'm here," I whisper to her. "I'm here."

I look up and I'm surrounded by love. Ava, Clara, and Delilah all stare back at me, face glistening with tears.

The room shifts and suddenly we are not in a hospital.

We are in sunlight.

A field I've never seen before. The grass is tall and soft, brushing against my legs. The sky is wide and endless, the kind of blue that doesn't belong to any season.

Clarabelle is no longer a newborn.

She's bigger now.

Maybe a year old.

Maybe two.

She stands in front of me in a pale-yellow dress, coils bouncing around her face. Her laugh rings out like wind chimes.

She runs toward me on unsteady legs.

"Mommy," she says. The word lands in my chest like a stone dropped into deep water. I kneel and catch her.

She fits against me like she was always meant to. Her arms wrap around my neck with complete trust. Complete certainty.

And that's when it hits me.

This possibility. This child could have existed outside of my fear.

I pull back slightly and look at her face. She looks like me.

But softer.

Like hope didn't have to fight so hard to survive.

"I'm sorry," I whisper, my voice breaking.

The wind moves through the grass around us, bending it gently.

"I wanted you," I tell her. "I *want* you."

Her small hand touches my cheek as she stares at me. She doesn't look confused. She doesn't look angry.

She just looks at me.

Like she understands something I don't.

The field begins to blur at the edges. The sky fading into white.

"Was I wrong?" I ask her. The question I never let myself say out loud. "Was I wrong for not wanting you to be raised by *him?*"

She tilts her head slightly, coils catching the sunlight. Then she presses her forehead to mine.

I know the answer.

It wasn't my decision to make. There are always choices. Always answers. I could have had the baby. I could have just left Leven. I didn't have to kill something that never asked to be brought in this world.

I didn't have to...

Suddenly I am back in the hospital room. Only this time it's quiet.

Too quiet. My arms are empty. The warmth is gone. I am alone, but the ache remains...

I wake up in Ava's apartment with my hand clutching at my chest.

The ceiling fan is still turning slow and unbothered.

My pillow is damp. There is no baby in my arms. No yellow dress. No field.

Just the echo of a word that never got to belong to me.

Mommy.

I lie there in the dark, staring at nothing, finally allowing myself to feel the truth I avoid when I'm awake.

There is no painless version of that choice.

There is only the version you survive.

And the version you grieve.

Chapter 7

Learning My Own Name

Friday is a great day when it's not the day you realize you have no idea how to pack for a trip you've never taken, for a woman you've never been.

My suitcase sits open on the bed like a hungry mouth waiting for direction.

I stand there staring at it, hands on my hips, trying to decide whether I should pack essentials or pack like I'm running away from my old life.

Should I bring hiking boots?

Cute outfits?

Sweats?

Do people who travel alone bring books?

Am I supposed to read on the plane like a functional adult?

I grab a stack of jeans. Put them in the suitcase.

Take them out.

Throw them on the floor.

Then put them back in again.

I swear packing should count as cardio.

When I go to grab shoes from the back of the closet, my hand brushes against something softer. Heavier. Familiar.

Leven's sweater.

The dark charcoal one he always wore when he was in a good mood. The one that smelled like him even after six washes. The one that hung off his broad shoulders and made him look softer than he ever acted.

I stare at it.

I pull it out slowly, like I'm disarming a bomb.

The moment it's in my hands, the scent hits me. Clean detergent, faint cologne, and something warm I can't understand, but I love. Memory rushes me like a wave breaking too close to shore. Before I can stop myself, I press it to my face.

God. Why does it still smell like him?

My fingers curl into the fabric. The ache in my chest comes fast, sharp, hard. I sit down on the edge of the bed, sweater clutched to my heart.

I don't mean to hug it.

But I do.

And instinctively, my eyes close.

I remember one morning, it was rare, quiet, one of the gentle days, when he sat on the edge of the bed sipping his coffee. He didn't smile often. His lips usually stayed straight or pressed or unreadable.

But that morning, I made a joke about his snoring. Something stupid, something light. And he actually smiled at me. A real one. Soft. Quick. A flash of warmth that felt like a sunrise.

I remember thinking: God, if I can make this man smile like that forever, I will be happy forever.

I hug the sweater tighter, the fabric pulled to my heart like it can resurrect something.

But then I open my eyes.

It's been a month.

A whole month without the silent treatment. Without the tension. Without his voice filling the room and my mind at the same time.

He is not here.

His sweater is just a sweater.

And I am about to take a trip for the first time in my life.

The thought terrifies me.

And thrills me.

And hurts like hell.

I lower the sweater into my lap, my hands still resting on it, not quite ready to let go.

"Okay," I whisper to myself. "Okay, Reya. You're allowed to remember the good. You're just not allowed to go back for it."

I pick up the sweater again.

This time, I fold it.

And I put it in the bottom drawer. Not the trash. Not the suitcase.

Just away.

Because healing doesn't mean burning everything that ever made me feel loved.

It means choosing not to live in the past anymore.

I stand, wipe my face, and return to the suitcase.

It's time to pack for the woman I'm trying to become.

Ava stands by the front door while I zip my suitcase closed for the hundredth time. She's watching me like she's memorizing me, like she wants to store every version of me in case I come back different. Maybe she knows I will.

When I open the door, she steps forward and pulls me into a hug.

A real one.

Not the half-armed side hug we used to give when we were pretending not to need each other.

A full-bodied, squeeze-the-lungs-out-of-you hug.

"Be safe," she murmurs into my shoulder. "And text me when you get there."

I smile. "I will."

"And text me when you land."

I snort. "Okay."

"And text me before you get on the plane so I know you're not running off with some random man…"

"Ava!"

She laughs, wiping her cheek like she's embarrassed for being emotional. "You know I'm just saying…you're an idiot magnet."

I shove her lightly. "I'm going into the woods, not Tinder."

"Still. Text me," she says again, softer this time. "Because I love you. And I want to know you're okay."

Something warm flickers in my chest, brighter than the shard, bigger than a spark, deeper than nostalgia.

This is love too.

A sister's love.

A safe love.

"I love you too," I whisper.

And I mean it in ways I didn't know I could.

***

Airports always smell like burnt coffee, tired people, and someone's spilled perfume. I move through security, through the loudspeaker announcements, through the slow-shuffling crowd with backpacks and neck pillows. Every sound echoes inside me like it's bouncing in a hollow canyon I'm still learning to fill.

When I find my seat on the plane, I slide into the window spot and rest my forehead against the cool glass. People file in. Bags thump overhead. Someone coughs. A baby is already fussing.

As the plane begins to taxi, my fingers drift to the book I tossed in my bag at the last second. Some self-help paperback I bought years ago but never opened. I flip through the first few pages, skimming words that all sound the same: healing, growth, inner child, boundaries.

But none of it hits me.

None of it feels like it's speaking to me.

I close the book and stare out the window instead. I fidget with the bracelet I haven't had the strength to take off.

As the plane lifts off the runway, the city shrinks beneath me. Las Vegas becoming a patchwork of lights and sand and heat. The desert looks small from up here. Manageable. Survivable. Almost beautiful in its emptiness.

My mind drifts. To the first fable, to Luma, to the forest where she lived and hid and pieced herself back together.

I wonder what kind of stories I would write now.

What kind of creatures would live in my mind if I let them come out. What kind of light I could create if I stopped running from myself. Maybe when I reach the forest, the real one, I'll try writing again.

Maybe I'll tell a story not about a girl hiding from a giant...but about a girl learning she never needed one in the first place.

Chapter 8

The Forest Finds Me

The cabin is smaller than I imagined.

Not cramped-small, but sacred-small. Like it was built for one person at a time. Like it's meant to hold only what you can carry inside you.

The moment I step in, the quiet hits me. Not empty, not eerie, but deep.

A kind of quiet that feels alive.

The floorboards creak softly under my steps. The air smells like cedar and old sunlight trapped in wood. There's a small fireplace built of smooth river stones, and a stack of chopped logs next to it. A single armchair sits beside a window that stretches almost from floor to ceiling, framing a view of trees. A tall, endless view of tress.

The whole place feels like it's inhaling with me.

Exhaling with me.

There's a bed tucked into one corner, covered in a quilt of burnt oranges and mossy greens. A tiny kitchen with copper pans hanging above the counter. A wooden table with scratches in it, like past visitors carved tiny pieces of their lives into it.

And it hits me, as sudden as a warm wave washing over my

ribs: I am alone. But I am not lonely.

Not in this cabin that feels like it's been waiting for me to shut the world out long enough to finally hear myself think.

I set my bag down like I'm unburdening more than just luggage.

I take off my shoes, the cold wood grounding my feet. My shoulders drop. My breath loosens. Something inside me, some tight, trembling coil inside me begins to unwind.

I don't rush to unpack. I don't fill the silence.

I just…exist.

A month ago, the quiet felt like punishment. Now it feels like permission.

Delilah would love this place, I think to myself.

After a few minutes, my body pulls me toward the door.

Not my mind…my body.

I slide the cabin door open and step onto the small porch. The air is crisp, sweet with pine and earth. The breeze is gentle, brushing the hair near my ears. I walk until my feet meet the soft patch of grass just beyond the porch.

Warmth sparks under my toes.

My breath slows because I remember this.

Not here, not this exact moment, but the sensation.

Dr. Jenson's office.

His hands folded.

He never asked me to go to my happy place. But I always wondered what it would be if he did ask.

Back then, sitting in the office of my therapist, I had to force the image.

Trees that weren't real. Sun I couldn't feel. Wind I couldn't touch.

Here, I feel everything.

The grass cushions my feet, velvety and cool.

The trees surround me, tall guardians swaying gently, whispering secrets through their leaves. A beam of sunlight breaks through the branches and lands on my skin, warm as a hand pressing reassurance into my shoulders.

I close my eyes.

My arms fall to my sides.

My mouth softens.

The warmth I imagined in his office, the warmth that flickered weakly, trembling, unsure, now builds inside me like a flame finally given oxygen.

I inhale, and the flame expands through my chest like sunlight breaking across a horizon.

I exhale, and it settles into my ribs, glowing in every crack, every scarred place, every hollowed-out ache that Leven dimmed.

That *I* dimmed.

The trees creak softly, like they're welcoming me. Like they've been waiting for me.

My eyes fill without breaking. This time, the tears don't burn. They warm.

They feel like proof.

This. This patch of grass. This wall of trees. This air that tastes like belonging. This is my happy place.

Not imagined.

Not guided.

Not forced.

Found.

I place a hand over my chest.

Over the place where the Luma-shard glows.

It burns bright now.

Not faint.

Not fragile. Here, in the trees, it finally has room to shine.

I keep my palm pressed against it, breathing slowly, letting the forest fill the parts of me I didn't know were empty and then my body gives up pretending. I drop to my knees so fast it knocks the breath out of me.

And then I break.

I cry ugly. Loud. Violent. My hands pressed into the dirt like I'm trying to keep myself from splitting open.

I cry for every man who ever made love feel like a transaction. Every apology that came with another bruise attached to it.

For every time I confused being chosen with being valued.

I cry for every woman who was shoved down the stairs because they just wanted to be accepted. For every woman who learned how to shrink herself before she learned her favorite color. For every woman who wanted to feel loved so fucking badly, she handed over pieces of herself like an offering. Her dignity. Her body. Her silence. Handed them over hoping somebody would finally hold them gently.

I cry because I understand that woman.

Because I *am* that woman.

Chapter 9

The Bird That Buried Her Wings

The porch creaks softly beneath my chair as I settle deeper into it, the chill of the evening brushing across my bare arms. The sky above the treetops shifts into deep golds and pinks, like the day is trying to apologize for ending too soon.

My journal rests open on my lap

Blank paper waiting.

Pen trembling lightly in my hand.

The forest hums around me. Crickets, wind, leaves brushing against one another like old friends.

Somewhere far off, an owl calls.

I inhale deeply.

And then, a story arrives like a soft knock on a door I forgot existed.

My pen touches the page.

> There once was a tree that did not grow fruit. It grew lanterns.

> The words fall out of me, slow but sure. And with each one, something unwinds inside my chest. I continue.

Hundreds of lanterns, hanging like little moons trapped in glass. But they didn't glow for everyone.
Only the broken could see them.
Only the ones who had lost something.
Only the ones who had buried pieces of themselves to survive.

I pause, fingers hovering.

Only the broken.

My eyes begin to sting as I begin to write the truth within me.

Each lantern held a story. Some were warm. Some were wild. Some were sorrow hidden behind colored glass.
And if you pressed your hand to one, you could feel your own memory breathing inside it.

The breeze moves across the porch, lifting the edge of the page.
It feels like the forest is listening.
I lean forward, elbows on knees, pen still moving.

The first lantern glowed a deep, aching blue, the color of a bird who had buried her own wings.

I swallow, soft and slow.
This is it. This is the story I'm supposed to write first.

My pen touches the page again and my phone explodes with sound.

I jump, dropping the journal.

The porch rattles beneath me.

For a split second, my heart plummets…because some part of me, some bruised and hungry part, thinks: Leven.

It's not.

It's Ava.

I blink slowly, remembering I never told her I made it. I pick up the phone, the cool metal grounding my fingers.

Before answering, I glance down at the page, my incomplete fable, my first lantern waiting.

Then I inhale, steadying myself.

And I swipe to answer still a little breathless from the interruption.

"Hello?"

"Reya!" Ava's voice is sharp at first, then softens into something exasperated and worried. "You didn't text me. You didn't call. I thought you got kidnapped in the woods by a raccoon or something."

A laugh slips out of me. Small, but real. "I'm alive. I promise."

"You made it?"

"I made it."

"Good." A pause. "Text me a picture of the place and check in tonight, okay?"

"I will."

"Love you."

"Love you too."

I hang up and the silence falls back over the porch like a warm blanket. Not heavy but comforting.

I pick up my journal again and stare at the last sentence I wrote about the lantern glowing blue. Something in my mind clicks open with a small, familiar hum I haven't felt in years.

Words.

Ideas.

Little sparks that want to become something.

I flip to the top of the page and scribble a messy list of thoughts, no structure, no plan, just things that drift through me like fireflies:

- Ava
- New beginnings
- Where is the moth?
- healing
- wings
- broken things
- Leven's shadow
- Leven
- Leven
- Leven
- Leven

-Lanterns that remember

The notes look chaotic, scattered, but something inside me warms at seeing them. At seeing his name. At seeing my ideas.

I sit back, pen tapping against my thigh, and then I return to the lantern.

The first one. The blue one.

I draw a soft circle around the sentence:

Lantern One: The Bird Who Buried Her Wings

My breath slows. The forest hushes. The world narrows into

the small, aching space between my chest and the page.

And I begin to write.

There once was a small bird who lived in a forest of tall, ancient trees.
Her feathers were white as winter frost, and her wings — oh, her wings — were the softest part of her, glowing faintly with a golden shimmer whenever she felt hope.

She didn't glow often.
Hope was rare in the forest she lived in.

But one spring morning, something miraculous happened.

A new pair of wings began to grow beneath her own.
Tiny and delicate.
Still folded, not yet ready to lift into the wind.

The wings pulsed with a warmth so new, so sweet, the bird would tuck herself into the crook of a tree branch and press her beak to them, humming lullabies she didn't know she remembered.

She dreamed of the day the wings would stretch on their own.
Of teaching them how to fly.
Of watching them catch sunlight for the first time.

For the first time in her life, the bird knew what it felt like to love something she hadn't even met yet.

But the forest she lived in was not safe.

There was a shadow that moved between the trees.
A presence that clipped her freedom, stole her breath, dimmed every bright thing she held inside her.
The shadow whispered that the forest was dangerous, that she could not protect her tiny wings, that she was too small and too fragile and too foolish to raise a new life in a world that belonged to someone else.

The bird tried to hide the new wings beneath her own. She tried to shelter them, warm them, keep them from the frigid wind that rattled the branches.

But the shadow grew darker. Larger. Hungrier.

And one night, trembling on a lonely branch, the little bird made a choice that shattered her.

She flew to the quietest place in the forest. A small clearing where the air stood still and the moon hid behind a cloud as if it could not bear to watch.

There, beneath the roots of an old oak tree, the bird buried the new wings.

She pressed her chest to the dirt.
She covered them gently with leaves, with moss, with the softest pieces of herself.

When she finished, she lay beside the fresh earth, her body shaking with sounds no creature in the forest had ever heard before.

It was not a song.
It was not a cry.
It was everything in between...a sound of breaking and loving and losing all at once.

For days, she did not fly.
Her golden shimmer went dark.
Her steps grew weak, uneven.

Sometimes she returned to the oak, touching the soil with her trembling beak, whispering apologies that the wind carried away.

"I wanted you," she would say to the earth.
"I wanted you so much."

The forest did not answer.
The oak tree remained still.

Seasons passed.
The bird learned to move again.

To breathe again.
But she never sang the same way.
Her voice carried a hollow space inside it, shaped like wings that never learned to open.

And yet…

One morning, as the bird sat beneath the old oak, the smallest, faintest glow rose from the ground.

At first, she thought it was a trick of sunlight.
A flicker on a dew drop.

But then the glow grew stronger.

A warmth touched her chest, gentle, like a memory leaning close to whisper:

I was here.
I sang your song.
I loved you too.

The bird folded her body over the glow, tears gathering in her eyes.

The wings she had buried would never rise, never beat, never soar across the sky…

but their light lived in her still.

A soft, golden shimmer returning not to her feathers, not to her flight, but to the broken place inside her heart.

Where it would stay.
Forever.

Not as pain.
Not as punishment.

But as the quiet proof that love, even brief, even unfinished, does not disappear.

It becomes a lantern.

And lanterns never stop glowing.

Chapter 10

I Can Mourn

When I finish writing the last line, my hand stays on the page long after the ink dries.

I don't move.

I don't breathe.

I just stare.

The forest around me seems to still in recognition, like it knows what I just pulled out of myself. Like the trees have stopped swaying out of respect.

A tear hits the paper.

Then another.

And before I realize I'm crying, my other hand lifts on its own, drifting toward the place it always goes when I let my guard down: My stomach.

My palm settles there gently, like apology and love folded together.

My breath breaks, soft and wet, and the ache behind my ribs swells until it feels too big for my chest.

The moon sits above the treetops, bright but quiet.

The kind of silence that doesn't weigh on me, the kind that holds space.

I close the journal, fingers trembling, and set it on the porch beside me as though it's fragile, sacred.

Because it is.

The pain doesn't feel like punishment.

It feels like mourning.

I wipe my face with the back of my hand and stand slowly, letting the night air cool the heat of my skin. My legs feel unsteady, but not weak. More like they're relearning how to carry me after shedding something heavy.

Inside the cabin, the quiet is thick and warm. The kind that invites you in, not traps you. I turn on a small lamp, its soft yellow glow filling the wooden walls with a gentle pulse.

I run a bath.

The water echoes as it fills the tub. A deep, soothing sound. Steam curls up in soft ribbons, fogging the edge of the mirror. I undress slowly, each layer feeling like a piece of old weight sliding off my body.

When I sink into the water, the warmth wraps around me instantly.

Not like a hug but like a home I forgot existed.

I let my head rest against the back of the tub.

I breathe.

In.

Out.

I don't push the thoughts away. I don't argue with them. I don't defend myself from myself.

I let the grief move.

Slow and honest.

Tears mix with the water, but I don't hide them. I don't

apologize for them. I don't shame myself for feeling too much. I let the warmth cradle my body. I let the ache exist without trying to fix it.

And eventually, the calm settles into my bones, heavy and soothing.

My eyes grow heavy.

My breathing slows.

The water laps gently at my skin like it's reminding me I'm here, I'm safe, I'm held.

I wrap myself in a cozy robe and sit on the couch next to the fireplace.

And before I realize it, the stillness, the warmth, the quiet, pull me softly into sleep.

The kind of sleep you fall into not because you're escaping the world, but because for the first time…you feel like you don't have to run from it.

Chapter 11

The First Night

I dream of salt.

In the dream, the air is warm and wet against my skin.

The first time Leven takes me to the beach; the sky is a pale gold that melts into soft blue. Not dramatic. Not stormy. Just open.

Endless.

The ocean stretches out like it doesn't care about anything we've ever argued about.

I remember stepping out of the car and the wind immediately tangling my hair. It tastes like salt when I lick my lips. It smells like sunscreen and seaweed and something clean.

Leven stands beside me, his fist clenched in his pockets, his lips pressed in thin lines, scanning the shoreline like he's assessing risk.

"You've never been to the beach?" He asks.

"Not like this," I say.

Not with someone who feels like possibility.

The sand is warm under my bare feet. It sinks slightly with every step, giving way without resistance. I laugh the first time a wave rushes over my toes. The water is colder than I expect, sharp enough to make me gasp.

Leven watches me like I'm unpredictable weather.

"Come in," I call to him.

He hesitates.

Then he takes off his shoes.

The water climbs his ankles, then his calves. His jaw tightens at the cold, but he doesn't retreat. I splash him.

He stares at me in disbelief. "You did not just do that."

I grin and do it again.

He lunges forward, grabbing me around the waist. The water explodes around us in silver arcs. My laughter echoes against the open sky. His hands are firm but not controlling. Just holding. Just there.

The sound of the ocean is constant. Waves folding into themselves. Seagulls crying overhead. The distant rhythm of someone's music drifting down the shore.

But when he looks at me, it feels quiet.

We walk along the shoreline until our feet are coated in wet sand. The wind presses my dress against my legs. His shirt ripples against his chest.

"Do you ever just…" I start, then stop.

"Just what?" He asks.

"Feel small, but in a good way?"

He looks out at the horizon. The water glitters under the sun like it's scattered with broken glass.

"Yeah," he says after a moment. "Out here, everything else feels…less important."

We sit down where the sand is dry and warm. I stretch my legs out in front of me. He leans back on his hands.

"The beach makes me feel free," I say. The sun kisses my

shoulders. The air wraps around us like a blanket. I can smell coconut sunscreen on my skin. I can feel grains of sand clinging to my calves.

The conversation drifts instead of moves.

He grows quiet for a moment, eyes tracing the horizon the way he did when we first arrived. Like he's looking for something he used to know by heart.

"I used to love this part," he says softly.

"This part?"

"Being surrounded by nothing." His voice is different now. Not guarded. Not instructive. Just remembering. "When I was in the Navy," he continues, "we'd be out at sea for days. Sometimes weeks. No land in sight. Just water in every direction."

He squints slightly, as if the sun in this memory is brighter than the one above us.

"At night, it was darker than anything you've ever seen. And during the day, the horizon just...disappeared into itself."

The waves roll in, steady and endless, like they're underscoring him.

"I loved standing at the edge of the ship," he says. "Feeling it rock under my feet. Not violently. Just enough to remind you that you're floating on something alive."

I can almost see it, the metal deck beneath him, the air thick with salt and diesel, the wind pressing against his chest.

"Sometimes," he adds, a small smile forming, "I'd close my eyes and stretch my arms out like this." He lifts his arms now, right here on the beach, palms open to the sky.

"Like I was flying..." His shoulders relax as he says it. "The breeze would hit my face. The ship moving beneath me. Nothing but open space ahead. It felt…" He pauses, searching.

"Free?" I offer.

He nods slowly. "Yeah. Free. Small. But not insignificant. Just…part of something bigger."

The wind catches his shirt, pulling it gently against his frame. The ocean glitters in front him, endless and unknowing.

I watch him there, arms open, eyes half-closed, salt air brushing his skin…and realize this is the most unguarded I've ever seen him.

Not because he's confessing. But because he's remembering.

We don't interrupt each other.

We don't compete.

We just talk.

At one point, he reaches over and brushes a piece of hair out of my face. His fingers graze my cheek, slow and absentminded.

The world doesn't shatter.

There's no dramatic music.

The sun lowers, turning everything honey-colored. The water shifts from blue to something deeper, almost purple. The wind cools slightly, carrying the faint scent of grilled food from somewhere down the beach.

I rest my head on his shoulder.

His skin is warm from the sun. Slightly salty. He smells like ocean and soap and something distinctly him.

"This feels easy," I whisper.

He nods. "It does."

And that's what I remember most about that time at the beach.

The way my body didn't feel braced.

The way I didn't feel like I had to earn the moment.

In the dream, I turn toward him. The light catches in his eyes. There's no shadow there. No guarded calculation. Just a man sitting beside me while the tide breathes in and out.

In the cabin, I shift in my sleep. The fire cracks softly.

In the dream, the waves keep coming.

I let myself relive it.

The taste of salt. The warmth of his shoulder.

The sound of our laughter dissolving into the wind.

Chapter 12

The First Morning

Morning comes gently.

Not with the frantic buzz of alarms or the heavy pull of dread, but with soft sunlight dripping through the cabin window, warm and golden, settling across my face like an invitation.

I open my eyes to quiet.

To calm.

To a new kind of clarity.

Emptier in a healing way. Like I've finally wrung out the stale thoughts and rotten memories that used to cling to me like damp clothes.

There is no ocean. No sunlight. Just the memory of how freeing it once felt to stand at the edge of something vast and not be afraid of it.

I lie there for a moment, staring at the wooden ceiling. Then I stretch beneath the quilt, listening to the creaks of the cabin as it wakes with me.

I dress simply: leggings, a hoodie, warm socks.

I undo the twists in my hair and pick out my afro so I can feel the breeze between my coils.

I pack a backpack with snacks, water, and the journal that now feels like a living thing.

Outside, the morning air meets me with a cool kiss. The forest smells like damp earth and pine sap and something ancient. Dew clings to the grass, glittering like tiny pieces of glass.

I step past the porch, past the soft patch of grass where I wrote last night, and venture deeper.

The further I go, the quieter the world becomes. Not silent, but full of sounds that don't rush me: the drip of water from leaves, the flutter of wings somewhere above, the distant murmur of a creek, the wind threading itself through branches.

I walk for a while with no destination in mind, just movement.

My thoughts drift, slow and free, like leaves floating down a stream.

My mind flashes with a memory, one of the first real conversations I had with Ava after Leven.

We were sitting on her couch.

She looked at me and said, "Do you even know what you like?"

At the time, I didn't know how to answer.

But somewhere between the bathwater last night and the path beneath my feet now, a soft truth begins forming.

Maybe I used to know.

Maybe I can know again.

A new story tugs at the edges of my thoughts: small, delicate, shy.

Not fully formed, but calling to me like a whispering breeze.

I follow the feeling.

After a few minutes, I find a spot that feels right. A patch of mossy earth beneath a wide cedar, its branches arching overhead like a protective canopy. The ground is damp, but soft. The kind of damp that smells alive.

I sit down, cross-legged, backpack beside me.

The moment my journal touches my lap, the forest shifts, leaning closer, quieter, like it knows what's coming.

I open to a fresh page.

I inhale the cool air.

I feel the damp earth beneath me.

I hear Ava's voice in the back of my mind: "*I was a kid too, Reya.*"

The beginning of a new lantern hums at the edge of my imagination.

Not ready for its full story but I press my pen to the page.

And in the middle of the quiet forest, with sunlight flickering through branches and the earth soft beneath me, I begin to write again.

Chapter 13

Ember And Ash

In a vast and dangerous forest, where winter came early and stayed too long, there lived two young wolves born under the same moon.

One was named Ember.
One was named Ash.

They were sisters.
Not just by blood, but by breath, by instinct, by the quiet way they curled around each other when the nights grew cold.

When they were small, the forest was not kind to them.
Storms came without warning.
Shadows moved in ways shadows shouldn't.
And there was a creature in the woods. A giant of muscle and rage, a beast who wore the shape of a father but never learned the heart of one.

He roamed their den, snarling, stomping, snapping his teeth too close to their ears. The ground trembled when he was angry. And he was angry often.

Ash, the older sister, learned to run early.

Not because she was afraid
but because she knew she had to survive long enough to save herself.

Ember, the younger, stayed behind.
Not by choice.
But because she didn't yet know the path out of the forest,
and because she still believed she had to be small to stay safe.

Years passed.

Ash wandered the woods alone.
She grew stronger.
Faster.
Wiser.

But every howl she released into the night carried a hollow note.
The ache of missing something she had left behind.

Ember stayed near the den, surviving storms she wasn't built for.
She learned to move quietly,
to breathe softly,
to hide the brightness of her fur beneath leaves and shadows.

But every night, she tilted her head back and listened.
She never forgot the sound of her sister's howl.

One night, after a storm so fierce it split a mountain tree in half,
Ash heard a distant cry.

Not a howl.
Not a scream.

A sound of breaking.

And without hesitation, without fear, without thought,
Ash ran.

Through briars.
Through thorn and mud.
Through the cold breath of winter.

She ran until her paws bled,
until she found the place where the sound had come from.

And there, beneath the twisted roots of an old oak, lay Ember.

Trembling.
Exhausted.
Trying to hide her wounds the way wolves hide weakness.

Ash approached slowly.

Ember lifted her head, confused.
"You came back for me?"

Ash pressed her furry forehead to Ember's.
"I never stopped looking for you."

And in that moment, the two wolves remembered something they had always known:

They were born with one heart between them.
Broken into two pieces at birth,
so they would always find their way back.

Ash lay beside Ember, shielding her from the cold with her body. The oak branches creaked overhead, bending like they were bowing to the reunion.

For the first time in years, the forest was quiet.

Safe.

Whole.

Together, the wolves rose.
Not as the frightened pups they once were
but as survivors
as warriors
as mirrors of each other's strength.

Ash taught Ember the paths out of the dark forest.
Ember taught Ash the courage it took to stay when running was easier.

Side by side, step by step,
they walked toward a new clearing,
a place untouched by giants or shadows.

And when they reached it,
they howled a long, rising cry that shook the moon awake.

Not a cry for help.

A cry of freedom.

Because the wolves had finally learned
what the forest had tried to steal from them:

They were always enough.
But together, even stronger.
And no matter how dark the woods became,
sisterhood was the light that could not be extinguished.

The one heart.
The fierce heart.
The unbreakable one.

Chapter 14

I Listen To Me

When I finish writing the last line of the wolves' story, my pen slowly slips from my fingers. The forest around me exhales, like it had been holding its breath while the lantern poured itself onto the page.

I sit there for a moment, letting the silence settle over me.

A silence that feels like peace.

I turn to a clean corner of the page and write, almost absentmindedly: Lantern Three: (grief? strength? identity?)

Then I stop.

Not because I'm out of ideas.

Not because the forest isn't feeding me a hundred small whispers.

But because my body sends a quiet message through my bones, a tiredness that isn't fatigue but closure.

A soft tug inward.

Enough. For now. You did what you needed to do today.

I don't force myself to write more.

I don't guilt myself into productivity.

I don't push creativity past where it wants to go.

I close the journal slow, holding the last page in place longer than I need to.

I slip it into my backpack and rise from the mossy ground, brushing the dampness from my leggings. The forest is still humming, but not in a rushed way. More like it's walking beside me.

I let my feet choose the path back.

I don't overthink it. I don't question myself.

I let instinct lead the way through the trees, a left here, a small hill there, a narrow trail wrapped in roots.

I trust the small, warm glow inside me that flickers like a lantern guiding my steps.

By the time the cabin comes into view, my breath feels different. Not forced, not shallow.

Mine.

Every step from the forest to the porch feels like learning a new language. A language written in intuition.

When to stop. When to rest. When to start again. When to breathe. When to speak. When to laugh.

All the things I didn't know how to control before, I'm learning now.

I pause at the door, hand resting on the frame, the air cool against my warmed skin.

And right there, with the forest at my back and the cabin glowing softly ahead, I make a promise to myself.

A quiet one, but a steady one.

I will listen to the still small voice inside me; the one I spent years silencing, the one I drowned at the feet of men who demanded to be louder, the one I ignored out of fear or confusion or misplaced devotion.

I will listen to it until it grows confident, until it grows bold, until it no longer whispers but roars.

When I reach the cabin, the quiet feels different than before.

It feels expectant, like it knows something is waiting for me inside.

I drop my backpack by the door and reach for my phone on the counter, wiping a bit of forest dirt from the screen.

Two missed calls.

Leven Mercer.

My chest tightens so fast it feels like a trap snapping shut.

My breathing stops and my fingers go numb.

Of course he called.

The moment I gained an inch of peace, he felt the distance, the shift, the space forming between us.

A small voice inside me whispers: He knows you're slipping away. He knows you're healing. He can feel it.

My thumb hovers over his name.

I can't breathe.

My heart pounds against my ribs like it's begging to be let out.

Am I strong enough to call him back?

I don't know.

I don't know anything except that the ache in my chest is rising in sharp, hot waves.

Instead of calling, I open a new text message.

My fingers move before my brain can stop them, pouring out everything I've tried to bury: How could you be so cruel when I loved you the most?

When I gave up every piece of myself?

When I emptied me to fill you up?

I loved you. I fucking loved you!

I still love you.

And I will probably love you for the rest of my life.

And if you said you would take me back right now, I would come running to you without question.

Because I still believe in you.

In us.

You told me we were connected in a way that was beyond our comprehension. You told me I was the only one that has ever made you feel loved. Was it true? If everything else was a lie, I cling to the only thing that was true was the love.

Because for me, it was real.

My thumb trembles over the send button.

And then, I hit it.

The message shoots off into the universe, carrying every piece of me I swore I wasn't going to give away anymore.

Instantly, my phone dings.

My heart leaps into my throat.

I open it quickly, desperate for any sign of him.

It's the same message.

Sent back to me. Along with a note I wrote to myself weeks ago, tied to an automation app I forgot I installed.

A reminder to journal honestly. A reminder that I am not ready to talk to Leven.

A mirror I never intended to look into this soon.

The text sits there on my screen, glowing like an accusation.

I read it again out loud. "I gave up every piece of me…emptied me to fill you…was it a lie?… I will always love you."

Every word sounds smaller when spoken. Every confession

sounds younger, needier, so unbelievably wounded.

My knees give out.

I slide down the kitchen cabinets and collapse onto the floor, the cool wood pressing against my legs as the sob rises raw, animal, unstoppable.

I cry until my face burns.

I cry until the room blurs.

I cry until the grief feels like it is clawing out of my chest.

"Healing is not linear." Dr. Jenson's voice echoes inside my head, gentle but firm.

A truth I didn't want to hear back then.

A truth I hate needing now.

I wipe my face with the back of my shaking hand and whisper, through broken breaths: "I am allowed to be vulnerable."

A pause.

A deeper breath.

"I am allowed to love him."

The tears fall harder, but they don't cut the same way.

"But I don't have to go back to him."

The words land in my chest like a stone.

I stand slowly, like I am relearning how to stand at all, fidgeting with the bracelet that still hangs on my wrist.

I open the door and step out into the night.

The trees stretch endlessly, their silhouettes piercing the sky. The moon hangs above them like a soft witness. A breeze sweeps across my face cool and real.

I walk onto the porch, grip the railing, and stare out at the endless forest.

And I cry, hard, messy, grieving the thought of him, grieving the loss of the addiction, grieving the parts of myself I gave him without understanding the cost.

The forest doesn't judge.

It doesn't interrupt.

It holds me the way I have never let anyone hold me.

And beneath the ache, beneath the heartbreak, beneath the longing that still tries to pull me backward, there is a flicker.

A tiny lantern-glow.

A reminder that healing is happening.

After crying to the moon until my lungs ache and my throat burns, I finally go back inside the cabin. The air is cool. The silence feels steady again. My eyes sting, my chest feels sore, but something inside me has shifted.

I lie on the bed, pulling the quilt up to my chin.

The forest hums outside, the crickets singing in uneven rhythms.

The window is cracked open, letting in the faint scent of pine and damp soil.

I fall asleep listening to myself breathe.

And as my eyes close, something miraculous happens: He doesn't come with me.

No dream of him appearing at the foot of the bed.

No illusions of his voice whispering my name.

No reliving the good moments trying to understand where I went wrong.

Just sleep.

Deep and uninterrupted and mine.

A sleep that feels like a small kind of victory.

Chapter 15

The Quiet Feels Different

When dawn slips into the room, soft, pale, stretching its fingers across the wooden walls, I wake with a strange, unfamiliar feeling.

Lightness.

The absence of him is suddenly not an ache.

It's air.

I sit up slowly, rubbing the sleep from my eyes, marveling at how my chest doesn't hurt the second I breathe.

I lace up my boots, grab water, a snack, and my journal, and I step into the morning.

The forest greets me like an old friend.

Warmer today.

Welcoming.

I walk deeper than I have before, letting the path narrow, letting the world around me grow thicker and greener. Ferns brush my calves. Shafts of sunlight pierce the canopy like golden ladders.

Every breath tastes alive.

Somewhere ahead, a creek bubbles softly.

Birds chirp overhead.

The ground turns softer, spongy with moss.

And then I see it.

A single green sprout. The sprout bright, impossibly bright, pushes up from the dark soil beside a fallen, decaying log.

It shouldn't be here.

Not in this patch of forest where sunlight barely penetrates.

Not in soil this damp and heavy.

But it is.

Small.

Stubborn.

Alive.

I crouch down, brushing my fingers lightly over the tender leaves. They quiver as though greeting me.

Something inside me warms.

New beginnings don't always look like beginnings, I think.

Sometimes they look like something growing out of the wrong place at the wrong time and surviving anyway.

The sprout leans slightly backward, toward the shadow of the dead log, like it's reaching for what once was, instead of what could be.

Backward.

Toward history.

Toward the past.

A seed that grew wrong…or perhaps right.

I take a deep inhale at the thought of it.

The start of a new lantern flickers in my chest.

I sit on a fallen trunk, the moss damp beneath me, and open my journal.

The forest quiets around me as the idea takes shape.

My pen touches the page, slow and certain.

> Lantern Three: The Seed That Grew Backward
> There once was a seed planted in the wrong direction…

I pause, feeling a softness in my chest, in my heart, in my bones. It feels something like recognition.

But this time, I don't push forward.

I write only the first line and close the journal and a hush washes over the trees, not silence but stillness.

I sit there on the moss-covered log, hands resting loosely on my journal, letting the quiet settle into the spaces that used to hold panic.

And then a soft crunch of leaves.

I look up.

Across a thin break in the trees, maybe twenty feet away, a deer stands perfectly still. A young doe, sleek and soft, with dark gentle eyes that seem to reflect everything back at me.

She's close enough that I can see her chest rise and fall. Close enough that her breath breaks in tiny puffs in the cool air. Close enough that I can hear the faintest flick of her ear as a fly drifts past.

We stare at each other.

She should be afraid.

Most wild animals are skittish, fleeting, always ready to run.

But she doesn't run.

She simply watches me. Calm, grounded, unbothered by my presence and I can't help but think about how much Delilah would drown in this. I can picture her eyes lighting up seeing a creature so beautiful.

The deer tilts her head, as if acknowledging this version of me. This quieter, braver, steadier version, the one learning how to be alone without being lonely.

For a moment, it feels like she's nodding.

Approving.

Recognizing something in me she understands.

And then, with the softest flick of her tail, the deer steps back into the trees.

Not running.

Not startled.

Just moving forward.

As she disappears into the shadows, a breeze sweeps through the clearing lifting my hair, brushing my cheek, stirring the leaves at my feet. It feels like a whisper.

Like a blessing.

Like a sign.

I place my hand over the warm place on my chest where the lantern glow lives.

And I feel proud of myself.

Not for being perfect.

Not for being healed.

Not for being strong.

But for continuing.

For choosing myself in the smallest, simplest, most sacred ways.

The forest around me seems to hum in agreement.

Chapter 16

I Forgive Myself

By the time I make it back to the cabin, the sun is already dipping behind the trees, turning the sky a bruised lavender. My legs ache in a good way. My chest feels cracked open, but not broken. Just spacious.

I set my backpack on the table, pour myself a glass of water, and pick up my phone. I don't check for Leven. I don't dread notifications. I don't brace for pain.

Instead, I scroll until I find Delilah's name.

My thumb hesitates only because I miss her.

I hit call.

She answers on the third ring.

"Hi, Mommy."

Mommy.

Her voice is deeper now, older, but still soft around the edges, still my little girl.

"Hey, baby. What are you doing?"

"Trying to train the cat to stop sleeping on my homework. It's not going well."

I chuckle, sinking into one of the cabin chairs. "Sounds like you're losing."

"I'm completely losing," she sighs dramatically. "I'm basically being bullied by a seven-pound animal."

Her voice makes something warm bloom in my chest. The soft, familiar glow of a lantern that only glows when she speaks. The glow of loving her without conditions.

We talk for a few minutes about school, her teacher who "needs to just retire already," and her best friend Jennifer who is "dramatic for no reason but hilarious."

Then, out of nowhere, I say, "I've been…taking a stab at writing fables."

There's a pause.

Then a gasp.

"YOU? Writing cute little animal stories? Mom, who are you?"

I laugh, leaning back in the chair. "I don't know. Someone with too much time and too many trees around her."

Delilah hums thoughtfully. "Okay, okay, so what's next? What should you write about?"

"I don't know," I say honestly. "That's why I'm asking you."

"Ooooh." She inhales like she's about to summon wisdom from the heavens. Or chaos from her teenage brain. Or both. "Okay. Hear me out."

I brace myself.

"A story…about a squirrel…" She pauses for dramatic effect. "…who's allergic to nuts."

I burst out laughing. "Delilah…what?"

"No, seriously!" She insists. "He's like, the world's worst squirrel. He has to carry an EpiPen made of, like, pine sap or whatever."

"An EpiPen made of pine sap?"

She laughs carelessly. "And…and…" Her voice is breathless with excitement. "He wants to fit in with the other squirrels but can't because they're always eating acorns, so he becomes best friends with a…" she pauses to think. "With a hummingbird."

This girl.

My hand covers my mouth to hide the smile stretching across my face.

"And what do they do?" I ask.

"They open a bakery," she says without missing a beat, "but all the pastries are tiny because hummingbirds are bad at portion control."

I laugh so hard tears prick the corners of my eyes.

She's ridiculous.

She's perfect.

She is every part of me that survived childhood and somehow grew sweeter.

"You know what?" I say when I finally catch my breath. "I think I'll try it."

"For real?"

"For real." I say. I can't help the tears forming in my eyes.

"Mom…" Her voice softens, the humor fading into something warm and proud. "I can't wait to read it.

Something inside my chest glows bright, steady, golden.

"Me either," I whisper because I'm trying to hide the crack in my voice.

After we hang up, I stay seated for a moment, letting the joy settle into all the places grief used to live.

Then I open my journal.

And on the next page, in Delilah's honor, I write:

Lantern Four: The Squirrel Who Was Allergic to Nuts

My smile isn't forced.
It's real.

Chapter 17

Pip And Zip

There once was a squirrel named Pip, and Pip had a problem.
A very serious, extremely tragic, undeniably ridiculous problem:

He was allergic to nuts.

Acorns made him sneeze.
Walnuts made his eyes swell shut.
If he so much as smelled a pecan, his tail puffed up like an angry dandelion.

None of this would've been a big deal
if he hadn't been born smack in the middle of Nutwood Forest,
where every squirrel ate nuts for breakfast, lunch, dinner,
and emotional support.

Pip tried to fit in.

He carried acorns under his arm like the others.
He practiced the classic squirrel head tilt.
He would stuff his cheeks with grass so his friends wouldn't notice.

He even tried nibbling a cashew one time.

He nearly died.

The other squirrels didn't understand.

"How can you be a squirrel and not eat nuts?"
"That's like being a fish that hates water!"
"That's like being a bird afraid of heights!"
"That's like being a teenager without mood swings!"

Pip tried to explain,
"I want to eat nuts…my body just hates me."

But the squirrels only shrugged and went back to their crunchy, nutty meals.

One day, frustrated and hungry and very much done with the nut-based oppression,
Pip wandered away from Nutwood and stumbled upon a tiny, shimmering bird
hovering over a patch of wildflowers.

The bird gasped when she saw him.

"Oh my gosh! Your tail looks like a broom! Are you okay?!"

Pip sighed dramatically. "I'm allergic to nuts."

The hummingbird, whose name was Zip, fluttered closer.
"That's terrible! Also, weird! Also…do you want some nectar?"

Pip blinked.
"Nectar?"

"Yes! It's sweet. It's soft. It doesn't try to murder you!"

Pip tasted a drop.

It was the best thing he'd ever eaten.
No sneezing.
No swelling.
No tail explosion.

In that moment, they became inseparable.

Pip taught Zip how to slow down long enough to see a sunrise.
Zip taught Pip how to drink from flowers without sticking his whole head inside.
They wandered the forest, two tiny misfits building a world where difference wasn't dangerous.

It was delicious.

And then one day, Zip had an idea.

"Pip! We should open a bakery!"

Pip tilted his broom-tail. "A bakery? Like…for what? Acorn-free pastries?"

"Exactly!" Zip chirped. "We'll make tiny treats! Small snacks! Mini muffins! Teensy cakes! Most squirrels won't even see them, they'll think they're sprinkles!"

They worked for weeks.

Zip mixed flower nectar with crushed petals.
Pip shaped the dough with his paws, humming little songs he didn't know he knew.
Together they baked the tiniest pastries the forest had ever seen.

When they opened The Teeny Tiny Bakery, the forest animals were skeptical.
But then they tasted the pastries.
They tasted sweetness they'd never tasted.
They tasted softness they'd never expected.
They tasted something made from a squirrel who couldn't eat nuts
and a hummingbird who couldn't sit still.

And everyone agreed:

It was the best food the forest had ever known.

From that day on, Pip wasn't the squirrel who didn't fit in.
He was the squirrel who created something new.

Something joyful.
Something that didn't exist before him.

Pip didn't overcome his allergy.
He didn't "fix" himself.
He didn't become normal.

He simply stopped trying to be what the world wanted and became exactly who he was…which turned out to be enough to feed an entire forest.

When I write the last line, I just stare at the page.

Then suddenly, a laugh slips out of me.

Not a polite little exhale. Not a forced giggle.

A real, full laugh that bubbles up so fast it surprises me.

I press my fingers to my lips, stunned.

Did that sound really come from me?

I read the fable again, shaking my head, and the laugh comes back, softer this time, but warm, sweet, alive.

God.

I forgot laughter could feel like this. Not the kind that covers pain. But the kind that actually isn't pain at all.

I sink back into the chair, holding the journal against my chest.

My eyes prick, but not from grief. From something gentler. Something I haven't felt in years.

Pride.

Joy.

Playfulness.

I whisper into the stillness of the cabin, almost afraid of the sound of my own voice:

"I forgot I could do joy."

The forest hums outside like it hears me, like it's nodding.

The lantern-warmth in my chest expands, glowing brighter than before.

I rest a hand over my heart and inhale deeply.

For once, for the first time in a very long time, I breathe without hurt.

Chapter 18

I Feel Warmth

Tonight is my last night here. My last night in the forest. My last night with nothing but trees, breath, and the heartbeat of the earth beneath me.

And something inside me whispers: Don't waste it.

So, I do something only a crazy person would do. Something that younger me would've judged. Something Leven would've mocked.

I decide to sleep outside.

Not on the porch. Not under the awning. Not with safety nearby.

But in the open, under the sky.

Where the air has teeth and wildlife roams free and I have absolutely no plan. I grab the sleeping bag from the closet and take it into the clearing behind the cabin. The moon hangs above me like a quiet witness. The stars are scattered across the sky like someone spilled diamonds.

I spread the sleeping bag on the grass and lie down. The earth is cool beneath me. The night smells like pine and dew and something ancient.

No protection.

Just me.

I don't feel scared.

I feel...*uncontained.*

The cold air brushes across my skin. The breeze lifts my hair. A nearby owl hoots. Something rustles far off, but I don't flinch.

This is freedom.

Raw and stupid and beautiful.

I place one hand over my chest.

The warm glow inside me flickers stronger, and I push my palm into it literally trying to force this feeling into my heart.

"Stay," I whisper. "Please stay forever."

It's the freest I've ever felt. The ground vibrates faintly with distant life. The sky stretches above me like possibility. And slowly, gently, I drift into sleep.

In the dream, I'm in a home I've never seen before.

It's small. Sunlight spills across the floor like it's been there all day. The walls are warm, soft, lived-in. Plants crowd the windows, reaching without apology. A candle burns on the counter, slow and steady. A bookshelf leans under the weight of stories I haven't read yet.

Delilah is there.

She's dancing in the middle of the living room, music too loud for the space, socks sliding across the floor. She is singing terribly into a wooden spoon like the world is her stage.

I try to follow her, but I miss every beat, spin the wrong way, almost fall...and it doesn't matter. Nothing about it has to be right.

The dream shifts.

I'm sitting alone in a restaurant. Dim lighting. Low music. The kind of place people come visit to feel like themselves.

The plate of pasta in front of me still steaming when I take a bite.

In the dream, I lift my hand and touch my own cheek like I'm checking to see if I'm really there.

I go grocery shopping next. Pushing a cart. Choosing oranges. Running my fingers along the cold metal freezer door. Existing in public.

Every mundane task feels like a miracle.

And the dream smiles back.

Chapter 19

New Beginnings

I wake up to sunlight warming my face, birds squabbling overhead, and the smell of damp grass clinging to my skin.

My back aches a little. My hair is wild. My cheeks are cold from the night air. I'm pretty sure ants crawled in my mouth while I was sleeping. And yet, I feel ready. Ready in a way I never have before. Ready in a way that feels like truth. Ready like something inside me finally clicked into place.

I sit up, stretch my arms toward the sky, and breathe in the morning.

I'm not healed.

I'm not finished.

But I am beginning.

I roll up the sleeping bag, sling it over my shoulder, and head toward the cabin.

Today, I'm walking into my life.

The moment my plane touches down in Las Vegas, the world feels louder than I remember. People dragging suitcases. Security guards shouting directions. Someone's baby screaming like it's offended by oxygen.

But underneath all that noise, inside me…there's a silence that wasn't there before.

I'm different.

Maybe only a little, but enough that I feel it with every step I take.

Ava meets me outside baggage claim, waving both hands like she's trying to land a helicopter.

When we hug, she squeezes tight, breathing me in like she's checking to make sure I really made it back in one piece.

"I missed you," she says into my shoulder.

"I missed you too."

"But girllllll, you stink," she says with a laugh.

She pulls away, her eyes bright with something she's trying to hide.

"What?" I ask.

She exhales. "Okay, so…" She bites her lip. "Don't be mad."

"Oh God."

"No, no, don't make that face."

"Ava…"

She throws her hands up.

"Fine! I got you an apartment."

I blink. "You WHAT?"

"Listen," she says quickly, stepping between me and the imaginary exit door I'm about to take. "Not because I didn't want you with me. I did. I do. You know I do. But…I think living on your own will be good for you." She says. "You were with Tim for a decade. Then you moved in with Leven. I just think…" She keeps talking, rambling in true Ava fashion. "And before you start stressing out, don't worry, I put down the deposit, paid first month's rent, and started a tab for you. A small tab. Like, a baby tab. Teeny-tiny tab that includes your freedom-forest trip, this apartment, and all the pain and suffering you caused by making me worry about you. You'll pay me back one day when you're rich and famous writing fables about squirrels with allergies."

I laugh that real laugh again. Delilah must have told her about her idea.

"Ava," I say softly, voice catching a little. "Thank you. For everything. Not just the apartment. For letting me crash with you. For being here. For…showing up."

Her face softens.

She pulls me in for another hug.

"That's what sisters are for," she whispers.

Before I even look at the apartment, I drive to Mom's house.

Because nothing makes you feel like you're starting over quite like stealing your mother's groceries.

When I walk in, she's standing at the stove, stirring something that smells like too much paprika and a mom-level amount of love.

I give Luther the driest, "Hello, Luther," I can muster before I smile at my mom.

Also, fuck you, Luther.

Mom turns and she smiles so big her eyes disappear.

"Well look who's back," she says. "You hungry?"

"Absolutely."

I grab a bag and start raiding the pantry like a raccoon at 3 a.m.

"Put those back," she says without looking. "Those are for the stew."

"Mom, you have six cans," I argue.

"I need all six."

"For what? Feeding the entire neighborhood?"

She shakes her head, grinning. "Don't start with me." But I'm already stuffing oatmeal, crackers, and a jar of peanut butter into my tote bag.

She pretends not to see.

Her own love language.

And for a moment, standing in her kitchen, I feel grounded again.

Chapter 20

The Plants Comes First

My new apartment is small, but it's mine.

The lock clicks behind me, and the sound echoes. Louder than it should in a place this size. The walls are bare. The floors are too clean.

The moment I walk in, the air feels different. Empty in a good way. Like a blank canvas waiting for me to fill it with a version of myself I haven't met yet.

There is no couch. No table. No soft place to land. And no roaches, so that's a plus.

Ava helped me carry in a few boxes earlier, but now I'm alone. Completely alone. And I can breathe.

I start by unpacking the plants.

All the plants. Too many plants.

Enough plants to make this tiny one-bedroom look like a rainforest having a midlife crisis.

I place a pothos on the kitchen counter.

A fiddle-leaf fig in the corner.

A prayer plant by the window because I like the way its leaves fold at night like little hands.

By the time I'm done, the air feels green.

Like the forest followed me home, but this time in manageable houseplant form.

I burn a candle. I put a blanket on the floor. I set out a mug next to the sink.

My space. My rules. My peace.

I look over what I feel is the start of something great, and scary, and priceless. It's quiet in a way that feels honest.

I slide down the wall until I'm sitting on the floor, my back pressed against it, my legs stretched out in front of me. The carpet is cool beneath my palms.

This is what starting over feels like.

Not dramatic. Not cinematic.

Just…empty.

Empty cabinets. Empty corners. Empty space where life is supposed to go.

I thought it would feel like freedom.

And it does, in a way.

But it also feels like standing in the middle of something unfinished, holding all the pieces and not knowing where to start.

I let out a breath I didn't realize I was holding and lean my back against the wall.

My phone is in my hand, but I don't know what I'm looking for. My thumb moves anyway, opening photos like muscle memory. Like maybe if I scroll long enough, something will explain itself.

Or undo itself.

I don't even realize I start deleting at first.

Tap.

Delete.

Tap.

Delete.

Screenshots I don't need. Blurry pictures. Random moments that meant something at the time but mean nothing now.

It feels...productive.

I scroll faster.

Then slower.

Then...I stop.

A group photo I almost don't recognize at first.

Everyone standing close together, the sun too bright, shadows cutting across faces like the camera couldn't decide what mattered.

Dusty ground and open sky.

Wendy is mid-laugh, head tilted back like she doesn't care how she looks. Michael is squinting, one arm thrown around someone's shoulder like he's known them his whole life.

The picture is of a group hike Dr. Jenson suggested I go on to have genuine encounters. And I'm glad I listened.

And then, I see myself. In the middle of all of it. Not posed. Not trying. Just there.

My eyes move to the dreadlocks and I smile a little. I see Brandon, doing some pose that I'm sure he thought was cool but wasn't. I made friends that day. Genuine friends.

My phone buzzes in my hand.

Delilah.

I don't think. I just answer.

Her face fills the screen, a little blurry at first before it adjusts. She is stretched out somewhere, probably her bed, braids pulled back, glasses slightly crooked like she forgot she had them on.

"Hey," she says into the camera.

"Hey, baby."

She studies me for a second, head tilting slightly. "Did you already move in?"

"Yeah," I turn the camera slightly so she can see behind me. "Don't judge me. I have nothing."

She squints. "You literally have nothing."

"But I have plants."

"That's not the same thing."

I laugh, and it surprises me a little. "I'm working on it."

She nods like she is considering it seriously. "It's cute though. Like...minimalist. Intentional."

"Intentional?" I raise an eyebrow.

"Yeah," she laughs back. "Like you didn't just leave your entire life behind and start over from scratch."

I blink at her.

Kids.

They say things so casually.

"I mean," she adds quickly, "you kinda did, but like...in a cool way."

"A cool way," I repeat.

"Yeah. Growth," she says, like it's obvious. "People pay for that aesthetic."

She laughs and I can't tell if she is making fun of me, or if she is proud of me. Either way, I will take it.

"So, tell me about this squirrel story," she says, changing the topic. "Because it looks like you may have a squirrel living with you considering all the plants you have,"

Okay, she's making fun of me. Got it.

But I laugh and happily explain Pip and Zip.

"I'm proud of you, mommy." She says after I finish telling her the story.

And I can't help but smile.

I can't help but to feel full of warmth.

When the call ends, the apartment feels different again.

Not full. But not emptier either.

Just...possible.

Chapter 21

I Watch Him Walk Away

Even though I stole some thing's from mom, I still need groceries. So, I grab my keys and sunglasses and head out the door.

As I push a cart through the grocery store, I feel like a functioning adult for the first time in…years.

Grocery shopping is better when you're not trying to accommodate a crazy person.

I stand in front of the bread section and do the most radical thing I've done all day:

I grab a loaf of white bread.

White. Fluffy. Processed. Borderline offensive to nutrition.

I toss it in my cart with a smirk.

"Take THAT, Leven The-Love-of-My-Life-Mercer," I mumble under my breath.

The bread does not protest and I feel victorious.

I'm scanning the produce when something catches my eye.

Not something, someone.

Tim.

And next to him is a gorgeous woman with long curls, smooth brown skin, and a sundress that's probably illegal in three states.

"Oh, God," I whisper.

My first instinct?

Run.

My second instinct?

Also run.

I turn my cart around too quickly and WHAM.

I crash straight into a display of canned green beans.

Cans scatter everywhere.

Rolling.

Clanking.

Rattling across the floor like tiny metal grenades.

The store goes silent.

Of course it does.

Because the universe LOVES to embarrass me.

Then, "Hey, lady!" Tim's voice booms across the aisle.

I freeze.

He sounds…happy? I turn around slowly. Tim is smiling at me. The soft, warm, no-resentment smile. The smile he used to give me when I made him laugh or ate the last cookie or told him a stupid story about my day.

"Tim," I breathe. I fidget with the finger that used to hold my engagement ring.

He walks over and pulls me into a hug.

A real one. All comfort, no tension, nothing held back. His arms feel familiar. Not in a romantic way, but in a safe-human way. When he lets go, he gestures to the stunning woman beside him.

"This is Briana," he says proudly. "Babe, this is Reya."

Briana steps forward with a warm smile that somehow isn't threatening in the slightest.

"Hi! Tim talks about you all the time."

I blink. "He does?"

Tim laughs. "All good things. I swear."

For some reason, that makes it worse.

I smile at Briana. "You're beautiful." I say to her. Then I look at the two of them. "I'm so happy for you guys." She beams and hugs me like she's known me for years.

I hug her back. It's easy.

Then I turn to Tim and hug him again. Longer this time, because now I'm letting myself feel it.

"Thank you," I whisper. "For everything you were for me."

He squeezes my shoulder. "You don't have to thank me, Reya. Loving you was never a burden."

I want to cry. I don't.

Instead, I step back, look at both of them, and feel something I didn't expect: Pure happiness.

The kind without jealousy.

The kind without ache.

The kind that wishes someone you once cared about the very best life possible.

I wave goodbye, pushing my cart toward the fallen cans.

Tim laughs. "Let me help you pick those up."

"No, no," I say, waving him off dramatically. "I need the humility."

They both laugh.

"I hope you found what you were always looking for." He says as he looks at me a second too long.

One unbearable second too long.

I watch as they walk down the aisle without looking back.

Chapter 22

I Asked For One Thing

I don't know if it was seeing Tim with someone else, or just how quiet my apartment felt after, but I answered the phone last night.

And now I'm standing outside the restaurant I always told him I wanted to try.

The sign glows warm against the dark, soft gold light spilling onto the sidewalk like an invitation I shouldn't accept. I check my reflection against the glass, then immediately regret it. I don't look different. I don't look stronger. I just look…here.

Inside, he's already seated.

Of course he is.

Leven stands the second he sees me, like he's been waiting, like he hasn't moved since he got here. For a moment, we just look at each other. Not long. Just enough to remember.

"Hey," he says.

"Hey," I say.

There is a small pause, and then he steps forward slightly, uncertain.

"Can I…" He hesitates. "Can I have a hug?"

I should say no.

But I don't.

I step into him, and it's familiar in a way that makes me relax my shoulders. Not overwhelming. Not electric. Just...known. Like my body remembers him before my mind can argue with it. His arms wrap around me, firm but careful, like he's trying not to scare me away.

"Hi," he says into me, softer this time.

"Hi." I say as I breathe him in.

We stand there swaying with each other for a moment too long before we pull apart, but not completely.

Then we sit.

The table between us feels smaller than it should.

"You look good," he says, studying me like he is trying to memorize something.

"Thank you."

"I mean it."

I nod, not trusting myself to say anything else but I smile big inside.

He is dressed like this matters.

A crisp button-down, the kind that still holds its shape at the shoulders, tucked neatly into dark slacks that fit him better than I remember. His shoes are clean. Polished, not flashy. And his watch catches the light every time he moves his hand, subtle but not intentional.

His head is freshly shaved, smooth, like he stood in the mirror a little longer than usual this morning. Even his beard is lined up, precise, controlled. Everything about him says effort without him trying too hard.

Everything but the ear hairs.

They curl just slightly past where they should, unruly and untouched, like they refuse to be part of whatever version of himself he put together tonight. And I hate how much I notice them.

How familiar they feel.

I hate how something so small, so imperfect, makes my heart reach for him in a way his polished shoes never could.

God, I love those hairs.

A server comes, asks if we want water, if we've been here before. I answer automatically. He lets me. He always lets me talk first when he doesn't know how to start.

When we're alone again, he leans back slightly, exhaling.

"I've missed you," he says.

It lands exactly where it used to.

I hate that.

"I miss..." He pauses, searching. His eyes dart from my left to my right eye, and back to my left. "I miss the way you think. The questions you used to ask. Nobody asks questions like you do, Reya."

I look down at the table, tracing the edge of my napkin with my fingers. Smiling on the inside wider than the span of the world.

"I miss your stories," he continues. "The way you told them like they were happening all over again. Like I was right there with you."

My chest turns inside.

"I miss your laugh," he says, quieter now. "The real one. The uncovered one."

I swallow and breathe deep. Tears forming in my eye because I miss him. I miss him so fucking much.

"That's specific," I say, trying to keep my voice even.

He shrugs slightly. "I notice things."

I look up at the ceiling and blink rapidly trying to keep the tears at bay. I nod, but I don't respond.

"I know I hurt you," he says.

There it is.

The apology.

I let it sit, still breathing.

"I know I should have told you I didn't file for divorce," he continues. "I know I should've been honest from the beginning."

"You should have," I say, not looking at him,

"I know."

Silence stretches between us, but it doesn't feel awkward. It feels…fragile.

"I was honest about Tim," I say finally, lifting my eyes to meet his. "When we met, you knew I was in a relationship. And we still chose each other."

He nods slowly.

"Do you think I would have thought differently," I continue, "if you would've told me you were married?"

He doesn't answer right away.

"I don't know…" He admits.

"That's honest."

"I'm trying to be."

I hold his gaze for a second longer, then I look away.

"And I stayed." I say, my voice barely above a whisper. "Even after I found out about Talia."

He doesn't interrupt.

"I didn't leave. I asked questions, I gave you time. I tried to understand what I was even standing in, and you still lied." My hand hits the table with all the built-up emotion.

"I know," he says softly.

I shake my head, letting the tears fall now. "No…you don't."

I fight the thought of it. The thought that having a piece of this man was better than not having him at all.

He exhales, leaning forward slightly. "Reya…"

"You let me sit in that, Karma," I cut in finally fully looking at him. "You let me believe whatever version of the truth made it easier for *you*."

"That's not fair," he says. But there is no real push behind it.

"It is," I say. "Because you didn't just lie in the beginning. You kept lying after I already knew something was wrong."

His jaw tightens. "I never meant to hurt you."

"I don't think you meant not to," I respond.

"Listen. I'm not asking you to forget," he says. "I'm not asking you to pretend it didn't happen. I just…" He exhales. "I want to do this right. With you."

My stomach flips.

"I want to be all about you. No confusion. No lies. No half-truths. Just you. Just me." He grabs my hand from across the table. "Reya, I'm sorry. I didn't realize how much you meant to me until you left. And I feel like shit that it had to go that far."

I feel it.

That pull.

That familiar shift in my chest where everything softens just enough to make space for him.

"This time would be different. I see what my life is like without you, and that's not the life I want."

I look at him.

Really look at him. And I believe him.

I can imagine what it could be.

What it almost was.

"Reya," he brushes my knuckles with his thumb and I melt inside. "Come here."

I don't move.

But I don't pull away either.

I can feel myself leaning. Not physically. Not yet. But something inside me already stepping forward. Already closing the distance.

Maybe it wasn't all bad.

Maybe I made it worse in my head.

Maybe…

"What's my daughter's name?"

The words come out before I can stop them.

His hands become still against mine.

"What?"

"My daughter," I say. Thinking about all the times he never even asked about her. "What's her name?"

A pause.

Not long.

But long enough.

"Reya…" He exhales, leaning back slightly. "Why are we doing this right now?"

Something in my chest shifts.

"It's a normal question."

"You're doing too much," he replies, shaking his head slightly. "We're here to fix things, not…whatever this is."

"I'm asking you one thing."

"And I'm telling you I don't need to prove that to you."

There it is.

Dismissal.

Like she was never part of the story to begin with.

My hand slips from under his.

And just like that, everything settles.

Not in relief.

In clarity.

I nod once, more to myself than to him, and push my chair back.

"Reya…"

"I'm good," I say, standing before he can finish.

He watches me, something unreadable passes across his face, but he doesn't reach for me again.

Of course he doesn't.

I grab my bag, turning toward the door, the warm light from the restaurant suddenly too much, too soft, too late.

Behind me, he doesn't call my name.

He just lets me leave.

And I don't turn back.

Chapter 23

I Am Not That Woman Anymore

Ava decides we're "going outside."

Not for groceries.

Not for errands.

Outside-outside.

"Put on something that says 'emotionally stable but still mysterious,'" she calls from her bedroom.

"I don't own that," I yell back. "I own 'I went through some shit but at least I'm not ashy.'"

She appears in my doorway five minutes later in a fitted sage dress that hugs every curve like it signed a lease agreement. Her curls are wild but intentional, cascading around her face.

Her skin is glowing. Not shiny. Just glowing. Like she drinks water and minds her business.

"Okay," I say, staring at her. "You look illegal."

She grins. "And you look expensive."

I look down at myself.

High-waisted black jeans. A soft cream bodysuit that makes my waist look like I have discipline. Gold hoops. My birthmark under my eye lighter because I didn't cover it. I let my hair fall natural, big, unapologetic, framing my face.

We both pause.

"No competition," Ava says, holding up her hand.

"None," I confirm. "If someone hits on you, I'm hyping you."

"And if someone hits on you, I'm conducting the interview."

We fist bump.

The comedy club smells like spilled beer, fried food, and bad decisions. The lights are dim and purple. The stage is small, brick wall backdrop, microphone standing alone like it's waiting for someone brave.

We squeeze into a two-top near the front.

"Front row?" I whisper. "You trying to get roasted?"

"You need exposure therapy," Ava says calmly.

The first comedian comes out and immediately starts roasting a man in cargo shorts.

"Sir, you look like you clap when the plane lands."

I choke on my drink.

Ava grabs my thigh. "Girllllll, do not make eye contact."

Halfway through the set, the host squints at our table.

"Oh no," Ava whispers.

"Yes," I whisper back.

"You two look like sisters."

"We are," Ava says confidently.

"Which one is the bad influence?" He asks.

We both point at each other.

The crowd laughs.

He grins. "Alright, I need one of y'all to come up here. Five minutes. Tell me something embarrassing."

Ava squeezes my hand. "Don't."

But I'm already standing.

Because of course I am.

The stage lights hit hot and bright. The mic is heavier than I expect. The room looks darker from up here.

"Hi," I say. "I was not prepared for this."

"That's obvious," someone yells.

"Sir," I respond without missing a beat, "you're wearing flip flops in February. We were both unprepared."

The crowd erupts.

Okay.

Okay.

Breathe.

"I just got out of a relationship," I continue. "And by 'just,' I mean recently enough that my algorithm still thinks I want couples therapy ads."

Laughter.

"Why does Instagram immediately start showing you '10 signs he's a narcissist' *after* the relationship has ended like it was just waiting for *you* to catch up? These 10 signs sure would have helped before I cheated on my fiancé with his no-good ass, red-flag having ass, don't know if he wants chocolate or crackers having ass…

"Anyway, yea, so again, I just got out of a relationship," I continue. "And when I say 'got out,' I mean escaped like I had to shimmy down emotional bedsheets tied together."

Bigger laugh.

"He cheated on me," I say plainly.

The crowd goes, "Ooooo."

"Yeah. He cheated on me with *his wife*. The audacity of that man."

Gasps from the audience.

"But let me tell you where he really drew the line," I say, leaning into the mic. "Not when I found the lies. Not when I left him stranded in San Diego."

Pause.

"No, when I took him off my YouTube Premium."

The room goes quiet for half a second.

"Yes," I nod. "He cheated on me. But apparently removing him from ad-free access was where I crossed it."

Huge laughter.

"This man betrayed me…but when those ads started playing again? You would've thought I canceled his citizenship."

I pace a little.

"He texted me while I was on vacation, 'Really, Reya? You took me off YouTube Premium?'"

I widen my eyes dramatically.

"Yes, really. You really cheated. You really lied. You really tried to gaslight me. And now you're really watching ads about Grammarly and mattress sales, *yes…*"

The crowd loses it.

"I'm sorry you had to watch two unskippable ads before your podcast. I had to watch you build a whole other relationship."

Standing applause level laughter.

"And the audacity," I continue. "He said, 'You didn't have to do that.'"

I tilt my head.

"So yeah," I say into the mic, pacing a little. "I just got out of a complicated relationship."

The crowd groans in solidarity.

"But let's not act like I walked into that relationship with clean hands."

Pause.

"I was in a nine-year commitment before him."

The audience goes, "Ohhhhh."

"Yes," I nod. "Nine years. I had stability. A fiancé. A man who paid bills *on* time. A man who communicated. A man who used spreadsheets for vacation planning."

Applause from the responsible adults.

"And what did I do?" I point to myself dramatically.

"I cheated on him with some bullshit."

The crowd loses it.

"I left peace for adrenaline. I said, 'You know what? This is wayyyy too healthy for me. Let me ruin my credit right quick.'"

Huge laugh.

"I looked at a man who color-coded his calendar and said, 'No thank you. I want a man who argues with me about white bread.'"

The host is bent over.

"I left a 401(k) for a situationship."

The room explodes.

"And honestly?" I shrug. "I got what I deserved."

Pause.

"I left a man who said, 'Let's build a future,' for a man who just needed a little work." I hold my thumb and index finger together to show how "little" the work was. "My own personal project.'" I continue.

Applause and screams.

"And what happened?"

I spread my hands.

"Consequences."

The crowd howls.

"I really thought I was choosing passion. Turns out this man had a whole construction crew of women trying to fix him."

Standing applause energy.

"But here's the thing," I lean in closer to the mic. "You ever notice how when you cheat with someone, you romanticize it?"

The crowd murmurs.

"You're like, 'This is destiny, we were meant to be together.' No ma'am. That is dopamine and poor decision-making."

More laughter.

"And then when it blew up, I had the audacity to be shocked."

I widen my eyes dramatically.

"Me? Facing consequences? After making reckless emotional decisions? And now I'm single, healing, and apparently funding ads on YouTube, because yes, I did put him back on my YouTube Premium, y'all. Don't judge me."

Callback laughter.

"I had a fiancé who brought me peace," I add, shaking my head. "And I said, 'No thank you. I want character development.'"

The audience screams.

"And baby…I got it."

I shrug.

"So yeah. He cheated. He lied. He made me the villain."

I point to myself.

"But I auditioned for the role."

Standing ovation energy.

I hand the mic back while they're still clapping.

Because growth is acknowledging your chaos…And monetizing it.

And the story doesn't feel heavy.

As I step off stage, Ava grabs my face.

"You did not tell me you were funny-funny."

"I didn't know," I admit, breathless. My hands shaking with adrenaline and nerves.

Back at the table, strangers are smiling at us. One woman leans over. "That was the most relatable thing I've heard all week."

I shrug. "I had material."

We laugh until our stomachs hurt. We critique the comedians like we're producers. Ava orders fries we don't need. I steal half of them.

Easy.

Chapter 24

I Choose Myself Again

Walking into work feels surreal.

The noise hits first. Impacts. Steel on steel. The hum of a lift backing up. Someone yelling measurements across the yard. The air smells like metal shavings, diesel, and that dry desert dust that never fully leaves your boots.

It's loud and chaotic and familiar.

It feels like stepping into an old version of myself.

Only now I'm wearing it differently.

"Look who decided to come back…again." Someone shouts from across the lay-down yard.

I look up to see Greg grinning at me from behind a stack of strut.

"You get lost in the woods?" John calls out. "We almost sent a search party."

"Did you fight a bear?" Wayne adds. "You look like you fought a bear."

I'm not sure if I should take it as a compliment or disrespect. But I laugh, anyway, adjusting my hard hat. "No bears. Just myself."

That earns a few confused looks and a couple of nods like

they don't fully understand it, but they respect it.

Normally, this is where I would step in like I never left. Clipboard. Directives. Delegating before the coffee even hits.

Instead, I clock in quietly.

I put on my gloves, and I go find a pallet that needs moving.

Jason walks over while I'm strapping material down.

"So," he says casually, "We could use a yard foreman, and you are the most organized person I know. You wanna run a crew?"

It's automatic. The old version of me would have said yes before he finished the sentence. Being needed used to feel like oxygen. Instead, I tighten the strap and shake my head.

"I've been gone too long," I say. "Nina would do a better job."

He studies me, surprised. "You sure?"

"Yeah," I nod. "I'll back her up. Just tell me where you need me." There's no dramatic speech. No declaration. Just a small shift.

He shrugs. "Alright. I'll talk to her."

And just like that, I'm not in charge. And nothing falls apart.

I spend the morning moving conduit with Wayne. He tells me about his daughter's soccer tournament, how she ran the wrong direction and scored a goal for the other team.

"She celebrated at the other team's net," he says, shaking his head.

I laugh. "That's confidence."

He grins. "That's my kid."

Later, while we're unloading a truck, I walk over to Greg.

"How's Melissa doing?" I ask.

He pauses mid-lift, surprised I remembered his wife's name.

"She's good," he says slowly. "Her back's still bothering her, but physical therapy's helping."

"I'm glad," I say. "Tell her I hope she keeps improving."

It's small and it costs me nothing.

But I see the way his shoulders soften.

Midday, I'm on the ground with Adam, organizing hardware into bins. Dust sticks to my forearms. My knees ache against the concrete.

And I don't hate it.

No one is watching me to see if I'm leading correctly. No one is waiting for my next command.

I ask Jason how his mom's doing after her surgery.

I ask Will if he ever finished that motorcycle rebuild.

I let Nina explain her system for labeling crates instead of correcting it.

And I listen. Not to respond. Not to redirect.

Just to hear them.

At one point, Greg walks over with a set of prints.

"Hey," he says, "can you double check this layout? Just want another set of eyes."

He doesn't say it like he's deferring. He says it like we're equal. I look it over, point out a minor adjustment, and hand it back.

"Looks solid," I say. "You've got it."

He nods once, appreciative. There's no power struggle. No proving.

Just work.

By the end of the shift, my body is tired in a clean way. My hands smell like metal. There's dust in my hairline and sweat at the back of my neck.

When my alarm goes off, the yard settles into that end-of-day shuffle. Lifts parking. Tools locking up. Laughter drifting across the lot.

I step outside into the sunlight and take a deep breath.

The kind that fills my lungs and stretches my ribs. The kind that reminds me that nothing here is trying to consume me.

The forest wasn't magic. It didn't change my job. It didn't change these people. It didn't silence the noise.

It just made me quiet enough to hear myself inside it.

Jason walks past, bumping my shoulder lightly. "Good to have you back."

"Good to be back," I reply.

Being here doesn't feel like something I have to conquer.

It feels like something I get to belong to.

And I bring that version of me home.

My apartment still smells faintly like new paint and the lemon candle Ava bought me "to make the place smell like hope."

The plants spill across the windowsill, leaning toward the late afternoon sun like they already know they're home.

I stand in the center of the room for a moment, just listening to the quiet.

The safe kind.

The chosen kind.

My apartment feels calmer tonight.

Like the air is settling into the walls.

Like the plants have rooted themselves deeper.

Like even the silence is breathing differently.

I sit on the floor in my dining room with my journal open, pen tapping softly against the page.

I stare at the lantern fables I've written: the bird, the wolves, the seed, the squirrel and something inside me stirs.

There's one story I never finished.

One I ran away from.

Moth and flame.

I turn to a blank page and let the words move through me.

Before I write anything, I whisper to myself: "I'd like to think it didn't die."

My heart thumps softly at the thought.

My hand moves.

And I write.

Chapter 25

The Moth

Everyone assumed the moth died.
After all, that's how the story usually ends.
A warning, a tragedy, a lesson about desire.

But this moth...was different.

When the flame burned too bright, when its heat became a prison, when the moth's wings began to curl from the intensity, the little creature realized something:

It wasn't in love.
It was in danger.

The flame didn't warm it.
Didn't feed it.
Didn't nurture it.

It only consumed.

And so, one night, when the flame crackled too fiercely, when the air grew too thin to breathe, the moth made a choice no one expected:

It flew upward.

Not away, but above.

Past the heat.
Past the pull.
Past the hypnotic glow.

Higher and higher until the flame was just a flicker on the ground below.

The moth's wings were singed, yes.
Its body exhausted, yes.
But it was alive.

It rose until the night air cooled its burns and wrapped around it like a soft blanket.
And the moth realized something the flame never taught it: there were other lights in the world.

Moonlight.
Starlight.
Sunlight.
Warmth.
The soft glow of things that didn't destroy but guided.

The moth fluttered toward a lantern tree far in the distance. A tree filled with tiny lights that shimmered like hope. And when it landed on a branch, wings trembling, heart aching but steady, the tree whispered: "You were never meant to burn. You were meant to glow."

And the moth believed it.

I set the pen down and close the journal gently, like a heart I've finally stopped breaking.

And that's when I walk to the bathroom.

The mirror waits for me.

My reflection meets me immediately: same face, same eyes, same mouth.

But not the same woman.

I lean closer to the mirror, studying myself like I'm meeting a stranger I want to know deeply.

My hair is messy.

My cheeks are warm.

My eyes look clear.

I place both hands on the counter and inhale slowly.

"This is who I am," I whisper to my reflection. "And I am going to learn to love every part of me."

My voice doesn't shake.

It settles into the room like truth.

"And I am allowed to be proud of myself."

I walk into my dining room, where my journal sits open. My lantern stories. My truths. My rebirths. The pieces of me I buried and dug up again.

I sit. I breathe. I let the moment linger because I earned it.

And then a thought drifts into my mind soft and unexpected.

Brandon.

Not the fantasy of him.

Not some imagined hero.

Nothing romantic or sexual.

Just the man who shared breath with me on a trail one morning when I needed a stranger to be kind.

A man who looked at me like I wasn't broken.

I scroll to his name and pause, thumb hovering. I haven't spoken to him in almost two years, I wonder if he even still remembers me.

I reach out anyway.

I just want simple, human connection. I want to talk to someone who met me in the middle of my storm and didn't flinch.

I type: Hey. Want to get lunch sometime? It'd be nice to catch up.

I sit with the message for a breath.

Two.

Three.

And I press send.

No expectation.

No desperation.

Just an open door.

Whatever comes next…I know I'll be okay.

Because I finally choose me.

Chapter 26

Brandon Washington
The One Where Reya Shows Up

I burst through the hospital doors so fast I nearly slip on the tile.

My chest is burning.

My hands won't stop shaking.

One minute Mom was standing at the kitchen counter giving me grief about my shirt.

"Brandon, my son, you look like you're going on a job interview for Target," and the next she was gripping the countertop like the floor was dropping out from under her.

I caught her before she hit the ground.

I yelled for help.

Everything after that is a blur of paramedics and sirens and me saying, "Stay with me, stay with me," over and over like my voice alone could keep her alive.

Now she's behind double doors that slam in my face every time a nurse passes through.

They told me to wait. "Someone will come talk to you shortly."

Shortly feels like a lifetime.

I sit.

I stand.

I pace.

My knee bounces uncontrollably.

My palms are slick with sweat.

My heart feels like it's trying to punch its way out of my body.

I can't lose her.

I can't…

I can't even finish the thought.

I lean forward, elbows on my knees, pressing my hands to my face, trying to breathe through the panic when my phone vibrates in my pocket.

I ignore it at first.

Whatever it is, it doesn't matter right now.

But when it buzzes again, I pull it out, only halfway paying attention until I see her name.

Reya.

I freeze.

For a second, the whole chaotic waiting room seems to dim around me.

I haven't stopped thinking about her since the morning we met on that trail.

She was a hurricane held together by sheer willpower, and somehow, she still found space to smile at me.

I swipe the message open; my breath caught in my throat.

Reya: Hey. Want to get lunch sometime? It'd be nice to catch up.

Relief washes over me.

It feels like the universe is tossing me a rope when I'm drowning.

I type with shaking fingers: Actually…I could really use a friend.

I barely have time to inhale before the response pops up.

Reya: I'll be there in 10.

My eyes sting.

I swallow hard.

I press a shaking hand to my face, and something unknots in me I hadn't realized was tied.

She's coming.

Someone is coming.

I won't be alone in this.

Ten minutes feels like one. It feels like one hundred.

I look up when the door opens, and she's there.

Reya.

Afro on full effect.

No makeup.

Wearing a hoodie like she ran out the door without thinking about anything except getting here.

Her eyes find mine immediately.

"Brandon?" Her voice is soft but strong enough to cut through the noise in my head.

I stand, and the moment she reaches me, something in me breaks.

I fold into her, not collapsing, not crumbling. Just…letting go of the weight I've been holding by myself.

She wraps her arms around me, firm and steady, grounding me in a way I didn't know I needed.

Her voice is warm against my ear. "I'm here."

I nod because I can't speak.

My throat is too tight.

My chest is too full.

A doctor steps into the hallway, scanning the room. "Mr. Washington?"

Reya's hand stays on my back, keeping me in this moment.

I straighten, inhale shakily, and walk toward the doctor.

I don't know what he's about to say.

I don't know what's waiting behind those doors.

But I do know this: I'm not facing it alone.

Reya is here.

And for the first time today, the panic loosens its grip.

Even if just a little.

Acknowledgments

Thank you for continuing the story with me.

As always, thank you to my mom, my daughter, my love, and my editor.

And to the people who gave me space to create, and understood that when I disappeared, I was just writing…thank you.

Coming Winter 2026

The Promise Within Me

She's done chasing love.
Now love has to meet her where she stands…
Or lose her for good.

For the first time, Reya Carter is choosing herself.
No more settling. No more shrinking. No more confusing chaos with connection.

And *he* sees it.

He sees the difference in the way she walks.
The way she no longer reaches.
The way she lets herself breathe.

But loving Reya has never been simple.

He doesn't move off impulse.
He doesn't fall recklessly.
And he doesn't give pieces of himself without knowing what it will cost him.

And Reya?
She's no longer waiting to be chosen.

Now, the question isn't whether he wants her.
It's whether he's willing to meet her where she stands.

Will he put aside his logic for her?
Will he choose what's easy…or what's real?

The Promise Within Me is a story about rising to meet love…
Or risk losing it altogether.

www.ingramcontent.com/pod-product-compliance
Lightning Source LLC
LaVergne TN
LVHW091248150826
845673LV00006B/1357
* 9 7 9 8 9 9 8 9 2 3 1 5 9 *